JAN 1 4 1993

New & Selected Essays

BOOKS BY DENISE LEVERTOV

POETRY
The Double Image
Here and Now
Overland to the Islands
With Eyes at the Back of Our Heads
The Jacob's Ladder
O Taste and See
The Sorrow Dance
Relearning the Alphabet
To Stay Alive
Footprints
The Freeing of the Dust
Life in the Forest
Collected Earlier Poems 1940–1960
Candles in Babylon
Poems 1960–1967
Oblique Prayers
Poems 1968–1972
Breathing the Water
A Door in the Hive
Evening Train

PROSE
The Poet in the World
Light Up the Cave
New & Selected Essays

TRANSLATIONS
Guillevic/Selected Poems
Joubert/Black Iris (Copper Canyon Press)

Denise Levertov

New & Selected Essays

A New Directions Book

Grateful acknowledgment is made to the editors of magazines and anthologies in which some of these essays previously appeared: *American Poetry, Avril, The Bloodaxe Book of Contemporary Women Poets: Eleven British Writers, Celebrating the Peace: Volume II, Chicago Review, Conversant Essays: Contemporary Poets on Poetry, Ezra Pound and William Carlos Williams: The University of Pennsylvania Conference Papers, Ironwood, Minnesota Review, New Directions in Prose & Poetry 20, Ohio Review, Poetry, Poetry East, Real Paper, Religion & Intellectual Life, Robert Duncan: Scales of the Marvelous, Spring, What Is a Poet?*. Due to space limitations, additional acknowledgment for permission to reprint quoted material in these essays will be found on page 265.

Publisher's Note: "Williams and the Duende," "Some Notes on Organic Form," "Linebreaks, Stanza-Spaces, and the Inner Voice," and "Great Possessions" were originally collected in Denise Levertov's 1973 prose volume *The Poet in the World* (New Directions); "On the Function of the Line," "Technique and Tune-up," "'News That Stays News,'" "Anne Sexton: Light Up the Cave," and "Rilke as Mentor" were first collected in her *Light Up the Cave* (New Directions, 1981).

Book design by Sylvia Frezzolini
Manufactured in the United States of America
New Directions books are printed on acid-free paper
First published clothbound and as New Directions Paperbook 749 in 1992
Published simultaneously in Canada by Penguin Books Canada Limited

Library of Congress Cataloging-in-Publication Data
Levertov, Denise, 1923–
New & selected essays / Denise Levertov.
p. cm.
ISBN 0–8112–1217–3 (cloth):—ISBN 0–8112–1218–1
I. Title. II. Title: New and selected essays.
PS3562.E8876N48 1992
814′ .54—dc20
                                                                  92–17887
                                                                     CIP

New Directions Books are published for James Laughlin
by New Directions Publishing Corporation,
80 Eighth Avenue, New York 10011

Contents

Some Affinities of Content

(1991)

IN THE FALL OF 1990, I realized that my own preferred reading in current poetry as the last decade of the century began was of two kinds: a certain kind of poem about the world of nature written predominantly by poets of the Pacific Northwest, and poems of various provenance that were concerned more or less with matters of religious faith. And as I thought about them, I realized that there was a similarity of direction in these two kinds of poem, though their manner of approach differed. I recognized that I felt a personal affinity with both, which stemmed from a shared preoccupation with that direction; and I was reminded of a Hans Christian Andersen story I had always loved, called "The Bell," which tells how a beggar-boy and a prince, taking different paths through the forest in quest of the place from which a mysterious and beautiful bell could be heard ringing, emerged at last, at the same moment, at the shore of a remote lake beside which stood the chapel and its golden-voiced bell.

There were, of course, many other kinds of poem which interested me too, but these two predominated; and my sense of affinity with them and of their parallel movement was not one of formal structure but of content or concern. I note a difference here which may be familiar to others of my age, in that what drew me to the work of various poets when I was in my twenties and thirties was often the shape of their poems, their diction, their rhythmic organization, whether or not I cared deeply, or understood, *what* they were saying. We have long assumed that it is an aesthetic truism to assert the indivisibility of form and content—but there is a certain amount of hypocrisy in the statement, after all. Perhaps it needs to be reformulated, to say that although inadequate formal expression always diminishes or distorts content, yet form itself can be perceived, admired, and experienced as pleasure or stimulus even when the reader's attention is not held by content. Thus, while content cannot be fully apprehended without a fusion with form equal to its task, form can be apprehended and absorbed in and of itself. The assertion of indivisibility does not cover this contingency. At all events, I as a younger poet was often drawn primarily to the structure or technique of poems I read, and paid less attention to what was being said; whereas the older I grow the more I find myself concerned with content, and drawn towards poems that articulate some of my own interests. This primary importance given to *what* doesn't imply a loss of interest in *how;* if a poem strikes me as banal, trite, flabby, pretentious or in any other respect badly written, I'm unlikely to read further no matter what its subject matter. But the poems to which I look for nourishment and stimulus are more and more those with which I feel an affinity that is not necessarily stylistic at all.

What then are these thematic affinities? And how do they differ from the thematic tendencies of the poems that most interested me when I was younger, before I came to America and became, for a while, more interested in form than content? When I think of the poets among whom my own work first appeared, the English poets of the phase Kenneth Rexroth anthologized in 1948 as The New Romantics, I would say that their appeal to me and to others was chiefly on an emotional level: they tended to convey, with varying degrees of musicality and through evocative but not very precise images, a certain rather narrow range of emotional *moods*. The poets with whom I was soon associated after I came to America (and who came to be known as the Black Mountain School—though I myself was never at Black Mountain in my life—and who were strongly influenced by Williams and Pound and by the Objectivists) were, however, a great deal more concerned with language itself, with formal concepts, and with history, than the English poets of the '40s. In Williams, likewise, who was for me the primary influence on my own development at that time, I found those formal concerns, along with that more than descriptive, that *evocative* sense of *how things are* which can be so keenly felt in his work. Transcending the merely documentary, that sense conveys a strong flavor or aroma of Williams' values, his love for a tenacious life-force, for qualities of daring, imagination, persistence, perceived in weeds and birds or in some rickety building embodying in its fragile means some idea or aspiration, as well as in the humans, obscure or known to history, of whom he also wrote.

All of this—what I found and loved and went on finding in Williams, as well as what excited me in the ideas and practices of those poets of my own generation who in the '50s were published in *Origin* and *The Black Mountain Review* (such as "composition by field" and a far more democratic diction than I had been accustomed to in England)—all of this was just what I instinctively needed at the time. What I did not find (and was not looking for) was an impulse of spiritual quest (though if I had been looking for it I could have found it in my great friend Robert Duncan, or in Margaret Avison, that profound Canadian poet who, though even more detached from actual connection with Black Mountain than I was, did correspond with Olson and Cid Corman and was published in *Origin* for a time). I was not looking for it because in the 1950s I was preoccupied with my technical development. Yet a sense of quest, of life as a pilgrimage, was, I believe, a part of me from the start, and by

1967, when Robert Duncan and I (along with Hollis Summers) participated in a symposium on *Myth in Religion and Poetry* in Washington, I had recognized that this was so.

Being the child of a socially conscious family, conscience and circumstance virtually forced me into the politics of the anti-war movement of the 1960s and on into the broader anti-nuclear, environmental, and social justice concerns which evolved from it, so that I found myself frequently acting as apologist for "engaged" writing in response to external demands as well as (initially) to explain to myself what I was doing. Thus I have spent a lot of time attempting to define what qualities can make "political" poetry work as poetry, to defend such poetry from attacks made from a position of rigid, general aesthetic objection rather than on a case by case basis, and to point out the honorable precedents for such literary "engagement." But this didactic role (which, once having taken on, I probably shall never be able to avoid) was undertaken as a further obligation of social conscience, not from personal choice; for my underlying interest has always been elsewhere. The tragic and fearful character of our times is not something from which we can detach ourselves; we are *in* it, as fish are in the sea, whether we speak about it in our poems or not. Sometimes the nagging, unceasing ache of a keen awareness of current history and of its impact on one's daily life deflects one's energies away from creative work; at other times it may stimulate them, and some of the results may be of lasting value. But more and more, what I have sought as *a reading writer*, is a poetry that, while it does not attempt to ignore or deny the ocean of crisis in which we swim, is itself "on pilgrimage," as it were, in search of significance underneath and beyond the succession of temporal events: a poetry which attests to the "deep spiritual longing" that Jorie Graham, in her very interesting essay of introduction to *The Best American Poetry, 1990* says is increasingly manifest in recent American verse.

One of the places where I have found what I needed is in

some of the poets of the Northwest, with whose work I was somewhat familiar long before I moved there. They are poets who usually have experienced a long-standing relationship to non-urban nature. The character of this relationship is clarified by contrasting what the word *Nature* tends to evoke on the Northwest coast and in the Northeast. In the latter, and in all states that were settled relatively early, the word "Nature," calls up a landscape of farms, of old cellar-holes, forgotten family burying-grounds, overgrown stone walls, appletrees lost in the woods; of barns and cows and tidy village greens, carpentered white churches, and here and there a just-surviving elm. In many places the cut-over woods look more venerable than they are, for they are largely mixed hardwood and were not systematically replanted in rigid rows for quick harvesting. It is a humanly populated landscape that comes to mind, and the typical poems that emerge from it are populated too. The relationship of the individual poet to the non-human environment in the East is always in some degree mediated through the presence of other humans even when they are not specifically referred to. And so it is natural that the focus often is on the poet's response rather than primarily on what is responded to; a focus that can reflect mere egotism, or else be a positive and illuminating introspection, as in, for instance, Hayden Carruth's *North Winter* or *From Snow and Rock, from Chaos*. In the Northwest the word "Nature," however, evokes Wilderness, notwithstanding that nature is being despoiled there in even swifter and more dramatically visible ways, as the lumber companies race to destroy the oldgrowth forests of Oregon, Washington, and British Columbia, than good farmland is being destroyed in the East. That the Northwestern poets I am speaking of have had or still have a genuine—and often a working, not only recreational—relationship to wild nature, leads to poems seldom frequented by other humans, and in which, even where the personal pronoun is present, we are given more of *what is seen* (or otherwise apprehended) and less emphasis on

5

the poet's reaction to it. Am I simply saying that such poems are more objective; those from the East Coast more subjective? Not quite, for the Western poems are introspective too—but in a different way, it seems to me: the strong influence of Chinese and Japanese poetry and of Buddhism on a people dwelling in a landscape which, with its mists and snowy mountains, often seems to resemble one of those great scroll paintings of Asian art, comes into play in much Northwestern poetry, and gives rise to a more conscious attentiveness to the non-human and to a more or less conscious desire to immerse the self in that larger whole. It is this which gives these poems that element I have called spiritual quest. It takes their poems beyond what for me, as a city-dweller, would otherwise be merely a sort of tourism, to a universal dimension that speaks to the inner life. Such poems communicate not just the appearance of phenomena but the presence of spirit *within* those phenomena. I have referred to an Asian influence, but the assumption of such spiritual presence in landscape and in all life-forms is even more closely related to Native American beliefs.

Let me give you some examples of such poems. People say that every poet of the Pacific Northwest has to write a heron poem now and then; this one is by Sam Hamill:

Black Marsh Eclogue

Although it is midsummer, the great blue heron
holds darkest winter in his hunched shoulders,
those blue-turning-gray clouds
rising over him like a storm from the Pacific.

He stands in the black marsh
more monument than bird, a wizened prophet
returned from a vanished mythology.
He watches the hearts of things

and does not move or speak. But when
at last he flies, his great wings

> cover the darkening sky, and slowly,
> as though praying, he lifts, almost motionless,
>
> as he pushes the world away.

That heron is observed with more than an ornithologist's eye, and is more than a mobile bundle of bones and feathers. Nor is it anthropomorphized, though it is impossible for us to avoid some human terms of analogy. A kind of animism informs such a vision. Hamill, a Buddhist, disclaims belief in God and is profoundly skeptical of human redeemability; but he is far too deeply a man of poetic imagination to espouse a crass rationalism, blind to the mystery of being. And if the world is "pushed away," another world, that is to say another dimension of being, is implied.

Wendell Berry has an equally wonderful heron poem, the last lines of which say that, after he finds himself close to the bird, "suddenly I know I have passed across/to a shore where I do not live." Berry's poem illustrates my point about Eastern U.S. poets, for it is as much concerned—though not in an egotistic or narcissistic way—with the shift in the poet himself from busy-ness and anxiety to stillness and openness brought about by the encounter, as it is with the heron himself.

An untitled poem by the Estonian poet Jaan Kaplinski, whose work Sam Hamill has translated, does something similar:

> I do not know whether each believer
> is as joyful that God exists
> as I was upon hearing
> the wood owl call from the ash tree
> where his next box
> has already rested a dozen years. Now
> he has nested there
> four or five years himself.
> He is.

Here again we have a bird whose spirit is invoked in that triumphant and awestruck last line; and again we have a reference to belief from outside of belief—here in the opening lines, and in Hamill's poem in the phrase, "as though praying." In both cases the birds are regarded with respect, even with humility. An owl poem by the wonderful poet John Haines goes further in this direction:

> Prayer to the Snowy Owl
>
> Descend, silent spirit;
>
> you whose golden eyes
> pierce the grey
> shroud of the world—
>
> Marvelous ghost!
>
> Drifter of the arctic night,
> destroyer of those
> who gnaw in the dark—
>
> preserver of whiteness.

Sam Green, who lives on an island in the San Juans where he and his wife and son built their house with their own hands, living in a tent year-round for two or three years while they did so, has a poem called "Covenant: Saying Hello to the Land We Will Live With," which is full of a sense of respect for place. One perceives that these people intend to fit themselves into the place they have come to, modestly, rather than planning to impose their wills upon it. The covenant is with the spirit of the place as well as with one another.

> Covenant: Saying Hello to the Land
> We Will Live With
>
> We pace off boundaries in a light rain
> wondering whether the air

slips over us, or we slip
into the air. We have only
the compass of how we walk here
how our feet move
over the soil that will feed us.

Everywhere there are gestures of
welcome, the intricate calligraphy
of branches, the slow traffic of summer
birds, the million plants giving up
their oxygen, our lungs filling.

There was the voice in your head the first time
we came

 I will die here

like a benediction, light as the first
leaf fall, and you unafraid.

I watch you kneel & smell
a handful of soil, the cornerstone
of wonder. The elements
of a future assemble inside us
though we worry where water is
whether we can build before
winter, how to find the longest light
for the labor we will do here.

Neither of us speaks it

 I will stay with you
 here, here I will love you

made good by the doing,
a contract signed & witnessed
with each breath as we keep faith
with the land, the names
we will learn, passing into each season
passing through in turn.

Emily Warn, writing of working all day in the wet woods with a friend to clear some scrub alder, saw it, and carry it up out of a ravine to dry for firewood, ends her poem "Axis Mundi" with lines that also convey a sense of respect and connectedness: they cease work just after dusk and

> watch the clearing we broke
> out of the woods, watch how it
>   holds the wet sky
> like a cupped palm, or a well, rounded and scooped
> by rain falling, slowly carving a basin
> where the animals can drink from the net of rain we love.

Tim McNulty is a poet who has worked in the woods for years, and has published some first-rate ecological essays as well as poetry. In a series called *Reflected Light* he pays homage to paintings by Morris Graves, but he is so steeped in direct knowledge of the area that in responding to Graves' titles and images he is simultaneously responding to his own accrued experiences which share Graves' sources of inspiration. It is as a poet whose hands have planted thousands of trees that he writes such a companion piece to one of Graves' tree paintings as this:

Joyous Young Pine

> The flushed glow of new life
> hidden in bud
>   and early gold-green leafage
> quickens a young pine
>   with a thousand warm
>   and radiant leaves.

> It's the spring of its
>   fourth year.
> Shallow roots deepen
>   in the temperate earth,
> and a smooth skein of bark
>   sheathes its stem. . . .

It's as if Graves' vision were not so much a revelation to him as a confirmation. Such poems, although full of sensory data, imply the presence of spirit in nature, of the natural world as material manifestation of the supramaterial.

The other category of poems of which I want to speak dares to approach spiritual longing and spiritual experience in a way that is more direct, since it is frankly about the quest for or the encounter with God. It might be called more abstract—except that it is a mistake to suppose an experience is abstract merely because it is not predominantly sensory. Predominantly is a key word, for it is not that these poems eschew concrete and sensuous imagery. But their focus is different. More of the poets who come to mind in relation to this kind of poem are well-known. Milosz, probably the greatest of living poets, is among them, as are R. S. Thomas, another profound older voice, Wendell Berry (whose range includes both my categories and often combines them, though his country is rural rather than wild), and Charles Wright, a poet whose diction incorporates many theological terms and references and whose exciting poetry is permeated by a longing for mystical revelation, for ecstasy, "I want to be bruised by God," he wrote in "China Trace" a few years ago:

> I want to be strung up in a strong light and singled out
> I want to be stretched, like music wrung from a dropped seed.
> I want to be entered and picked clean.

Other poets I'm thinking of are little-known.

While, if any known belief-system provides the center for the poems of wild nature, it would be Buddhist or Native American, the poems I am thinking of now have a Christian or Jewish context. Their authors don't necessarily claim faith, but that is the frame of reference. Some of these poems deal with the struggle between faith and doubt, some with moments of epiphany; some are explorations and illuminations of Biblical

11

scenes or sayings. And unlike the poems in the first group (with the exception of Kaplinski), some of these poems are known to me only through translations—but translations which truly appear to have ferried poetry safely across from language to language. There is considerable variety of style and tone among them, whether translated or written in English.

The Chicano poet Ben Sáenz, in his collection *Calendar of Dust* (Broken Moon, 1991) writes in "Easter: Mesilla, N.M., 1962," of a childhood encounter with a grandmother's certitude that marked him for life. He has told of the ride to Mass:

> in a red pickup, bright and red and waxed
> for the special occasion. Clean, polished as
> apples, the yellow-dressed girls in front
> with Mom and Dad; the boys in back, our
> hair blowing free

and of the Mass itself. Then:

> Mass ending, we running to the truck,
> shiny as shoes going dancing. Dad
> driving us to see my grandmother. There,
> at her house, I asked about the new word
> I'd heard: *resurrection*. "Death,
> death," she said, her hands moving downward,
> "the cross—*that* is death." And then she
> laughed: "The dead will rise." Her upturned
> palms moved skyward as she spoke. "The dead
> will rise." She moved her hands toward me,
> wrapped my face with touches, and
> laughed again. *The dead will rise.*

Lucille Clifton is one of the illuminators of scripture. She has written, for example, a whole series of short poems on the life of the Virgin Mary, others on the life of Jesus or in the voices of

other personages of the Gospels, all translated into a diction
that enables us to see them as Black—whether African American or West Indian—just as the icons from Solentiname in
Guatemala enable us to see them as Central American, restor-
ing universality to what has too often been depicted in wholly
Northern European terms—those blond, bland, Holy Families
of undertakers' Christmas calendars. Her St. John the Baptist
says (in a poem just called "john"):

> somebody coming in blackness
> like a star
> and the world be a great bush
> on his head
> and his eyes be fire
> in the city
> and his mouth be true as time
>
> he be calling the people brother
> even in the prison
> even in the jail
>
> i'm just only a baptist preacher
> somebody bigger than me coming
> in blackness like a star

In her poem "good friday" Christ says:

> i rise up above my self
> like a fish flying
>
> men will be gods
> if they want it

The polish poet Adam Zagajewski's poem, "Kierkegaard on
Hegel," implies that men, humans, do *not* want it—they don't
dare to want it.

Kierkegaard said of Hegel: He reminds me of someone
who builds an enormous castle but lives himself
in a storehouse next to the construction.
The mind, by the same token, dwells in
the modest quarters of the skull,
and those glorious states
which were promised us are covered
with spiderwebs, for the time being we should enjoy
a cramped cell in the jailhouse, a prisoner's song,
the good mood of a customs officer, the fist
of a cop. We live in longing. In our dreams,
locks and bolts open up. Who didn't find shelter
in the huge looks to the small. God
is the smallest poppy seed in the world,
bursting with greatness.

As I myself have tried to say in a poem or two, our wings hang
unused on our shoulders, a dead weight. Only in dreams,
Zagajewski seems to be saying, do we approach God, who is at
once minute and vast, an unreleased potentiality like the unparalleled power to grow contained in the mustard-seed of the
parable. We "live in longing," not present to ourselves and
therefore not present to the divine—this is what afflicts our
species. That at least is my reading of this poem after looking at
what Kierkegaard wrote of Hegel in *Either/Or*. In another
poem, "He Acts," Zagajewski seems to envision God not as
absent, and certainly not dead, but not to be found in the
familiar places of Judeo-Christian tradition.

He Acts

He acts, in splendor and in darkness,
in the roar of waterfalls and in the silence of sleep,
but not as your well-protected shepherds
would have it. He looks for the longest line,
the road so circuitous

it is barely visible, and fades away
in suffering. Only blind men, only
owls feel sometimes its dwindling trace
under their eyelids.

A number of David Shaddock's poems take up the ancient
Jewish tradition which Arthur Waskow (who wrote an afterword for a group of them) has called "God-wrestling." In section XI of "In This Place Where *Something's Missing* Lives"
Shaddock writes:

In the space between the pink plum-blossoms
and the thick leaves of the loquat tree,
a grey February sky is burst by beams of gold light.

I want to leave off this dialogue
with a God I can't be sure exists
and go into that light.

But I cannot. Inside my chest
is a fist, clenching darkness,
that has been shaking for a thousand years.

Towhees dive past the window.
Their God is not the God of the Jews.
No Hasid, laughing and dancing,

is as oblivious as a bird.
And no bird shoulders the world's sorrow
like a Zaddik, lifting the bride's chair at a wedding.

I want to lay down my burden.
But even joy remembers and burns
like a Yahrtzeit candle in my chest.

And in Section VII:

The white phosphorous bombs.
The bone-seeking fire.

The rubber bullets and swinging batons,
the trainwheels cutting a man's legs.

I do not accuse You.
I live uneasily with my despair.

Yet some days I am still moved to hope,
against the news of perpetual pogrom,
that something other than this fist
in men's hearts will prevail.

Elohim, God of mercy,
is it in hoping that You exist,
that You exist,
this longing itself
Your in-dwelling spark?

Czeslaw Milosz's profound doubt is one face of the gold coin of his great poems; the other face is the whole culture of belief in which his life, with its studies and affiliations, is rooted. The doubts of a wholly secular mind and its life-experience have no context, no ground, no substantial referents. Belief has to accompany doubt for doubt to be serious. "It is better to praise God in misfortune, thinking He did not act, though He could have," Milosz writes in "Before Majesty": "Unanswered is our prayer. . . ." Another stanza of this poem says, "A weak human mercy walks in the corridors of hospitals and is like a half-thawed winter"—and the last line is, "And I, who am I, a believer, dancing before the All Holy?" In the poem "On Prayer" he writes:

You ask me how to pray to someone who is not.
All I know is that prayer constructs a velvet bridge
And walking it we are aloft, as on a springboard,
Above landscapes the color of ripe gold
Transformed by a magic stopping of the sun.
That bridge leads to the shore of Reversal
Where everything is just the opposite and the word *is*

Unveils a meaning we hardly envisioned.
Notice: I say *we*; there, every one, separately,
Feels compassion for others entangled in the flesh
And knows that if there is no other shore
They will walk that aerial bridge all the same.

And he follows this in *Unattainable Earth*, published in 1986, with a quote from his uncle Oscar de Lubicz Milosz: "To wait for faith in order to be able to pray is to put the cart before the horse. Our way leads from the physical to the spiritual." This is reminiscent of that prayer of St. Anselm which says, "I do not seek to understand so that I may believe, but I believe so that I may understand; and what is more, I believe that unless I do believe I shall not understand."

Amid the savagery, stupidity, and corruption we of the late 20th century see around us, confronted with an over-expanded technology and an atrophied sense of moral responsibility, the poetic vision of God is almost always a somber, shadowed one even in those most committed to faith. The Welsh poet R. S. Thomas, who is an Anglican priest, ends "Pilgrimages" with the question,

> . . . Was the pilgrimage
> I made to come to my own
> self, to learn that in times
> like these and for one like me
> God will never be plain and
> out there, but dark rather and
> inexplicable, as though he were in here?

Harlow Clark, a young Western poet living in Utah, has written of the olive tree in a way that moved me:

The Olive

> This Tree is light to the world,
> Its fruit light to the mind,

Fire to the lamp, calm to troubled waters.
The fruit bears its fire by being crushed:
Salt well in a stone box.
Add purgatives—vinegar is good.
Let sit.
Crush between two grinding stones driven by a mule
Kissed by a whip
Till the skins break
Repeat to the lees, then burn the mash on a torch.
If the oil enlightens your soul
You will see the beaten traveller
There, by the side of the road, as you head down to Jericho.
Pour it on his broken skin.

This man, light of endless worlds,
Praying near the trunk
Feels the branches enfolding him,
Folding him in—kneading, pressing
Till the skin breaks and it is not oil
Which will spill on ground that will shake tomorrow
Like waves tossing the boat
His nearby friends dream they are sleeping in—unaware
A friend will whip him with a kiss
Enemies whip nails through his palms and wrists
and spear him up a sponge of vinegar through his ribs.

After the healing has all flowed out
Layer him in linen
Salt him away in a stone room
Post sentinels to guard the rock that guards the room
That guards the shroud that keeps the dead
Dead—till the earth rolls the death stone like a boat
Tossed in stormy dreams and the empty cloths fold themselves
And Mary hears her name spoken
Not by the gardener.

But first, now, the tree draws him closer, tighter
Glowing in the approaching torchlight
As if dripping oil.

Opening with the properties of all olive trees, the poem zeroes in on a particular tree in the Garden of Gethsemane; and from there moves to focus on Jesus *in* the garden, close to the tree; by the end of the poem, so closely have He and the tree been mutually embraced, we are led not only to see in the tree an archetype of the Cross, but, as it opposes its own glow to "the approaching torchlight" (to return to the opening line), to see Jesus *as* olive tree, "light to the world"—so that the composition has a kind of circularity.

Eugene Warren (who also publishes as Gene Doty) writes of the fear that *doesn't want to know* about the Passion, that just doesn't want to have to hear about it:

A *signature*

—went into the world like a shining knife—

they don't like the blood,
the rusty nails crookt
with gore
                    the hot gush
out of split skin

& the hot wind like boild sand,
a bath of grainy steam

the wildness, a black sun
& the shaking
is terrific
                    they don't like
the stench of death,
not even rich heaped manure
rotting for the garden

(delicate glaze of blossom formed
of dung translated into cells of sweet)

they don't like the body coming
back like that, wounds open

19

to sun & air, walking around,
they don't like not being able to vanish

Another poet not widely known, Kathleen Norris, has a poem called "Imperatives" in which she simply—and brilliantly—collages essential words and phrases from what Jesus is recorded to have said:

Imperatives

Look at the birds
Consider the lilies
Drink ye all of it

Ask
Seek
Knock
Enter by the narrow gate

Do not be anxious
Judge not; do not give dogs what is holy

Go: be it done for you
Do not be afraid
Maiden, arise
Young man, I say, arise

Stretch out your hand
Stand up, be still
Rise, let us be going . . .

Love.
Forgive.
Remember me.

It brings the "found poem" to a level one never expected it to aspire to, much less reach.

The fact that poems such as any of these (both those of homage to wild nature and those of doubt and faith) are being written and are being read, and that there is indeed, in so many writers and readers, that "deep spiritual longing" Jorie Graham speaks of, seems to underscore the irrelevance to literature, for both writer and reader, of the kind of criticism currently prevalent in the academic world—a criticism which treats works of art as if they were diagrams or merely means provided for the exercise of analysis, rather than what they are: testimonies of lived life, which is what writers have a vocation to give, and readers (including those who write) have a need to receive. Those I have cited provide only a scant sampling of what I, as one hungry reader, have been happy to receive in the last year or two; and I have no anxiety about the supply of such nourishment. There will be more.

Given as the 1991 Paul Zweig Memorial Lecture at Poets' House, New York City.

On Williams' Triadic Line, or How to Dance on Variable Feet

(1984)

ALTHOUGH SO MUCH CRITICAL literature on William Carlos Williams has accumulated and continues to proliferate, that part of it which concerns his prosody typically applies a tin ear, or no ear at all, to the sounds of his poems and to the relation of sound, and especially rhythm, to the nuances of significant expression. The common reader who approaches Williams without the intervention of critical mediators frequently responds with instinctive understanding; but a great many persons first encounter him in the classroom, where—if the instructor is strongly influenced by the secondary material—mistaken concepts, confidently asserted, too often lead them astray.

The old evaluation of Williams as a homespun Imagist dies hard: the red wheelbarrow is trundled on stage at every "Introduction to Modern Poetry" course, year after year, at college after college. And "The Yachts," admired by the academics of twenty or more years ago less for itself than for its atypicality, which enabled them to patronize Williams with a "can do good work if he tries" school-report, retains its contrasting place in the anthologies. In recent years, his stock having risen so far above what it was in his lifetime, the focus has shifted to his prosodic theories and to the poems, from *The Desert Music* on, in which he demonstrated them. But just what constitutes a "variable foot" evidently puzzles the critics, often to the point where it is dismissed, after a brief *pro forma* attempt to define it, as an obsessive illusion of his old age.

I have not read the entire body of Williams criticism, but from the books and articles I have read I derive the impression that this bafflement is due primarily to a failure to recognize that the variable foot is not a matter of stress patterns but of duration in time.

Reed Whittemore for example (*Willam Carlos Williams: Poet from Jersey*) seems to come closer than many to understanding this measure when he quotes Yvor Winters on "the foot in free verse"—"one heavily accented syllable, an unlimited number of unaccented syllables, and an unlimited number of syllables of secondary accent"—in a context which assumes that this clustering of a variable number of syllables around a central beat, though it was to be found in poems written long before Williams proclaimed the variable foot as a discovery, nevertheless describes the phenomenon. But this formulation is at best only a partial description; and Winters' assumption that the focus of such a cluster was the central heavily accented syllable, while applicable to "free verse" and perhaps (as I shall set forth later) to Williams' earlier poems, does not apply—as Whittemore tries to make it do—to the consciously written variable foot and triadic line of the later Williams. Winters, in his 1947 *In Defense of Reason* had chosen to scan Williams' "The Widow's Lament in Springtime," from the early 1920s; he did so by marking what he heard as its strong stresses (which to his ear turn out to be consistently two to a line). Whittemore comments that by 1955 the major change Williams would have made in those lines "would not have been in the syllable count but the spacing" (into triads), because by the 1950s Williams "was not thinking syllable by syllable* but unit by unit so that each triad was really a threesome of ones." And he then proceeds to more or less dismiss this "spatial" arrangement, as he calls it, as less significant than Williams liked to think. But whether or not Williams' concept and practice of the variable foot are of vital importance for modern poets and poetry in general, their significance is *not* "spatial" (and thus visual) but temporal and auditory. (Perhaps that's what Whittemore means by saying Williams was "thinking unit by unit" but I don't think he makes it clear.)

Again, Alan Stephens, as quoted by Louis Simpson (in *Three on the Tower*), said that though there was "no definite and recurrent combination of stressed and unstressed syllables" and therefore no possibility of that "measurement" Williams desired and claimed, yet his line "is a line because, relative to its neighboring lines, it contains that which makes it in its own right a unit of the attention," and because it "has a norm against which it almost constantly varies . . . the formal architecture of the sentence." Simpson comments, "He [Alan Stephens] goes on to say that this principle also underlies verse in meter; 'audible rhythm' is not the 'supreme fact' of the line of verse, and so 'Dr. Williams will have been working in the tradition all along.' . . . Dr. Williams would not have been happy to hear it," says Simpson, "for he insisted on the variable foot's being a measurement in time . . . a unit of rhythm, not a form of sentence structure." But Simpson does not commit himself further; instead he questions, at this point, whether or not there is indeed an "American measure."

Williams himself tended to cloud the understanding of his prosodic ideas by linking them too closely to his emphasis on notating American, not English, speech patterns; but the variable foot itself is a principle equally applicable to other idioms, not only to American speech. Simpson, however, a page or so

---

*Williams never *had* been a counter of syllables and a pattern of stresses is not the same as syllables anyway!

earlier, *had* reiterated some of Williams' own clearer definitions of the measured line he was after—"auditory measure" and the assertion that "the passage of time (not stress) is the proper . . . key to the foot. . . ." In the face of such evidence it is particularly distressing to read that so astute a critic as Hugh Kenner (whose close reading of "Young Sycamore Tree" and the little poem about the cat stepping over the jam-pot are models of what such analyses can be—and rarely are) could write to Mike Weaver (as quoted in *Three on the Tower*) that Williams' use of the triadic line was merely a visual aid to reading aloud after strokes had affected his visual coordination. Perhaps Kenner was merely trying to account for why the variable feet were arranged in three's rather than four's, let's say. I would find no argument with that attempt: it's a good question; but Kenner's remarks *can* be read as a relegation of what was a deliberate auditory notation to the level of merely visual typographical convenience; and in *The Pound Era* he does say the term "variable foot" suggests "a rubber inch."

As for Marjorie Perloff, she claims that Williams scored his lines for the eye, not the ear (in *"To Give a Design": Williams & the Visualization of Poetry* from *William Carlos Williams: Man & Poet*)—something I know, from my own conversations with him and his approval of my way of reading his own work back to him (at his request), was not the case. Unfortunately, Flossie Williams was the only witness to those occasions, so you have only my word for it. Among the writers on Williams whose expositions of the variable foot I've read, only James Breslin approaches clarity and understanding, for he does write (in *William Carlos Williams: An American Artist*) of "uniform intervals of lapsed time," with variable syllable count and "pauses used to fill out the intervals in the shorter lines." But even this does not seem to adequately acknowledge the variations in *speed* which I hear in these units, nor, to my mind, are pauses merely fillers: they are not resorted to, as it were, but have expressive functions to fulfill—waiting, pondering, or hesitating.

What then is my own sense of how to read the variable feet in their (usually) triadic line-clusters? It is so simple, if I am right, that one wonders at all the confusion and mystification. Each segment of a triadic cluster is a foot, and each has the same *duration*. Thus a foot (or segment) with few syllables, if it is to occupy the same amount of time as one with many, must by the reader be accorded, in the enunciation of those syllables, a slowness (or marked "quantity"). If that would in any particular instance distort the words or impart a weird mouthing effect, then the reader must give full value to the spaces between the words—especially in a foot with syntax and expression (punctuated or not) calling for some degree of pause in any case. Conversely, a foot (or line-segment) of many syllables must be uttered with whatever rapidity will give it equal duration with a few-syllabled line. What sets the norm? Just as the tempo at which a piece of music will be played is established in the first bar (so that if, in practicing the piano, one starts very fast, one will be obliged to play the designedly quickest passages all the faster) so, in reading aloud a poem of Williams' written in this relative mode, the opening segment (many or few syllabled) is the determinant. As one moves through a poem, the consistency of *duration in time*, though not absolute, can be felt, registered, experienced—not in a blatant or obtrusive way, but in much the same way that the consistency of traditional metric patterns is felt: as a *cohesive* factor. In *The Pound Era* Kenner records a conversation with William Carlos Williams in 1957. Kenner asks (conversant though he was with Pound's definition of rhythm as "a form cut in TIME"), "Did he mean . . . each line to take up the same time?" Williams, he recounts, "at once said Yes; then he said, More or less."

That "Yes" is clear and unequivocal; nor does the added "more or less" take it back, but simply qualifies it in the same degree that any traditional prosodist would note that an absolutely unvarying rhythm, with no inverted feet, no departures

26

of any kind from a rigid norm, is deadly dull and inexpressive: some "give," some "more-or-less-ness" is required.

If duration in time, not number of syllables nor of stresses (or accents), is the simple, open secret of the variable foot, what determines which words go into which foot? *Why* are some words—being few or of few syllables, or even monosyllables—stretched, or their surrounding silences given more than average importance, so that they may, taken together, form a foot as long as another which contains a larger number of polysyllabic words uttered with rippling rapidity? Why should not some of the latter have gone into the preceding few-syllabled segment? The answer is no different from that with which the same question would (by my lights) be met had it been asked concerning any modern poem written in non-traditional forms: the ultimate determinant of what goes into a line is the totality of the demands of expressiveness, comprising intellectually comprehensible syntax, sensuous and expressive musicality (including variation of pace), and above all the emotional charge—delicate or forceful—of content. Each of these interpenetrates the others. The more fully wrought the poem, the less discrete each of its strands.

This assertion leads me to consider in what way the poems written before the triadic line became Williams' prevailing mode differ from the latter in rhythmic organization. If duration in time was not, in these, the cohesive structural factor, what was? One finds in them that "pulse"—a rhythm experienced underneath all else, yet rarely "heard," just like our heartbeats—which is essential to any good poem (and which distinguishes non-traditional, non-re-useable forms from mere formless free verse, though the latter term is widely employed to allude to poems which deserve a better definition). And it is my conviction that the source of this pulse, this subliminally registered ground-bass, this verbal analogue for such unifying elements in visual art as an unobtrusively recurring hue or a subtly echoing series of diagonals, is a *dominant* (not a relentless) number of strong stresses per line, often with an alternation—usually irregular in frequency of occurrence—of another number of strong stresses. So that (rather than the steady march of two strong stresses in each line that Winters, juggling natural enunciation a bit to demonstrate his point, claimed for "The Widow's Lament in Springtime") we get in one poem, if we count strong stresses only, a definite dominance of three, let's say, with a goodly number of twos and a *sprinkling* of ones or fours or even more disparate numbers per line; or in another poem, fives may dominate, with threes a strong second and here and there the odd six or four; and so forth. The shorter the poem the less variation, otherwise a sense of dominant stress will have no chance to accrue. And in a longer poem the balance may shift, gradually, to a different figure.

This unifying pattern of stresses is written by ear and out of the feeling-tone of the content, not by conscious scansion; but the vigilance of ear and sensitivity are as "crafty" as in the work of syllable-counting or the maintenance of traditional meters. In the case of Williams, his aural alertness was towards the speech around him, but this focus of his attention as listener and as maker was held in tension with a peculiarly distinctive high rhetoric very different from common speech. I think this tension contributes greatly to the abiding interest of his diction, rhythms and syntax, which are both more intense and more lofty than so much contemporary work supposedly influenced by him but which is flat and flabby, devoid of that aristocratic and eccentric inner voice Williams engages in counterpoint with the notation of external voices. His typical use, within a generally demotic phraseology—which is unobtrusive as *diction* even when its images startle—of such turns as "save only" ("lifeless/save only in / beauty, the kernel / of all seeking" . . .), "by what" ("passionately biased / by what errors of conviction"), "were it not" ("Were it not for the March within me, . . . I could not endure"), contribute, along with other syntactic idiosyncrasies, to this important stylistic tension.

An example—not outstanding but representative—can be found in "Approach to a City" (*Collected Poems, Volume II, 1939–1962*). The poem begins with the vernacular "*Getting through with** the world"; moves through four stanzas of images, simple in diction but giving, in their precision, the "shock of recognition." Then, in the last stanza, though without recourse to a recherché vocabulary, the whole poem lifts, culminating in the language of the inner voice:

> I never tire of these sights
> but refresh myself there
> always for *there is small holiness*
> *to be found in braver things**

To demonstrate the kinds of stress-dominance I've spoken about I've chosen a poem which does not clearly manifest this peculiar counterpoint of diction since it is an intimate conversation between Williams and his ancient mother—two very articulate people.

The Horse Show

4	Cónstantly néar you, I néver in my entíre
5	síxty-four yeárs knéw you so wéll as yésterday
4	or hálf so wéll. We tálked. You were néver
3	so lúcid, so disengáged from all éxigencies
4	of pláce and tíme. We tálked of oursélves,
4	íntimately, a thíng never heárd of betweén us.
5	How lóng have we wáited? álmost a húndred yéars.
3	You saíd, Unléss there is some spárk, some
4	spírit we keép within oursélves, lífe, a
4	contínuing lífe's impóssible—and it is áll
4	we háve. There is no óther life, ónly the óne.

*(My italics)

4   The wórld of the spírits that cómes áfterward
5   is the sáme as our ówn, júst like yóu sítting
4   thére they come and tálk to me, júst the sáme.

4   They come to bóther us. Whý? I sáid. I dón't
4   knów. Perhaps to fínd out whát we are dóing.
3   Jeálous, do you thínk? I dón't know. I
4   dón't know whý they should wánt to come báck.
2   I was réading about some mén who had been
3   búried under a moúntain, I sáid to her, and
4   óne of them came báck after twó mónths,

3   dígging himself oút. It was in Swítzerland,
3   you remémber? Of coúrse I remémber. The
4   víllagers thó't it was a ghóst coming dówn
2   to compláin. They were fríghtened. They
3   dó come, she saíd, what you cáll
3   my "vísions." I tálk to them júst as I
4   am tálking to yóu. I sée them pláinly.

4   Óh if I could ónly reád! you don't knów
3   what adjústments I have máde. Áll
4   I can dó is to trý to live óver agaín
3   what I knéw when your bróther and yóu
4   were chíldren—but I cán't álways succéed.
2   Téll me about the hórse show. I have
3   been wáiting all wéek to héar about it.

4   Móther dárling, I wasn't áble to get awáy.
4   Óh that's too bád. It was júst a shów;
4   they máke the hórses wálk up and dówn
3   to júdge them by their fórm. Oh is thát
3   all? I thó't it was something élse. Óh
4   they júmp and rún tóo. I wísh you had been
4   thére, I was só ínterested to heár about it.

Here I find 4 to be the dominant number of strong stresses
per line: 23 out of 42 lines; 3 is the secondary dominance, with
13 lines, and there are 3 each of 5 and 2.

Read the poem aloud without any thought of traditional prosodic feet or of counted syllables, but paying minute attention to *what* is being said and in what mood, in this poignant dialogue; I hope the logic of my scansion will then be apparent.

It may be helpful, in studying the rhythms of this or other poems, to mark off with a musical "phrasing mark" those cadences which override syntactic units, especially those which "swallow" some words, giving them minimal emphasis. (Such cadences, in common speech as well as poetry, run counter to syntactic logic, or coincide with it only incidentally.) Here for instance are a few examples of this method:

Cónstantly néar you, I néver in my entíre

(Note that though I've marked 4 strong stresses for this line, it has 3 cadence units.)

You sáid, Unléss there is some spárk, some

(Again: 3 stresses, but only 2 cadence units.)

You remémber? Of cóurse I re mémber. The

víllagers thó't it was a ghóst coming dówn

(Note that the speech cadence break in the penultimate example cuts right through the word "remember," in the same way that a line-break occasionally divides a word in modern poems.) A principle that emerges from this phrase-marking seems to be that the end of the cadence unit occurs just before one of the strong stresses and just after a "swallowed," minimally stressed syllable—in other words, when that particular combination (of the extremes of unstressed and strong-stressed) appears. Not all strong stresses follow notably unstressed syllables.

Unless the poem is given physical embodiment—voiced reading—it is not possible to fully evaluate, to weigh and measure, the components of its sonic character. This does not imply that silent reading (if "sounded out" in the mind) should be abandoned as inferior; but its limitations (and virtues) need to be more clearly recognized by most readers. Both silent and voiced reading are needed for the fullest experience of a poem.

How do Williams' pre-triadic line poems differ from the triadic ones? An effect of the triadic line seems to me to be a certain stateliness of pace, even though individual line-segments may move swiftly. Thus they seem peculiarly appropriate to his late years, expressing formally a hard-earned wisdom. But wherein lies the principal difference between the two kinds of Williams poem when we consider them with a view to better comprehension of his prosodic theories? Clearly the cadences I have pointed out partake of the character of what he later named the variable foot. However, rather than the organizing principle being parity of *duration* as in the triadic lines, the earlier poems depend upon the less conscious phenomenon of focal stresses around which the syllables cluster in variable (or as Winters called them, unlimited) numbers. But this does not imply that the "pulse" provided by focal strong stresses is absent from the triadic, duration-organized structures. Williams did not abandon it, but absorbed it into the triadic mode. An examination of that process is not within the scope of this essay. My hope for the preceding pages is simply to clarify a subject which has been considered more difficult than it is or else contemptuously dismissed as illusory. Williams *did* know what he was doing, and it worked.

Williams and the Duende

(1972)

THOUGH IN WILLIAM CARLOS WILLIAMS there is what I
have thought of sometimes as a Franciscan sense of wonder that
illumines what is accounted ordinary—

> I never tire of the mystery
> of these streets: the three baskets
> of dried fruit in the high
>
> bar-room window, the gulls wheeling
> above the factory, the dirty
> snow—the humility of the snow that
> silvers everything and is
>
> trampled and lined with use.
>
> *(Approach to a City)*

—an illumination reminiscent of Chardin's still-lifes and his
paintings of servants among their kitchen utensils (indeed parts
of Proust's beautiful essay on Chardin read like a description of
this aspect of Williams); and though, as I first read him, this
quiet and tender celebration deepened for me, as a great writer
always does for his readers, some latent capacity in myself to
see the world more freshly: yet my strongest sense of his vision, as I grow older, is of the way it encompasses the dark, the
painful, the fierce.

33

This is the time of year
when boys fifteen and seventeen
wear two horned lilac blossoms
in their caps—or over one ear

. . .
They have stolen them
broken the bushes apart
with a curse for the owner—

Lilacs—

They stand in the doorways
on the business streets with a sneer
on their faces

adorned with blossoms

Out of their sweet heads
dark kisses— . . .

(*Horned Purple*)

Williams's fierce delight in the contradictions of life is not a passive acceptance, a kind of fatalism. He is anguished, he rails against stupidity and gracelessness and man's inhumanity to man. "The Mind's Games" is one of his little-known political poems; he writes in it that to a human being at a moment of ecstasy and completion, the world

. . . is radiant and even the fact
of poverty is wholly without despair.

So it seems until there rouse
to him pictures of the systematically
starved—for a purpose, at the mind's
proposal. . . .

. . .
Beauty should make us paupers,
should blind us, rob us—for it
does not feed the sufferer but makes

> his suffering a fly-blown putrescence
> and ourselves decay—unless
> the ecstasy be general.

There are many other poems of his which, in differing degrees
of overtness, are of political import; so pervasive was the historical sense in him that there is virtually nothing he wrote
that does not—especially within the context of his work as a
whole—have social implications. "In Chains" (from *The Wedge*,
1944) seems to me one of the most interesting, and least known,
of twentieth-century political poems:

> When blackguards and murderers
> under cover of their offices
> accuse the world of those villainies
> which they themselves invent to
> torture it—we have no choice
> but to bend to their designs,
> buck them or be trampled while
> our thoughts gnaw, snap and bite
> within us helplessly—unless
> we learn from that to avoid
> being as they are, how love
> will rise out of its ashes if
> we water it, tie up the slender
> stem and keep the image of its
> lively flower chiseled upon our minds.

It has, however, a flaw of logic: he poses as choices, (1) to bend
to their designs, to go along with the system and be a party to
its crimes; (2) to buck them; (3) to neither buck them, that is,
struggle in rebellion against their designs, nor become complicit, but suffer ourselves to be trampled while inwardly—
helpless—our thoughts gnaw at us; or (4) to learn "from that"—
i.e., apparently from the equal negativity of the first three
alternatives—to "avoid being as they are." The lapse in logic

occurs when Williams fails to develop a definition of what "bucking them"—resistance—might be and why he is treating it as a negative. It cannot be because he sees it has small chance of succeeding; Williams consistently manifested a love of "pure grit," putting a high value on boldness, daring, a refusal to resignedly anticipate defeat. He loved generosity, and was moved not by the ingenious prudence of Ben Franklin but by the rash and adventurous Aaron Burr. The shad making their way "unrelenting" upstream, the two starlings landing backward, facing "into the wind's teeth," are images central to Williams; and one finds throughout his work variations on that theme of defiance—as, for example, in the little poem that forms part one of the three-part "A History of Love"—

> And would you gather turds
> for your grandmother's garden?
> Out with you then, dustpan and broom;
> she has seen the horse passing!
>
> Out you go, bold again
> as you promise always to be.
> Stick your tongue out at the neighbors
> that her flowers may grow.

Is it then, as the fourth choice implies, that resistance *without* keeping the image of love's "lively flower chiseled on our minds" is self-defeating, because a struggle uninformed by love and compassion makes of the rebel a mirror image of the executioner—the ultimate irony of co-option? This is what it means to me—and I like to think Williams, though he was never a political revolutionary (except in the *implications* of much of his work) and was rather repelled than enthused by the left-wing politics of his day, meant it to convey to the reader that meaning I attribute to it. But the way in which he lets the syntax slide him past "buck them" without defining qualification deflects some of the impact. It is a flaw of form, of form considered as *revelation* of content, not as something imposed upon it, and which should therefore not stop short of all possible lucidity consonant with not oversimplifying. Not seldom Williams, in the prose as well as the poetry—or perhaps oftener, indeed, in prose—gives inadequate attention to detail, fails to follow all the way through, as if he were in too much haste to get on to the next matter. This may have been the price paid for his amazing productivity as an artist even while leading to the full the busy life of a doctor. Given the wealth and vigor of his artistic output, I have always found petty and unresponsive to the point of absurdity the caviling of those critics who have loftily characterized him as "lacking in intellectual force" and so on. He had in fact a sweep and depth of original intellectual insight. If one takes a close look, what gave a handle to even his sympathetic, "favorable" critics when they dismissed him as "even less logical than the average good poet . . . an 'intellectual' in neither the good nor the bad sense of the word" (Randall Jarrell) or as a man whose "pronouncements on poetry and poetics are almost never of such a quality as would force us to take them seriously" (Hyatt Waggoner) was not the invalidity of his concepts (and certainly not the *absence* of concepts, as some anthologists who try to reduce him to a sort of witless imagist miniaturist would have one suppose), but simply the occasional impulsive abandonment of a piece of writing before checking out all of its nuts and bolts. In its positive aspect this can be regarded as a manifestation of his largeness, his boldness, in contrast to the compulsive perfectionism of many a smaller, less fertile imagination, though it results in a good deal of frustration for his admirers.

But in speaking of his vision as encompassing the darkness, wildness, fierceness of life as well as celebrating the ordinary, I'm thinking not only of his political/historical/social understanding, his grappling with America, his constantly taking up the challenge to deal with his time and place, but also of the deep and equally pervasive sense of loneliness and strangeness I find in his poetry. The fairly early "Lighthearted William" "twirls his November moustaches" and sighs "gaily" (this delightful poem has a certain kinship with some of Stevens's short poems), but the world on which he looks out is the same "fearful" one of the even earlier "Winter Sunset," where

> Then I raised my head
> and stared out over
> the blue February waste
> to the blue bank of hill
> with stars on it
> in strings and festoons—
> but above that:
> one opaque
> stone of a cloud
> just on the hill
> left and right
> as far as I could see;
> and above that
> a red streak, then
> icy blue sky!
>
> It was a fearful thing
> to come into a man's heart
> at that time; that stone
> over the little blinking stars
> they'd set there.

Nowadays Williams is "taught" in the colleges and presumably widely read—but what does this teaching and reading amount to? I am constantly meeting people who have been taken, bewildered, on a tour of *Paterson* without any reference to *The Wanderer*, the early poem in which so many clues to the understanding of *Paterson* are embedded (which is in fact one of those early works in which the whole subsequent development of an artist is shadowed forth prophetically), and equally without reference to the rest of his work except for the tiresomely familiar and basically unrevealing anthology "specimens," such as "The Red Wheelbarrow" and "The Yachts." Or else they have read some of the really late poems—"Asphodel, That Greeny Flower," perhaps—again with no sense of what led up to them during a whole lifetime. I don't mean to imply that "Asphodel," for example, does not very firmly stand as a work of art on its own supreme merits; nor that a student eighteen or nineteen years old has not the ability to respond to it; but surely few readers of any age are likely to receive Williams most rewardingly by beginning with a poem whose content is a summing up, a testament prepared for by a whole lifetime of other work, and whose formal structure has likewise grown slowly out of a long development, a long history of experimentation and exploration. A strictly chronological approach is not necessary; it is often fascinating and revealing to read concurrently works from different periods of any writer's life; but a tendency in the formal study of Williams—even among individuals reading him of their own free choice—has been a *reverse* chronology that does not even lead all the way back to the beginnings but leaves readers ignorant of all the earlier work except for the small selection Randall Jarrell edited.* Few students are brought to recognize, and rarely discover for themselves, the high degree of his relevance to contemporary concerns, to the daily questions of "how to live, what to do" that they have such a hungry need to ask and answer and for which they are given (in the childhood and student years) so poor a provision for doing so.

How different Williams, re-explored, is from the stereotypes too often presented even by his supposedly sympathetic critics. These stereotypes give the impression of a poet of inadequate intellectual underpinnings, essentially prosaic—a leveller who,

---

* In 1985 a more comprehensive *Selected Poems*, edited by Charles Tomlinson, superceded that volume.

determinedly democratic, pulled language down from lyric heights; they imply that a reader hungering for illumination rather than information, for numinous song rather than flat, if precise, statement, or for challenging ideas rather than depictions, had best look elsewhere.

One can indeed find information and statement in his poems, and many instances of isolated or assembled reportages, consciously and deliberately undertaken, sometimes as exercises (he never ceased training himself to listen to the rhythms of common speech), sometimes as parts of an "ideogrammic," Poundian construction (the prose quotations in *Paterson* can be perceived as Williams' adaptation of Pound's method of demonstration by documentary collage rather than by authorial discourse). And those elements of his work have their own value. But there is so much more to him!—more music, more magic, more *duende*. Perhaps "soul," in the Afro-American sense, is the closest approximation to the word *duende*, which a standard Spanish dictionary translates merely as "elf, hobgoblin, ghost." It was *soul* that, as Garcia Lorca tells in his famous essay on the *duende*, the famous Flamenco singer lacked as she sang with such skill, but which fired her later as she flung herself, hoarse and strident, into the song beyond song. Williams' not very well-known poem "The Sound of Waves" suggests a whole exploratory poetics, leading to such *goings-beyond*—beyond the brilliantly conceived and perfectly executed, beyond facile closures. It is a poem not so much about poetry as about experiencing the creative venture: the poet-voyager comes to that place where he asks himself the eternal human/artistic question, "How to proceed? How, and where, do I go from here?" Williams moves by a process of elimination towards an image in which the mist, rain, sea-spume of language is blown against jutting rock, and by the encounter is changed, as if the impact shocks the vague drift of inchoate words into granite utterance. It is as if for every projection and

crevice in the rock a converse crevice and projection takes substantial form in the mist. But that transformation (brought
about by a confrontation with a level of reality arrived at in the
course of the questing journey—a reality that may be the recognition of mortality) is perceived by the voyager as the journey's *end* only for a long moment. There is a line of dots across
the page—and then the dynamic of exploration resumes, not as
further movement across a space but as a deepening of listening
attention *in* the place to which movement has brought it:

> . . . . .
>
> Past that, past the image:
> a voice!
> out of the mist
> above the waves and
>
> the sound of waves, a
> voice   .   speaking!

It is a poem that, starting dubiously with the question, "A
quatrain? Is that / the end I envision?" propels itself from point
to point, awkward and hesitant at first, then picking up speed
and direction, pulling the reader along with it to a place where
(by shared revelation, not by exposition) it is discovered that an
end can—or must—precede a beginning. (Who would have
expected to find such consonance between Williams and Eliot!)
Beyond and above known image, known sound, there opens to
us the prospect of the poem beyond the poem. . . .

The poetics implied by "The Sound of Waves" is not a
matter of applied metrics but of *following through* the meta-
morphic stages of experience with a persistence that is open to
whatever may befall. It risks the abyss, it endures the cloud of
unknowing, it yields itself to fiery light. Doc Williams, shrewd,
practical, skeptical, as some admirers see him and as he liked

41

to present himself (even *to* himself), was at the same time a poet ("I am, I am a poet"—he repeats in "The Desert Music") with all of the archetypal poet's resemblance to the archetypal mystic.

"The Sound of Waves" embodies a poetics inseparable from the rest of human experience and—*not* because of its content but by its very nature, its forms, its sensuous forms that are its very essence—expresses and defines the nature of humanness; and in so doing arrives at the edge of the world, where all is unknown, undefined, the abyss of the gods. From there at last, beyond the human,

       a voice   speaks.

Like most artists of large scope and complex substance, Williams cannot be narrowly categorized as Apollonian or Dionysian, classic or romantic. His lifelong concern with structure and technique, his insistence on the need for "measure," a certain aristocratic elegance of gesture in the turn of phrases, the impeccable completeness and brevity of countless "little" poems, the tone of controlled passion, austere, sober, solemn, we hear tolling in the very late long poems—these could be called Apollonian. But if the Apollonian form-sense is the bones of an art, the intuitive, that which is pliant, receptive— but not docile!—rather abandoning itself fiercely, recklessly, to experience—is the flesh and blood of it, and this is Dionysian. As a young man he committed himself to the Muse; She had cried to him,

    . . . "Haia! Here I am, son!
    See how strong my little finger is!
    Can I not swim well?
    I can fly too!" And with that a great sea-gull
    Went to the left, vanishing with a wild cry—
    But in my mind all the persons of godhead
    Followed after . . .

42

and he responded with the realization that,

> I know all my time is forespent!
> For me one face is all the world!
>
> (*The Wanderer*)

—the face of a Muse who is both wild gull and godhead, "marvelous old woman" and "horrible old woman; mighty, crafty, feared and beloved." The reader who would know Williams must know his diversity and experience the plunge of the understanding into his frightening depths.

Written in 1972 and delivered as an Elliston Lecture at the University of Cincinnati in the spring of 1973.

The Ideas in the Things

(1983)

THERE ARE MANY MORE "ideas" in William Carlos Williams' "things" than he is commonly credited with even today; and this is true not only of *Paterson* and the post-Patersonian, clearly meditative poems in triadic lines, but also of a great deal of his earlier work. Because he did write numerous poems that are exercises in the notation of speech or in the taking of verbal Polaroid snapshots, it is assumed that many other short- or medium-length poems of his are likewise essays in the non-metaphorical, the wholly objective. And because he said (in his introduction to *The Wedge*, 1944), "Let the metaphysical take care of itself, the arts have nothing to do with it," it is forgotten that he immediately added: "They will concern themselves with it if they please." It is not noticed that he himself frequently *did* so please. Williams, for much of his life, did take on, it is true, the task of providing for himself and others a context of objective, anti-metaphysical aesthetic intent in order to free poetry from the entanglement of that sentimental intellectualism which only recognizes the incorporeal term of an analogy and scorns its literal, sensuous term. This view denies the equipoise of thing and idea, acknowledging only a utilitarian role for the literal (as if it were brought into existence expressly and merely to articulate the all-important abstract term), rather than perceiving concrete images as the very *incarnation* of thought. This view insults the imagination, for the imagination does not reject its own sensory origins but illuminates them, and connects them with intellectual and intuitive experience. Williams, working against that insult to imagination, needed to assert a confidence in the actuality and value of observable phenomena as well as a recognition of the necessity of sensory data to the life and health of poetry. But by so doing he incurred much misunderstanding from his admirers (not to speak of his detractors) and, I suspect, endured a good deal of (mainly unacknowledged) inner conflict; for he was frequently obliged to betray his stated principles in favor of the irresistible impulse toward metaphor, which is at the heart of *poiesis*.

I find it interesting to sort out, in the *Collected Poems: Vol. I, 1909–1939*, those poems which are indeed snapshots, descriptive vignettes, notations of idiom and emphasis (as are some of the very late short poems also), from those which have unobtrusively the resonance of metaphor and symbol.

The mystery and richness of *further significance* which such poems of his possess is akin to what R. H. Blyth delineated for us in his commentaries on Japanese haiku. The allusive nature of the Zen art, possible only in a culture alert to the ubiquity of correspondences and familiar with an elaborate symbology, has of course no exact parallel in twentieth-century America; yet Blyth could have been evoking the art of Williams when he quoted this haiku by Kyoroku,

> even to the saucepan
> where potatoes are boiling—
> a moonlit night

and commented, "It is only when we realize that the moon is in the saucepan with the potatoes that we know the grandeur of the moon in the highest heaven. It is only when we see a part that we know the whole."

Readers who come to Williams' pre-Patersonian or pre-*Desert Music* poems with the expectation of simple depictive Imagism or of a classic, ascetically single-visioned objectivity (which was not in fact the stated aim of the Objectivists, incidentally) miss these resonances, that sense of discovering, in a vivid part, the adumbration of an unnamed but intensely intuited whole. They forego the experience of becoming aware, precisely through the physical *presentness* of what is *de*noted, of the other presentness—invisible but palpable—of what is *con*noted. They come to the poems solely for the Things; but inherent in the Things are the Ideas.

I'd like to present two examples along with a running commentary on what I believe is to be found beneath their surfaces.

"The Farmer," the third poem from *Spring and All* is not a depiction of a farmer that compares him to an artist, but vice versa. Read thus, as a portrait of the artist, each of its images has a double meaning. The literal *is there*, vivid in every detail. But climate, landscape, everything takes on, along with (not instead of) its denotative significance, a symbolic one. The poet is a *farmer*, one who tends the land of language and imagination and its creatures, who makes things grow, poem-things, story-things, not out of nowhere but out of the ground on which he walks. At present the rain is falling, the climate is cold and wet, as was the critical climate of the time for Williams the poet; he is exposed to that wet and cold, and his fields—the fields of his art—are apparently empty. But he's trudging around *in* that climate and *in* the fields of language, calmly, hands in his pockets, intent on imagining the future poems; and the rain prepares the soil and the seeds. "On all sides / the world rolls coldly away"—he's left quite alone with his imagination. The orchard trees are black with the rain, but it is spring (the preceding prose has announced, "Meanwhile, SPRING, which has been approaching for several pages, is at last here," and the poem states that it is March). Soon those trees (the deep-rooted anatomy of what grows from his terrain) will be white with blossom: there are implied poems in this superficially unpromising landscape; and the very isolation in which the poet is left by the world gives him "room for thought." His dirt road (his own road among his fields) is sluiced (and thus deepened) by the rain that will help the seeds to sprout. He's not a small, lost figure in nature, this artist farmer—he "looms" as he moves along past the scratchy brushwood that, trimmed and dried, will make good tinder. The poet is *composing* as he goes, just as a farmer, pacing his fields on a Sunday at the end of winter, composes in his mind's eye a picture of spring growth and summer harvest. He is an *antagonist*—but to what? To the hostility of the environment, which, however, contains the elements that will nourish his crops. And in what sense? In the sense of the struggle to compose—not to *im*pose order but to *com*pose the passive elements into a harvest, to grow not tares but wheat.

"A Morning Imagination of Russia" is a poem I'm very fond of and which, besides being full of implication and resonances, has many of the qualities of a short story (indeed, as well as being set in Russia, it has a flavor or tone quite Chekhovian); it is a part of *The Descent of Winter*. Webster Schott's selection from Williams' prose and poetry, *Imaginations*, restored the full context of that series as well as of *Spring and All;* and Schott, unlike some of Williams' critics, doesn't treat him as wholly lacking in thought. Nevertheless, intent upon an enthusiastic but careless reading of this poem (which sees it as speaking figuratively of Williams' own situation vis-à-vis American poetry), Schott misses the clear drama of its narrative. He quite unjustifiably claims that it depicts Williams himself on an imaginary visit to Russia after the revolution, whereas (however much he may be a projection of the poet's sensibility) it seems to me quite clear that the protagonist is not intended as a persona in the sense of a mere mask for the self, but as a more fully projected fictive personage, a member of the intelligentsia who is casting his lot with the masses. The time is very early in the revolution. Nothing has yet settled down. No new repressive bureaucracy has yet replaced the old oppression. The whole atmosphere is like that of a convalescent's first walk in pale sunshine after a time when bitter storms in the world outside paralleled his inner storm of fever and life-and-death struggle. It begins:

> The earth and the sky were very close
> When the sun rose it rose in his heart

The dawn is, equally, an actual one and the dawn of an era. And he feels one with it.

> It bathed the red cold world of
> the dawn so that the chill was his own

The red is the red of sunrise *and* of revolution.

> The mists were sleep and sleep began
> to fade from his eyes . . . .

The mists are both morning mists and the mists of the past, of prerevolutionary sleep. His consciousness is changing.

> . . . . below him in the
> garden a few flowers were lying forward
> on the intense green grass where
> in the opalescent shadows oak leaves
> were pressed hard down upon it in patches
> by the night rain . . . .

The beauty of flowers and grass, opalescent shadows, patches of rain-soaked dead oak leaves, is vividly evoked. It can all be read with validity as pure, precise description. But it too has a doubleness; the whole scene has been through a night of storm, the flowers are bowed forward by it, the grass is more vividly green than it would have been without it, but parts of the grass

48

are hidden and half-smothered by the fallen brown leaves. All this is the counterpart of his own experience and of events in the historical moment. The flowers and common grass of his own life, after the storm, are more vivid and yet almost broken—and some of his life is gone, fallen like the leaves, gone with the lives and the ways of living fallen in war and revolution.

> . . . . There were no cities
> between him and his desires
> his hatreds and his loves were without walls
> without rooms, without elevators
> without files, delays of veiled murderers
> muffled thieves, the tailings of
> tedious, dead pavements, the walls
> against desire save only for him who can pay
> high, there were no cities—he was
> without money—

> Cities had faded richly
> into foreign countries, stolen from Russia—
> the richness of her cities—

Here, deep in rural Russia, deep into the attempt to construct a new society, he is not impeded by the complexities of urban, Westernized Russia. His nature, with its desires, hatreds, loves, is out in the open; and the "city" here clearly stands for more than an architectural and demographic agglomeration, but for the money values of capitalism. He has no money—but here and now he does not need it. All the desirable content of Russia's cities has been stolen away, gone West with the emigrés.

> Scattered wealth was close to his heart
> he felt it uncertainly beating at
> that moment in his wrists, scattered
> wealth—but there was not much at hand

The "scattered wealth" he feels (scattered like money and jewels dropped by fleeing thieves) is his own and Russia's—it has not been, and cannot be, wholly robbed, absconded with. He feels that, feels it close. But also he feels a tickling wave of nostalgia:

> Cities are full of light, fine clothes
> delicacies for the table, variety,
> novelty—fashion: all spent for *this*.
> Never to be like that again:
> the frame that was. It tickled his
> imagination. But it passed in a rising calm.

He feels a nostalgia for all which (for now, anyway, and perhaps forever) must be given up for the sake of the new thing yet to be defined. The old context, the frame, gone. But now "*this*": the "few flowers," the vividness he will know.

That wave of nostalgia passes in a *rising* calm—not the sinking calm of resignation, but a lift of the spirits.

> Tan dar a dei! Tan dar a dei!

> He was singing. Two miserable peasants
> very lazy and foolish
> seemed to have walked out from his own
> feet and were walking away with wooden rakes
> under the six nearly bare poplars, up the hill

> There go my feet.

Singing with lifted spirits (singing, one notices—and there is an irony in this—that medieval refrain we associate with spring, love and courtesy, ancient forests, knights errant, and troubadours), he feels as much one with the peasants he watches from his window as he had with the chill red dawn. He sees them as lazy and foolish, as well as miserable, just as he might have done from the viewpoint of prerevolutionary class privilege: he does not idealize them; but the difference is that now he identifies with them, lazy and foolish as they are, and with their task—to rake away rubbish, perhaps dead leaves—to which they must go *uphill*. "There go my feet."

> He stood still in the window forgetting
> to shave—
>
> The very old past was refound
> redirected. It had wandered into himself
> The world was himself, these were
> his own eyes that were seeing, his own mind
> that was straining to comprehend, his own
> hands that would be touching other hands
> They were his own!
> His own, feeble, uncertain . . .

In this new world—around him and within him—he finds ancient roots, not the immediate past which has been razed but the "*very old* past," taking new directions. Identified with what is happening historically, he feels himself a microcosm; the proposition invites reversal—it is not only that he is intimately and intensely involved but that, just as his mind strains to comprehend, so the mind of the peasants, the mind of all Russia collectively, strains to see, to comprehend. His hands, though, reaching out to touch others, are feeble and uncertain; and so are the hands of the multitude.

> . . . He would go
> out to pick herbs, he graduate of
> the old university. He would go out
> and ask that old woman, in the little
> village by the lake, to show him wild
> ginger. He himself would not know the plant.

He will go humbly, as pupil of the old peasant, the ancient root wisdom, not as teacher of others.

A horse was stepping up the dirt road
under his window

—a live thing moving on unpaved earth: not merely a descriptive detail but a metaphor.

He decided not to shave. Like those two [*the two peasants*]
that he knew now, as he had never
known them formerly. A city, fashion
had been between—

Nothing between now.

He would go to the soviet unshaven. This
was the day—and listen. Listen. That
was all he did, listen to them, weigh
for them. He was turning into
a pair of scales, the scales in the
zodiac.

This is evidently the day of the regular meeting of the local soviet, which he is attending not for the first time (as one can gather from the syntax), and it is also the day of a new access of consciousness and resolve, a *first* day in some sense. He puts his university education at the service of the community. Perhaps he weighs physical supplies—grain, fertilizer, medicines—bringing particular professional skills into play: that's not specified. But there's more to weighing than that. He not only feels, with a mixture of humility and amusement, that he becomes his function, becomes a pair of scales, but that they are the zodiacal scales, charged with moral, mythical, and psychological symbolism.

But closer, he was himself
the scales . . .

That is, not only did his work of weighing transform him into a function, but he was anyway, intrinsically, an evaluator, he realizes.

> . . . The local soviet. They could
> weigh . . .

In his new sense of identification with his fellows, others too become intrinsically, as humans, evaluators.

> . . . If it was not too late.

That is, if too much damage had not already been done; too much for the revolution to have a future; too much for that human ability to measure for themselves, to evaluate justly, to manifest itself among the many.

> . . . He felt
> uncertain many days. But all were uncertain
> together and he must weigh for them out
> of himself.

His "weighing" is a service he performs as an intellectual, contributing his ability to listen closely, which has been trained by education. But his judgments must be made out of a commitment, a center in himself, and not merely abstractly, perfunctorily. It is "out of himself," his very substance, that he must act.

> He took a small pair of scissors
> from the shelf and clipped his nails
> carefully. He himself served the fire.

He reasserts his education, maintains his standards of hygiene and decent appearance. But to attend to the fire in his hearth himself—this is new for him. To use his hands, with their clean, clipped nails. And that fire: it is literal, and it is the fire of life, hope, revolution. Now he soliloquizes:

> We have cut out the cancer but
> who knows? perhaps the patient will die.

He reiterates his own realistic uncertainty. Then he proceeds to define the "patient," which is not solely Russia, a country in the throes of total reorganization:

> The patient is anybody, anything
> worthless that I desire, my hands
> to have it— . . .

Lines which I would gloss thus: anybody, anything albeit *considered* "worthless" that I desire, my hands *desiring* to have it: that is to say, the "patient" is the sum of things that, though the world think them tawdry, assigning them no value, Williams consistently sees as having the glitter of life: cats' eyes in the dark: "Beautiful Thing," "Melon flowers that open/about the edge of refuse"; "the small/yellow cinquefoil in the /parched places." Or those starlings in the wind's teeth. And, too, the "patient" whose survival is in question is desire itself, the desire to touch that aliveness with bare hands,

> . . . —instead of the feeling
> that there is a piece of glazed paper
> between me and the paper—invisible
> but tough running through the legal
> processes of possession—

That glazed top sheet, a transparent obstacle to touch, covers the surface even of the documents that proclaim possession of what is desired, and thus cancels out the *experience* of possession.

54

>   —a city, that
>   we could possess—

That is, *my hands desire to have a city that we could possess*. (The syntax is clearer here if instead of dashes before the word "instead" and after the word "possession" we enclose those lines in parentheses.) A city, then—unlike the cities that have "faded richly / into foreign countries" and were only to be enjoyed by those who "can pay high"—that would embody an accessible life.

>   It's an art, it's in
>   the French school.

>   What we lacked was
>   everything. It is the middle of
>   everything. Not to have.

Here both "it's" refer back to the "patient" in the sense of that quality of immediacy which, in the prose passage immediately preceding "A Morning Imagination of Russia" in the *Descent of Winter* sequence and dated only one day before it, Williams had said was the very goal of poetry: "poetry should strive for nothing else, this vividness alone, *per se*, for itself," and further, "The vividness *which is* poetry." So, "*It's* in art, in the French school"—here he draws on his own educated knowledge and experience, on all that make him different from those two "miserable, lazy, and foolish" peasants—and also "*It* is the middle of everything"—*it* is not *only* in art but in all kinds of things, common experience, and here he reasserts his sense of brotherhood. But "What we lacked was everything . . . *Not to have*," was what, till now, we experienced. I am reminded here of Wallace Stevens' lines, "That's what misery is, / Nothing to have at heart." Both the intellectual (because of his sense of that invisible wall of glazed paper between him and life), and oppressed and ignorant people have hitherto been cut off from the "everything" in the middle of which are found the sparks of vivid beauty; they have experienced only *not having*, absence.

> We have little now but
> we have that

[The "it," the sparks, the poetry.]

> We are convalescents. Very
> feeble. Our hands shake. We need a
> transfusion. No one will give it to us,
> they are afraid of infection. I do not
> blame them. We have paid heavily. But we
> have gotten—touch. The eyes and the ears
> down on it. Close.

The whole people is convalescent from the convulsions of revolution. The transfusion they need is not forthcoming—seen historically, this would have meant international support for their experiment instead of an economic and psychological blockade. But other nations, other governments, were scared. The protagonist, like a true Chekhovian character, says he can't blame them; he sees what scares them, and why—he is not doctrinaire. And he recognizes that a great price has been paid and will perhaps be further exacted. But what has been gained is precisely what he has desired: touch itself. Williams the doctor knew how the touch of hand could diagnose, cure, bring to birth; his fictive Russian knows the imagination as an intimate form of touch without which all is dull, hopeless, ashen. What he celebrates here, at the end of the poem— returning to its opening, when earth and sky are close, known, touched with the imagination—is the sun rising in his heart.

The prose which immediately follows the poem and is dated four days later, begins with the words, "Russia is every country, here he must live. . . ." And a few pages further on Williams breaks off from diverse topics to return to the protagonist of the poem, in these sentences, "—He feels the richness, but a distressing feeling of loss is close upon it. He knows he must coordinate the villages for effectivenes in a flood, a famine." I see two ways of reading that, and they are complementary, not conflicting. If, as I've been doing, one reads the poem without disregard for its narrative reality, the truth of its fiction, and thus the universality of the poem's Russia—"every country; here he must live"—then the richness that "he," the protagonist, feels is the richness of new beginnings, the reassertion of the "very old" past and also the democratic "everything" of human experience. The "distressing feeling of loss" that comes close upon it concerns the equally real subtleties, nuances, desirable complexities—that "scattered wealth" he earlier felt "beating at his wrists"—which as yet we have not figured out how to attain in any social system without a sacrifice of justice and mercy. But one can also read "A Morning Imagination of Russia" somewhat as Webster Schott chose to do, that is, as a parable of Williams' poetic struggle in the 1920s (it was written in 1927). According to the first reading, the hero's recognition of the need to "coordinate the villages for effectiveness in a flood, a famine," reminds one of Chekhov's letters in the early 1890s when he was an unpaid local medical inspector during the cholera epidemic. If one looks beyond the Russian scene (set just a few years before the writing of *The Descent of Winter*) to an analogy in Williams' own struggles to establish a new sense of poetry and the imagination in the American 1920s, we may see in those words about coordinating the villages an almost Poundian missionary spirit; then one takes the "villages" to be outposts of intelligent poetry and the flood or famine as aspects of the hostile or uncomprehending world of readers, critics, other poets, and the public at large.

Webster Schott, reintroducing *The Descent of Winter* in 1970, saw it *entirely* as Williams' struggle "to verbalize a theory of contemporary poetry" and "to realize a clear conception of himself as an artist." That is partially true; but when Williams wrote the words, "We have paid heavily. But we/have gotten—touch," he was not speaking in a vacuum, as if from an airtight aesthetic island: the political images with which, in "A Morning Imagination," he had chosen to work, do not *only* have meaning as metaphor, as figurative ways to speak about literature. Those images work as Chekhovian narrative description; they work as implications of political ideas; *and* they work as analogies for the poet's need to act in society, humbly and with an understanding that in trying to serve the commonweal he will serve also his own need for intimate experience of the living mystery. Ideas without Things are vaporous, mere irritants of the detached and insensate intellect; but Things abound and are chockablock with the Ideas that, thus incorporate, dance and stumble, groan or sing, calling and beckoning to one another, throughout the decades of his poetry.

Williams and Eliot

(1989)

IN ENGLAND WHEN I was growing up, Eliot was compla-
cently counted as an *English* poet. Though I knew he was born
in America, it was quite a jolt to discover, when I first came
over here, that in the States he was claimed without qualification as an American. Although I learned to acknowledge this
many years ago, I have nevertheless continued to think of him
as in full possession of a kind of European urbanity that could
take the cultural palimpsest for granted. But perhaps in fact he
suffered in some degree from a lack of confidence under that
urbane shell, a self-consciousness detectable also in the even
more urbane Henry James (who analyzed it so beautifully in
others that one tends not to suspect it in *him*). I used to notice,
when I was new to America, how frequently the topic of conversation was *what it meant to be American, and what America
was*. This constant need for self-definition astonished me; in
England—or in France, Italy, Holland—I had never encountered a similar preoccupation. Now I have come to see that not
only Williams's overt concern for how to be a specifically *American* artist, but also Eliot's emphasis on the need to deliberately
learn a tradition, manifests that peculiarly American need.

This idea is of special interest to me, because it helps me
understand my own feeling, which increases as I grow older,
of being substantially "out of sync" with American culture
even though I've spent nearly four decades here, and was so

strongly—and I believe beneficially—influenced by William Carlos Williams. I'm "out of sync" because I have never related to European, or specifically English, literary tradition with that poignant concern and discomfort, that sting of self-consciousness. I don't say this smugly, for it seems to me that this sting can often be turned to advantage by individual artists. It can become the subject, if not the very ground, of a life's work. It's something which I've had to manage without, just as I've had to manage without the deep sense of roots in a particular town or countryside which is so valuable to many writers.

It has been suggested that if Williams had read Eliot without prejudice he might have seen in him a "comrade-in-arms" engaged in a process parallel to his own, impelled by as personal a need. If Williams and Eliot had simply been writing poems, without manifestoes, might they have learned to appreciate one another? Did the intellectual and aesthetic theories of each obstruct any mutual perception of their art itself? I don't think one can sweep away the grounds for conflict between them so easily, though one certainly wishes that open and fruitful engagement had occurred in place of sterile antagonism.

In a transcribed interview published in *Quarterly West* in 1976 my response to the question of what it was about Eliot that annoyed Williams so much was that I thought it had to do:

> less with Eliot's diction than with his *rhythmic* structures. It was that lack of rhythmic energy, that sort of slump of the line that has to drag itself wearily up into the next one; I think *that* was probably the thing about Eliot that Williams felt was setting back American poetry. He was talking about the structure of the poems, about language, and I think that that was the basic thing . . . not concepts, attitudes toward life, philosophy, ethics, politics, but what was actually happening from word to word and line to line in the language of Eliot's poems. . . .

Fifteen years later I see it as a more complex and less conscious matter. (I have also, in the meantime, been able to return to a more positive personal response to Eliot's poems, particularly the "Four Quartets." But that is because I can relate to Eliot's adopted Englishness in a way impossible for Williams.)

What Steven Friedman, in a paper given at the MLA in 1988, characterized as anxiety, even desperation, in Eliot's plea for the immolation of individuality on the altar of tradition, does indeed find an echo in Williams' lifelong, and perhaps no less anxious, search for an indigenous and modern set of formal principles: standards that would act as a preventative to just that formless "self-expressive" flow which too often, alas, has been taken as "Williams influence" in poets who have misunderstood what he was after, and who (like his antagonists) fail to see how principled his own prosody was.

But an inescapable contrast between Williams and Eliot is apparent in Eliot's insistence on the necessity for a poet to absorb "the whole literary history of Europe," while Williams, though also emphasizing the need to comprehend history, focuses on what happened on this continent, and therefore (despite the Eric the Red chapter of *In the American Grain*, which might be considered a somewhat irrelevant prelude) on relatively modern, post-Columbian history. For Eliot, the writer's education must begin with Homer. For Williams, it is not even *literary* history that the writer must know, but the story of the body politic in relation to the American continent. Both sought, in these contrasting ways, to avoid the fatal feebleness of a colonial culture's dependence on a distant mother-country; they recognized that every artist, or at least every Western or modern artist, must establish his or her own ground, must "prove upon the pulses," in Keats' phrase, the principles of poetic action. If this is not achieved, a debilitating provincialism will ensue.

Not only in *In the American Grain* but throughout his work

Williams struggles with this: how to grasp (and the tragedy of not grasping) the newness of the New World—how to make of it a sovereign ground and not a cultural colony. In "Against the Weather" he instances the naming by English Puritans of a large redbreasted thrush: robin, they called it, not really looking—just because the sparrow-sized European robin, so utterly different in personality, also is redbreasted. What he deplored was a lack of attention—and it is attention, fearless and objective, that he applauds in his idealized Daniel Boone. Williams' depiction of Daniel Boone (while I'm sure it bears little resemblance to the historical truth) exemplifies the determining characteristic for membership in his personal pantheon, which transcends both national and merely personal significance because it points to an essential quality: what he imagined in Boone was that Boone, with that intense attention, took what he saw for what it was, a pristine phenomenon, not imposing preconceptions formed upon another continent. Such attentiveness, with the respect for otherness which it implies, is essential to poets; but Williams sought, found, and valued it also in others. It was bound up with his idea of "how to be American," a personal variation of the myth of "the fresh start."

Here I'll digress for a moment to mention that I've come to feel a certain element is regrettably lacking in this program of Williams': whether in the chapters on Spanish conquistadores, on English Puritans and counter-Puritans, on a Père Sebastien Râsles or a Daniel Boone, Native Americans are evoked by Williams in a role subsidiary to that of the White main characters he chose to examine. Pocahontas remains as exotic as the Aztec empire. He never, unfortunately, attempted some respectful appropriation of Native American culture as a possible element of the ground for his art; and in failing to do so he committed the same error that he deplored in the colonists. Such appropriation can be offensive if it lacks humility—but if Williams were alive now he might empathize with the recogni-

tion that there is a wisdom in Native American spiritual traditions which Americans of any ethnic origin would do well to
learn from, in the same way that a few Australians of European
origin have begun to try and learn from Aboriginal culture. To
fault Williams for not including some focus on African-
American experience or on women would be unhistorical; *In
the American Grain* was, after all, written in 1925, not the 1980s.
But to have explored the Native American experience would
have been in line with his thesis and his studies, and such
minor writers as Mary Austin (in *The American Rhythm*) were
already trying to undertake such an exploration.

How wide the distance was between the cultural concerns of
Williams and Eliot is brought home by the fact that while one
may regret that Williams did not go deeper into the indigenous
life of the continent, such a concern would not even occur to
one in relation to Eliot, to whom Amerindian spirituality
would have seemed irrelevant precisely because it had *not* been
absorbed into Western art and culture.

But other kinds of loyalties also were a factor in their mutual
lack of regard—Williams' disdain so explicit, Eliot's implicit in
his silence. Surely Williams' negative attitude came in part
from simple jealousy of Ezra Pound's friendship with Eliot.
Ezra's decision to live in Europe did not seriously undermine
the warm personal affection Williams had for him as the pre-
eminently stimulating friend of his youth. Instead, the resent-
ment Williams felt at Pound's chosen exile was displaced onto
Eliot, all the more so because of Pound's enthusiastic view of
Eliot, whom he characterized to Harriet Monroe as "the *only*
contemporary poet who is adequately prepared for his task."
Williams may never have seen that particular remark, but the
spirit of it surely reached and stung him.

Then, too, even aside from intellectual disagreements, can
one discount temperamental differences which in themselves
might have made the two men dislike each other if they had
met? In contrast to Williams' gusto, at which he himself pokes

63

fun in "Smell" ("must you have a part in *everything?*" he says to his nose), Eliot describes himself, in his essay on "Goethe as the Sage," as combining "a Catholic cast of mind, a Calvinistic heritage, and a Puritanical temperament." He was by nature fastidious and patrician. There was a deeply felt ethical and emotional disharmony in the contrast between Williams' love for the courage and ingenuity he perceived in the poor and disenfranchised, his love for the untutored but vivid turns of phrase he heard among his patients (at a time when the originalities of folk speech were not yet eroded by the media), and the distaste with which the uneducated masses are presented in Eliot's poems. Williams was by temperament democratically expansive, and he relished the ingenuity of anyone who, having little or nothing, *makes do* and contrives solutions. "It's the anarchy of poverty / delights me," he wrote, and "I never tire of the mystery / of these streets . . . / . . . I never tire of these sights / but refresh myself there / always, for there is small holiness / to be found in braver things."

I recently heard Robert Giroux and others reminiscing about Eliot at a celebration of his centenary, and it is clear he was a man of great honor and urbane charm; I myself experienced this kindness when he took the trouble to write me quite a long letter of advice when I was only twelve. Williams could be charming too but not urbane. He would have found Eliot's smooth, scholarly, aristocratic ways pompous; and in all probability Eliot would have been equally irritated by some quality in Williams—perhaps by his enthusiasm and spontaneity, his very *lack* of urbanity. Williams was not a wild man, not a Bohemian; but he was rough, *craggy* in comparison with Eliot's polished surface, which is palpable not only in his recorded voice but in the rhythms of his prose—even if, as has been recorded, he did know the lyrics of pop songs by heart. Eliot was polished even at his most lighthearted, and his practical cats are surely denizens of a rather Edwardian London, where class differences are both important and accepted.

I dislike a too biographical approach to literature, the approach Proust criticized for subjecting the visions of creative imagination to impertinent analysis as mere reflections of personal psychology. But to talk about Eliot and Williams' lack of appreciation for each other as if it were exclusively a matter of intellect, of reasoned stance, is to ignore the reality of that lack of sympathy's social and emotional context. It may be true, as Michael Davidson has suggested, that if an Eliot had not existed Williams would have had to invent one; but the actual Eliot not only provided him with opposing *ideas* on which to test his own, but presented a personality I believe he would not have found congenial even in an intellectual ally.

To the temperamental predispositions of each was added the contrast of their youthful experiences. Eliot was a Harvard student at a period when that involved, to a much greater degree than today, a formative reenforcement of unquestioned privilege. Such an education causes a person to take certain conditions for granted, as if they were universal: an allusion to childhood, if made by economically and socially privileged person, may, for example, refer to "the nursery bedroom" as if all children were brought up with a night nursery and a daytime nursery and a nanny. Uneducated people who live in furnished rooms and spend their evenings in pubs will seem to them to be of another species. In a world of class privilege it is easy to indulge a temperamental reserve. This does not imply that Eliot was some kind of monster of insensitivity—only that he was much more representative of, and formed by, a well-defined background than Williams. While Williams was never poor, the contrasting backgrounds of his parents and, early and late, his close contact with the lives of those who *were* poor, freed his work from those tell-tale allusions and unconscious assumptions which occur in the writings of people who live within the limits of a defined class. Williams, going straight from Horace Mann to medical school, did not obtain a thorough classical, scholarly education like Eliot and Pound, but, following his nose, his lively and robust curiosity about people, plunged straight from medical school into the blood and guts of Hell's Kitchen and then to the years of GP and obstetric practice in New Jersey. All of this brought him into constant contact with a world unknown to Eliot. The ideas and aesthetics of each, then, existed in differing social contexts which each sometimes reflected and sometimes transcended. When we fail to take into account such contexts in examining works of literature, we are reflecting a similar failure prevalent in other spheres of life—a kind of parochialism which addresses symptoms not causes, or isolates a single cause from its interrelation with other causes. We can see this in medicine, in education, in the way social problems are addressed, and most of all in the way ecological disasters result from the disregard of the complex interdependence of all things.

To think about the antagonism between Williams and Eliot and their conflicting aesthetics may be useful not only in studying their work but in helping a person clarify his or her own aesthetic values—siding with one or the other or arriving at some personal synthesis. But one's understanding and evaluation will be skewed if their argument is divorced from a biographical and sociological context.

Some Notes on Organic Form

(1965)

FOR ME, BACK OF the idea of organic form is the concept that there is a form in all things (and in our experience) which the poet can discover and reveal. There are no doubt temperamental differences between poets who use prescribed forms and those who look for new ones—people who need a tight schedule to get anything done, and people who have to have a free hand—but the difference in their conception of "content" or "reality" is functionally more important. On the one hand is the idea that content, reality, experience, is essentially fluid and must be given form; on the other, this sense of seeking out inherent, though not immediately apparent, form. Gerard Manley Hopkins invented the word "inscape" to denote intrinsic form, the pattern of essential characteristics both in single objects and (what is more interesting) in objects in a state of relation to each other, and the word "instress" to denote the experiencing of the perception of inscape, the apperception of inscape. In thinking of the process of poetry as I know it, I extend the use of these words, which he seems to have used mainly in reference to sensory phenomena, to include intellectual and emotional experience as well; I would speak of the inscape of an experience (which might be composed of any and all of these elements, including the sensory) or of the inscape of a sequence or constellation of experiences.

A partial definition, then, of organic poetry might be that it is a method of apperception, i.e., of recognizing what we perceive, and is based on an intuition of an order, a form beyond forms, in which forms partake, and of which man's creative works are analogies, resemblances, natural allegories. Such poetry is exploratory.

How does one go about such a poetry? I think it's like this: first there must be an experience, a sequence or constellation of perceptions of sufficient interest, felt by the poet intensely enough to demand of him their equivalence in words: he is *brought to speech*. Suppose there's the sight of the sky through a dusty window, birds and clouds and bits of paper flying through the sky, the sound of music from his radio, feelings of anger and love and amusement roused by a letter just received, the memory of some long-past thought or event associated with what's seen or heard or felt, and an idea, a concept, he has been pondering, each qualifying the other; together with what he knows about history; and what he has been dreaming— whether or not he remembers it—working in him. This is only a rough outline of a possible moment in a life. But the condition of being a poet is that periodically such a cross section, or constellation, of experiences (in which one or another element may predominate) demands, or wakes in him this demand: the poem. The beginning of the fulfillment of this demand is to contemplate, to meditate; words which connote a state in which the heat of feeling warms the intellect. To contemplate comes from "*templum*, temple, a place, a space for observation, marked out by the augur." It means, not simply to observe, to regard, but to do these things in the presence of a god. And to meditate is "to keep the mind in a state of contemplation"; its synonym is "to muse," and to muse comes from a word meaning "to stand with open mouth"—not so comical if we think of "inspiration"—to breathe in.

So—as the poet stands open-mouthed in the temple of life, contemplating his experience, there come to him the first words of the poem: the words which are to be his way in to the poem, if there is to be a poem. The pressure of demand and the meditation on its elements culminate in a moment of vision, of crystallization, in which some inkling of the correspondence between those elements occurs; and it occurs as words. If he forces a beginning before this point, it won't work. These words sometimes remain the first, sometimes in the completed poem their eventual place may be elsewhere, or they may turn out to have been only forerunners, which fulfilled their function in bringing him to the words which are the actual beginning of the poem. It is faithful attention to the experience from the first moment of crystallization that allows those first or those forerunning words to rise to the surface: and with that same fidelity of attention the poet, from that moment of being let in to the possibility of the poem, must follow through, letting the experience lead him through the world of the poem, its unique inscape revealing itself as he goes.

During the writing of a poem the various elements of the poet's being are in communion with each other, and heightened. Ear and eye, intellect and passion, interrelate more subtly than at other times; and the "checking for accuracy," for precision of language, that must take place throughout the writing is not a matter of one element supervising the others but of intuitive interaction between all the elements involved.

In the same way, content and form are in a state of dynamic interaction; the understanding of whether an experience is a linear sequence or a constellation raying out from and into a central focus or axis, for instance, is discoverable only in the work, not before it.

Rhyme, chime, echo, reiteration: they not only serve to knit the elements of an experience but often are the very means, the sole means, by which the density of texture and the returning or circling of perception can be transmuted into language, apperceived. A may lead to E directly through B, C, and D: but if then there is the sharp remembrance or revisioning of A, this return must find its metric counterpart. It could do so by actual repetition of the words that spoke of A the first time (and if this return occurs more than once, one finds oneself with a refrain—not put there because one decided to write something with a refrain at the end of each stanza, but directly because of the demand of the content). Or it may be that since the return to A is now conditioned by the journey through B, C, and D, its words will not be a simple repetition but a variation . . . Again, if B and D are of a complementary nature, then their thought- or feeling-rhyme may find its corresponding word-rhyme. Corresponding images are a kind of nonaural rhyme. It usually happens that within the whole, that is between the point of crystallization that marks the beginning or onset of a poem and the point at which the intensity of contemplation has ceased, there are distinct units of awareness; and it is—for me anyway—these that indicate the duration of stanzas. Sometimes these units are of such equal duration that one gets a whole poem of, say, three-line stanzas, a regularity of pattern that looks, but is not, predetermined.

When my son was eight or nine I watched him make a crayon drawing of a tournament. He was not interested in the forms as such, but was grappling with the need to speak in graphic terms, to say, "And a great crowd of people were watching the jousting knights." There was a need to show the tiers of seats, all those people sitting in them. And out of the need arose a formal design that was beautiful—composed of the rows of shoulders and heads. It is in very much the same way that there can arise, out of fidelity to instress, a design that is the form of the poem—both its total form, its length and pace and tone, and the form of its parts (e.g., the rhythmic relationships of syllables within the line, and of line to line; the sonic relationships of vowels and consonants; the recurrence of images, the play of associations, etc.). "Form follows function" (Louis Sullivan).

Frank Lloyd Wright in his autobiography wrote that the idea of organic architecture is that "the reality of the building lies in

70

the space within it, to be lived in." And he quotes Coleridge: "Such as the life is, such is the form." (Emerson says in his essay "Poetry and Imagination," "Ask the fact for the form.") The *Oxford English Dictionary* quotes Huxley (Thomas, presumably) as stating that he used the word organic "almost as an equivalent for the word 'living.'"

In organic poetry the metric movement, the measure, is the direct expression of the movement of perception. And the sounds, acting together with the measure, are a kind of extended onomatopoeia—i.e., they imitate not the sounds of an experience (which may well be soundless, or to which sounds contribute only incidentally), but the feeling of an experience, its emotional tone, its texture. The varying speed and gait of different strands of perception within an experience (I think of strands of seaweed moving within a wave) result in counterpointed measures.

Thinking about how organic poetry differs from free verse, I wrote that "most free verse is failed organic poetry, that is, organic poetry from which the attention of the writer had been switched off too soon, before the intrinsic form of the experience had been revealed." But Robert Duncan pointed out to me that there is a "free verse" of which this is not true, because it is written not with any desire to seek a form, indeed perhaps with the longing to avoid form (if that were possible) and to express inchoate emotion as purely as possible.* There is a contradiction here, however, because if, as I suppose, there is an inscape of emotion, of feeling, it is impossible to avoid presenting something of it if the rhythm or tone of the feeling is given voice in the poem. But perhaps the difference is this: that free verse isolates the "rightness" of each line or cadence—if it seems expressive, then never mind the relation of it to the next; while in organic poetry the peculiar rhythms of the parts are in

---

*See, for instance, some of the forgotten poets of the early 20s—also, some of Amy Lowell—Sandburg—John Gould Fletcher. Some Imagist poems were written in "free verse" in this sense, but by no means all.

some degree modified, if necessary, in order to discover the rhythm of the whole.

But doesn't the character of the whole depend on, arise out of, the character of the parts? It does; but it is like painting from nature: suppose you absolutely imitate, on the palette, the separate colors of the various objects you are going to paint; yet when they are closely juxtaposed in the actual painting, you may have to lighten, darken, cloud, or sharpen each color in order to produce an effect equivalent to what you see in nature. Air, light, dust, shadow, and distance have to be taken into account.

Or one could put it this way: in organic poetry the form sense or "traffic sense," as Stefan Wolpe speaks of it, is ever present along with (yes, paradoxically) fidelity to the revelations of meditation. The form sense is a sort of Stanislavsky of the imagination: putting a chair two feet downstage there, thickening a knot of bystanders upstage left, getting this actor to raise his voice a little and that actress to enter more slowly; all in the interest of a total form he intuits. Or it is a sort of helicopter scout flying over the field of the poem, taking aerial photos and reporting on the state of the forest and its creatures—or over the sea to watch for the schools of herring and direct the fishing fleet toward them.

A manifestation of form sense is the sense the poet's ear has of some rhythmic norm peculiar to a particular poem, from which the individual lines depart and to which they return. I heard Henry Cowell tell that the drone in Indian music is known as the horizon note. Al Kresch, the painter, sent me a quotation from Emerson: "The health of the eye demands a horizon." This sense of the beat or pulse underlying the whole I think of as the horizon note of the poem. It interacts with the nuances or forces of feeling which determine emphasis on one word or another, and decides to a great extent what belongs to a given line. It relates the needs of that feeling-force which dominates the cadence to the needs of the surrounding parts and so to the whole.

Duncan also pointed to what is perhaps a variety of organic poetry: the poetry of linguistic impulse. It seems to me that the absorption in language itself, the awareness of the world of multiple meaning revealed in sound, word, syntax, and the entering into this world in the poem, is as much an experience or constellation of perceptions as the instress of nonverbal sensuous and psychic events. What might make the poet of linguistic impetus appear to be on another tack entirely is that the demands of his realization may seem in opposition to truth as we think of it; that is, in terms of sensual logic. But the apparent distortion of experience in such a poem for the sake of verbal effects is actually a precise adherence to truth, since the experience itself was a verbal one.

Form is never more than a *revelation* of content.

"The law—one perception must immediately and directly lead to a further perception" (Edward Dahlberg, as quoted by Charles Olson in "Projective Verse," *Selected Writings*). I've always taken this to mean, "no loading of the rifts with ore," because there are to be no rifts. Yet alongside this truth is another truth (that I've learned from Duncan more than from anyone else)—that there must be a place in the poem for rifts too—(never to be stuffed with imported ore). Great gaps between perception and perception which must be leapt across if they are to be crossed at all.

The *X*-factor, the magic, is when we come to those rifts and make those leaps. A religious devotion to the truth, to the splendor of the authentic, involves the writer in a process rewarding in itself; but when that devotion brings us to undreamed abysses and we find ourselves sailing slowly over them and landing on the other side—that's ecstasy.

First published in *Poetry*, Vol. 106, No. 6, September 1965; reprinted in *New Directions in Prose and Poetry 20*, 1968.

On the Need for
New Terms
(1986)

ALL DISCUSSION OF CONTEMPORARY poetics is vitiated by the lack of a more precise terminology. I constantly hear poets, teachers, and students refer to "writing in forms" on the one hand, by which they mean the traditional forms, and to "free verse" on the other, a term utilized for every kind of poem that is not written in a traditional form. The logical implication of this usage is that the non-traditional is formless; whereas in fact a sense of form is vital to the creation of any work of art. "Free verse" is an inappropriate term: instead of suggesting the inventive development and exploration of new forms (which are typically not re-usable, because expressive of a particular unique Gestalt), it implies the rejection of every restriction. But the sense of form, of composition, balance, inner harmony, always necessitates certain restrictions—selectivity, precise choices in every area of the poem (whether in cadence and lineation, diction, stanza length, etc.)—which, for the poet using non-reusable forms, are voluntary, not imposed by the established rules of preconceived forms. The closest analogy is the laws of conscience contrasted with the laws of the state. (Obviously, the two often coincide—but woe betide anyone who assumes they are necessarily identical, and thus loses his conscience!) Just as "free verse" is a misnomer for non-traditional poetry directed by a scrupulous aesthetic conscience, so "forms," unqualified by the word "traditional" or an equivalent, reflects a parallel misinterpretation of motive and practice: the logical implication is that only pre-decided forms partake of the *qualities* of form (such as balance, interior dynamic, auditory and intellectual shapelines, etc.) and that only their practitioners have a proper sense of composition. (It may even suggest that obeying the rules automatically imparts formal success.)

A refined terminology would benefit both those whose preference and natural bent is for the traditional, or closed, modes, and those whose bent and preference is for exploratory or open modes. And it would be equally useful to readers, not only to writers and teachers. I am not, and never have been, trying to align people on one side of an "open v. closed" controversy; my concern is to clean up the terminology, get some decent ground rules for discussion.

At the same time, of course, I would like people to better understand *how* the kind of poetry I and many others write *works*, so that it will be *heard* better (out loud or with the inner voice). When Richard Wilbur, who has written some of the most beautiful, supremely elegant and pleasurable poems of our time, visited a writing workshop at Stanford a few years ago, he revealed very clearly that he simply did not understand the structure of those poems by students that were written in open forms: he read them aloud with no regard to linebreaks, to tonal differentiations indicated by indentations, or to other non-traditional techniques; and so, though he sometimes picked out an image or a contextual approach for praise or blame, he missed the sounds and the rhythms entirely. Yet he has a most complete understanding of traditional prosody. I would like to see as much comprehension of the *standards* by which non-traditional forms can be evaluated—that is, of their *formal qualities*—as of those in traditional forms.

The existing gap in technical understanding between traditionalists and explorers is damaging to poetry itself, because it precludes the full experience of a great many wonderful poems.

75

A parallel phenomenon is the shocking inability of many students who have only read non-traditional poetry to scan traditional poetry properly. That evidence of aural insensitivity is something we all deplore; but when non-traditionally formed poems are equivalently mangled, it goes unrecognized and undeplored.

The inability to scan traditional poems correctly is due to ignorance and laziness: the rules are fully available, and if an individual has no natural "ear" he or she can at least learn to read correctly. The inability to scan non-traditional forms is due sometimes to inflexibilities of expectation on the part of those who are skilled in traditional prosody, but more often to the refusal of the non-traditional practitioners to adopt and utilize a common terminology and a common recognition of the *functions* of the various techniques they use. Many imitate their contemporaries without thinking, without consideration for the roots and *raisons d'etre* of their methods. Like sloppy amateur carpenters who use tools at random, hit or miss, they don't bother to find out what special properties their tools may have, what options their tool-chests offer. Knowing what the options are is not aesthetically prescriptive or partisan, but simply a basis for artistic action.

An adequate terminology is clearly necessary to these understandings. A refined terminology can only evolve out of serious contemplation, study, and practice; but for that to occur we need at least an adequate working vocabulary. Can we not agree to begin by always qualifying the word "form" or "forms" by the words "traditional" or "classical" or "reusable," and by dropping the term "free verse" except in a particular historical context (the *vers libre* movement and its English-language followers) or critically, to describe a certain invertebrate sort of poem that meanders along in search, perhaps, of its still undiscovered form? What then would we substitute for the term "free verse"? I have almost given up using the word "organic" since it has been taken up by the shampoo manufacturers; it may be some time before it is restored to its proper place. "Open forms," the term proposed by Stephen Berg and Robert Mezey in *Naked Poetry*, is vague and does not apply precisely to non-traditional forms which have a strong sense of closure. "Nonce forms," a term used by the editors of the anthology-textbook, *Strong Measures*, is not bad—though I've already discovered that my students are unfamiliar (O tempora . . . !) with the expression "for the nonce," so it will seem obscure to many. I think the best word that I've come up with so far, other than the temporarily incapacitated "organic," is "exploratory." The inscape of the subject, the instress of its perception, the options for their articulation, are *explored* by the non-traditionalist in ways which result in a form peculiar to that occasion. But I have no rigid adherence to "exploratory form" as the best possible substitute for "free verse" and would be delighted to adopt a better one if someone would provide it.

My passion is for the vertebrate and cohesive in all art. I believe any distinction between form and that which lacks form can only be a distinction of art from non-art, not of kinds of art. That some forms are not reusable does not mean that they are not forms, i.e., possessed of formal qualities equal to those of the reusable. This simple truth will never be clearly recognized until we cease to lump the inept with the intricately evolved— until we develop, and consistently use, an appropriate terminology.

On the Function of the Line

(1979)

NOT ONLY HAPLESS ADOLESCENTS, but many gifted and justly esteemed poets writing in contemporary nonmetrical forms, have only the vaguest concept, and the most haphazard use, of the line. Yet there is at our disposal no tool of the poetic craft more important, none that yields more subtle and precise effects, than the linebreak if it is properly understood.

If I say that its function in the development of modern poetry in English is evolutionary I do not mean to imply that I consider modern, nonmetrical poetry "better" or "superior" to the great poetry of the past, which I love and honor. That would obviously be absurd. But I do feel that there are few poets today whose sensibility naturally expresses itself in the traditional forms (except for satire or pronounced irony), and that those who do so are somewhat anachronistic. The closed, contained quality of such forms has less relation to the relativistic sense of life which unavoidably prevails in the late twentieth century than modes that are more exploratory, more open-ended. A sonnet may end with a question; but its essential, underlying structure arrives at *resolution*. "Open forms" do not necessarily terminate inconclusively, but their degree of conclusion is—structurally, and thereby expressively—less pronounced, and partakes of the open quality of the whole. They do not, typically, imply a dogmatic certitude; whereas, under a surface, perhaps, of individual doubts, the structure of the sonnet or the heroic couplet bears witness to the certitudes of these forms' respective epochs of origin. The forms more apt to express the sensibility of our age are the exploratory, open ones.

In what way is contemporary, nonmetrical poetry exploratory? What I mean by that word is that such poetry, more than most poetry of the past, incorporates and reveals the *process* of thinking/feeling, feeling/thinking, rather than focusing more exclusively on its *results;* and in so doing it can explore human experience in a way that is not wholly new but is (or can be) valuable in its subtle difference of approach: valuable both as human testimony and as aesthetic experience. And the crucial precision tool for creating this exploratory mode is the linebreak. The most obvious function of the linebreak is rhythmic: it can record the slight (but meaningful) hesitations between word and word that are characteristic of the mind's dance among perceptions but which are not noted by grammatical punctuation. Regular punctuation is a part of regular sentence structure, that is, of the expression of completed thoughts; and this expression is typical of prose, even though prose is not at all times bound by its logic. But in poems one has the opportunity not only, as in expressive prose, to depart from the syntactic norm, but to make manifest, by an intrinsic structural means, the interplay or counterpoint of process and completion—in other words, to present the dynamics of perception *along with* its arrival at full expression. The linebreak is a form of punctuation *additional* to the punctuation that forms part of the logic of completed thoughts. Linebreaks—together with intelligent use of indentation and other devices of scoring—represent a peculiarly *poetic*, alogical, parallel (not competitive) punctuation.

What is the nature of the alogical pauses the linebreak records? If readers will think of their own speech, or their silent inner monologue, when describing thoughts, feelings, perceptions, scenes or events, they will, I think, recognize that they frequently hesitate—albeit very briefly—as if with an unspoken question—a "what?" or a "who?" or a "how?"—before nouns, adjectives, verbs, adverbs, none of which require to be preceded by a comma or other regular punctuation in the course of syntactic logic. To incorporate these pauses in the rhythmic structure of the poem can do several things: for example, it allows the reader to share more intimately the experience that is being articulated; and by introducing an alogical counter-rhythm into the logical rhythm of syntax it causes, as they interact, an effect closer to song than to statement, closer to dance than to walking. Thus the emotional experience of empathy or identification plus the sonic complexity of the language structure synthesize in an intense aesthetic order that is different from that which is received from a poetry in which metric forms are combined with logical syntax alone. (Of course, the management of the line in *metrical* forms may also permit the recording of such alogical pauses; Gerard Manlèy Hopkins provides an abundance of evidence for that. But Hopkins, in this as in other matters, seems to be "the exception that proves the rule"; and the alliance of metric forms and the similarly "closed" or "complete" character of logical syntax seems natural and appropriate, inversions notwithstanding. Inversions of normal prose word order were, after all, a stylistic convention, adopted from choice, not technical ineptitude, for centuries; although if utilized after a certain date they strike one as admissions of lack of skill, and indeed are the first signs of the waning of a tradition's viability.) It is not that the dance of alogical thinking/feeling in process *cannot* be registered in metric forms, but rather that to do so seems to go against the natural grain of such forms, to be a forcing of an intractable medium into inappropriate use—whereas the potential for such use is implicit in the constantly evolving nature of open forms.

But the most particular, precise, and exciting function of the linebreak, and the least understood, is its effect on the *melos* of the poem. It is in this, and not only in *rhythmic* effects, that its greatest potential lies, both in the exploration of areas of human consciousness and in creating new aesthetic experiences. *How* do the linebreaks affect the melodic element of a poem? So simply that it seems amazing that this aspect of their function is disregarded—yet not only student poetry workshops but any magazine or anthology of contemporary poetry provides evidence of a general lack of understanding of this factor; and even when individual poets manifest an intuitive sense of how to break their lines it seems rarely to be accompanied by any theoretical comprehension of what they've done right. Yet it is not hard to demonstrate to students that—given that the deployment of the poem on the page is regarded as a score, that is, as the visual instructions for auditory effects—the way the lines are broken affects not only rhythm but *pitch patterns*.

Rhythm can be sounded on a monotone, a single pitch; melody is the result of pitch patterns combined with rhythmic patterns. The way in which linebreaks, observed respectfully as a part of a score (and regarded as, say, roughly a half comma in duration), determine the pitch pattern of a sentence, can clearly be seen if a poem, or a few lines of it, is written out in a variety of ways (changing the linebreaks but nothing else) and read aloud. Take, for instance, these lines of my own (picked at random from *Relearning the Alphabet:* Four Embroideries: III Red Snow):

> Crippled with desire, he questioned it.
> Evening upon the heights, juice of the pomegranate:
> who could connect it with sunlight?

Read them aloud. Now try reading the same words aloud from this score:

> Crippled with desire, he
> questioned it. Evening
> upon the heights,

> juice of the pomegranate:
> who
> could connect it with sunlight?

Or:

> Crippled
> with desire, he questioned
> it. Evening
> upon the heights, juice
> of the pomegranate:
> who could
> connect it with sunlight?

Etc.

The intonation, the ups and downs of the voice, involuntarily change as the rhythm (altered by the place where the tiny pause or musical "rest" takes place) changes. These changes could be recorded in graph form by some instrument, as heartbeats or brain waves are graphed. The point is not whether the lines, as I wrote them, are divided in the best possible way; as to that, readers must judge for themselves. I am simply pointing out that, read naturally but with respect for the linebreak's fractional pause, a pitch pattern change *does occur* with each variation of lineation. A beautiful example of expressive lineation is William Carlos Williams' well known poem about the old woman eating plums:

> They taste good to her.
> They taste good
> to her. They taste
> good to her.

First the statement is made; then the word *good* is (without the clumsy overemphasis a change of typeface would give) brought to the center of our (and her) attention for an instant;

then the word *taste* is given similar momentary prominence, with *good* sounding on a new note, reaffirmed—so that we have first the general recognition of well-being, then the intensification of that sensation, then its voluptuous location in the sense of taste. And all this is presented through indicated pitches, that is, by melody, not by rhythm alone.

I have always been thrilled by the way in which the musicality of a poem could arise from what I called "fidelity to experience," but it took me some time to realize what the mechanics of such precision were as they related to this matter of pitch pattern. The point is that, just as vowels and consonants affect the music of poetry not by mere euphony but by expressive, significant interrelationship, so the nuances of meaning apprehended in variations of pitch create *significant, expressive melody* in the close tone range of speech, not just a pretty "tune."

One of the ways in which many poets reveal their lack of awareness about the function of the linebreak is the way in which they will begin a line with the word "it," for instance, even when it is clear from the context that they don't want the extra emphasis—relating to both rhythm and pitch—this gives it. Thus, if one writes,

> He did not know
> it, but at this very moment
> his house was burning,

the word "it" is given undue importance. Another example is given in my second variant of the lines from "Red Snow." The "it" in the third line is given a prominence entirely without significance—obtrusive and absurd. When a poet places a word meaninglessly from the sonic point of view it seems clear that he or she doesn't understand the effect of doing so—or is confusedly tied to the idea of "enjambement." Enjambement is useful in preventing the monotony of too many end-stopped lines in a metrical poem, but the desired variety can be attained by various other means in contemporary open forms; and to take away from the contemporary line its fractional pause (which, as I've said, represents, or rather manifests, a comparable minuscule but affective hesitation in the thinking/feeling process) is to rob a precision tool of its principal use. Often the poet unsure of any principle according to which to end a line will write as if the real break comes after the first word of the next line, e.g.:

> As children in their night
> gowns go upstairs . . . ,

where *if one observes the score* an awkward and inexpressive "rest" occurs between two words that the poet, reading aloud, links naturally as "nightgowns." X. J. Kennedy's definition of a *run-on* line (*Introduction to Poetry*, 1966) is that "it does not end in punctuation and therefore is read with only a *slight pause* after it," whereas "if it ends in a full pause—usually indicated by some mark of punctuation—we call it *end-stopped*." (My italics on "slight pause.") Poets who write nonmetrical poems but treat the linebreak as nonexistent are not even respecting the traditional "slight pause" of the run-on line. The fact is, they are confused about what the line is at all, and consequently some of our best and most influential poets have increasingly turned to the prose paragraph for what I feel are the wrong reasons—i.e., less from a sense of the peculiar virtues of the prose poem than from a despair of making sense of the line.

One of the important virtues of comprehending the function of the linebreak, that is, of the line itself, is that such comprehension by no means causes poets to write like one another. It is a *tool*, not a style. As a tool, its use can be incorporated into any style. Students in a workshop who grasp the idea of *accurate scoring* do not begin to all sound alike. Instead, each one's individual voice sounds more clearly, because each one has gained a degree of control over how they want a poem to sound. Sometimes a student scores a poem one way on paper, but reads it aloud differently. My concern—and that of his or her fellow students once they have understood the problem—is to determine which way the author wants the poem to sound. Someone will read it back to him or her *as written* and someone else will point out the ways in which the text, the score, was ignored in the reading. "Here you ran on,"—"Here you paused, but it's in the middle of a line and there's no indication for a 'rest' there." Then the student poet can decide, or feel out, whether he or she wrote it down wrong but read it right, or vice versa. That decision is a very personal one and has quite as much to do with the individual sensibility of the writer and the unique character of the experience embodied in the words of the poem, as with universally recognizable rationality—though that may play a part, too. The outcome, in any case, is rather to define and clarify individual voices than to homogenize them; because *reasons* for halts and checks, emphases and expressive pitch changes, will be as various as the persons writing. Comprehension of the function of the linebreak gives to each unique creator the power to be more precise, and thereby more, not less, individuated. The voice thus revealed will be, not necessarily the recognizable "outer" one heard in poets who have taken Olson's breath theory all too literally, but rather the inner voice, the voice of each one's solitude made audible and singing to the multitude of other solitudes.

Excess of subjectivity (and hence incommunicability) in the making of structural decisions in open forms is a problem only when the writer has an inadequate form sense. When the written score precisely notates perceptions, a whole—an inscape or gestalt—begins to emerge; and the gifted writer is not so submerged in the parts that the sum goes unseen. The sum is objective—relatively, at least; it has presence, character, and— as it develops—needs. The parts of the poem are instinctively adjusted in some degree to serve the needs of the whole. And as this adjustment takes place, excess subjectivity is avoided. Details of a private, as distinct from personal, nature may be deleted, for example, in the interests of a fuller, clearer, more communicable whole. (By private I mean those which have associations for the writer that are inaccessible to readers without a special explanation from the writer which does not form part of the poem; whereas the personal, though it may incorporate the private, has an energy derived from associations that are shareable with the reader and *are* so shared within the poem itself.)

Another way to approach the problem of subjective/objective is to say that while traditional modes provide certain standards for objective comparison and evaluation of poems as effective structures (technically, at any rate), open forms, used with comprehension of their technical opportunities, *build unique contexts* which likewise provide for such evaluation. In other words, though the "rightness" of its lines can't be judged by a preconceived method of scansion, each such poem, if well written, presents a composed whole in which false lines (or other lapses) can be heard by any attentive ear—not as failing to conform to an external rule, but as failures to contribute to the grace or strength implicit in a system peculiar to that poem, and stemming from the inscape of which it is the verbal manifestation.

The *melos* of metrical poetry was not easy of attainment, but there were guidelines and models, even if in the last resort nothing could substitute for the gifted "ear." The *melos* of open forms is even harder to study if we look for models; its secret lies not in models but in that "fidelity to experience" of which I have written elsewhere; and, in turn, that fidelity demands a delicate and precise comprehension of the technical means at our disposal. A general recognition of the primary importance of the line and of the way in which rhythm relates to melody would be useful to the state of the art of poetry in the way general acceptance of the bar line and other musical notations were useful to the art of music. A fully adequate latitude in the matter of interpretation of a musical score was retained (as anyone listening to different pianists playing the same sonata, for instance, can hear) but at the same time the composer acquired a finer degree of control. Only if writers agree about the nature and function of this tool can readers fully cooperate, so that the poem shall have the fullest degree of autonomous life.

Published in *Chicago Review*, Vol. 30, No. 3, 1979.

Linebreaks, Stanza-Spaces, and the Inner Voice

(1965)

IN AN INTERVIEW WITH me in 1964, Walter Sutton asked me to talk at some length about a short poem of mine. I chose "The Tulips" from *The Jacob's Ladder:*

> Red tulips
> living into their death
> flushed with a wild blue
>
> tulips
> becoming wings
> ears of the wind
> jackrabbits rolling their eyes
>
> west wind
> shaking the loose pane
>
> some petals fall
> with that sound one
> listens for

First, there was the given fact of having received a bunch of red tulips, which I put in a vase on the window sill. In general I tend to throw out flowers when they begin to wither, because their beauty is partly in their *short* life, and I don't like to cling to them. I thought of that sentence of Rilke's about the unlived life of which one can die (*Letters to a Young Poet:* Rilke speaks of "unlived, disdained lost life, of which one can die," August 12, 1904); and, looking at these tulips, I thought of how they were continuing to be fully alive, right on into their last moments. They hadn't given up before the end. As red tulips die, some chemical change takes place which makes them turn blue, and this blue seems like the flush on the cheeks of someone with fever. I said "wild blue" because, as I looked at it, it seemed to be a shade of blue that suggested to me perhaps far-off parts of sky at sunset that seemed untamed, wild. There seem to be blues that are tame and blues that are daring. Well, these three lines constitute the first stanza . . . Then came a pause. A silence within myself when I didn't see or feel more, but was simply resting on this sequence that had already taken place. Then, as I looked, this process continued. You can think of it as going on throughout a day; but when cut flowers are in that state, things happen quite fast; you can almost see them move. The petals begin to turn back. As they turn back, they seem to me to be winglike. The flowers are almost going to take off on their winglike petals. Then "ears of the wind." They seem also like long ears, like jack rabbits' ears turned back and flowing in the wind, but also as if they were the wind's own ears listening to itself. The idea of their being jack rabbits' ears led me to the next line, which is the last line of this stanza, "jackrabbits rolling their eyes," because as they turn still further back they suggest, perhaps, ecstasy. Well, this was the second unit. Then another pause. The next stanza, "west wind / shaking the loose pane," is a sequence which is pure observation without all that complex of associations that entered into the others. The flowers were on the window sill, and the pane of glass was loose, and the wind blew and rattled the pane. This is background.

Is it part of the sound that comes in, as you mentioned earlier?

Yes, although it doesn't really get into the poem quite as sound. Then again a short pause, and then, "some petals fall / with that sound one / listens for." Now, the petals fall, not only because the flowers are dying and the petals have loosened themselves, in death, but also because perhaps that death was hastened by the blowing of the west wind, by external circumstances. And there is a little sound when a petal falls. Now why does the line end on "one"? Why isn't the next line "one listens for"? That is because into the sequence of events entered a pause in which was an unspoken question, "with that sound one," and suddenly I was stopped: "one what?" Oh, "one listens for." It's a sound like the breath of a human being who is dying; it stops, and one has been sitting by the bedside, and one didn't even know it, but one was in fact waiting for just that sound, and the sound is the equivalent of that silence. And one doesn't discover that one was waiting for it, was listening for it, until one comes to it. I think that's all.

I think the line also turns back with the "one." There is a kind of reflexive movement for me, as you read it, emphasizing the solitary nature of the sound. Now in your comments on this poem you have talked mostly about the meanings, the associations of the experience, and their relation to images.

Also, though, about their relation to rhythm, about where the lines are broken and where the silence is, about the rests.

Where the silences fall. Now, "variable foot" is a difficult term. Williams said that it involves not just the words or the phrases but also the spaces between them. Is that your meaning also? That a pause complementing a verbal unit is a part of the sequence of events?

Yes, and the line-end pause is a very important one; I regard it as equal to half a comma, but the pauses between stanzas come into it too, and they are much harder to evaluate, to measure. I think that what the idea of the variable foot, which is so difficult to understand, really depends on is a sense of a pulse, a pulse behind the words, a pulse that is actually sort of tapped out by a drum in the poem. Yes, there's an implied beat, as in music; there is such a beat, and you can have in one bar just two notes, and in another bar ten notes, and yet the bar length is the same. I suppose that is what Williams was talking about, that you don't measure a foot in the old way by its syllables but by its beat.

Though not by what Pound called the rhythm of the metronome?

Well, there is a metronome in back, too.

Is it like the mechanical beat of the metronome or the necessarily variable beat of a pulse? Is it a constant beat? Or is it a beat that accelerates and slows?

Oh, it accelerates and slows, but it has a regularity, I would say. I'm thinking of *The Clock* symphony of Haydn. Well, there's where the pulse behind the bars is actually heard—*pum*-pum, p*um*-pum, and so on. But then, winding around that pum-pum, it's going *dee*, dee-*dee*-dum, and so forth. Well, I think perhaps in a poem you've got that melody, and not the metronomic pum-pum; but the pum-pum, pum-pum is implied.

When you think of the variable foot, then, you think of beats rather than of the spacing of phrases or of breath-spaced units of expression?

I've never fully gone along with Charles Olson's idea of the use of the breath. It seems to me that it doesn't work out in practice.

Of course, he thinks of this as one of the achievements of the modernist revolution—that Pound and Williams inaugurated the use of breath-spaced lines.

But I don't think they really are breath-spaced. There are a lot of poems where you actually have to draw a big breath to read the phrase as it's written. But so what? Why shouldn't one, if one is capable of drawing a deep breath? It's too easy to take this breath idea to mean literally that a poet's poems *ought* by some moral law to sound very much like what he sounds like when he's talking. But I think this is unfair and untrue, because in fact they may reflect his *inner* voice, and he may just not be a person able to express his inner voice in actual speech.

You think, then, that the rhythm of the inner voice controls the rhythm of the poem?

Absolutely, the rhythm of the inner voice. And I think that

the breath idea is taken by a lot of young poets to mean the rhythm of the outer voice. They take that in conjunction with Williams's insistence upon the American idiom, and they produce poems which are purely documentary.

What do you mean by the inner voice?

What it means to me is that a poet, a verbal kind of person, is constantly talking to himself, inside of himself, constantly approximating and evaluating and trying to grasp his experience in words. And the "sound," inside his head, of that voice is not necessarily identical with his literal speaking voice, nor is his inner vocabulary identical with that which he uses in conversation. At their best sound and words are song, not speech. The written poem is then a record of that inner song.

Published in *Minnesota Review*, No. 5, 1965, as "A Conversation with Denise Levertov." This article is an extract from that interview conducted by Walter Sutton.

Technique and Tune-up

(1979)

A LOT OF PEOPLE write in what have come to be called "open forms" without much sense of why they do so or of what those forms demand. Or if they do think, it seems mainly to recognize that they are confused. They are sailing without the pilots and charts that traditional forms provide. If one is interested in *exploration* one knows the risks are part of the adventure; nevertheless, as explorers travel they do make charts, and though each subsequent journey over the same stretch of ocean will be a separate adventure (weather and crew and passing birds and whales or monsters all being variables) nevertheless rocks and shallows, good channels and useful islands will have been noted and this information can be used by other voyagers. But though people have been exploring open forms for a long time now, from the free verse pioneered by Whitman and picked up later by Sandburg or the very different free verse of the Imagists through to the various modes of the last two decades (so that nowadays it is rare to find a college freshman writing in traditional forms) there has been a curious lack of chart-reading. People not only have their personal and proper adventures with the infinite variables—the adventures which make it all worthwhile and exciting—but also they keep bumping unnecessarily into the same old rocks, which isn't interesting at all. (And incidentally, when they do attempt traditional forms, college students often display an inability to scan, revealing how untrained their *ears* are even in the simplest repetitive rhythmic structures.) Since, judging from my experience as a teacher and also as a reader, this general confusion seems to me to be so prevalent, I'm going to try to note some common problems of technique as well as ways to get the written score of nontraditionally formed poems down on paper efficiently. Because there's no consensus about some of the tools of scoring—just as up till the eighteenth century there was virtually no consensus about musical scoring techniques—one can detect uncertainty and a hit-or-miss approach to these matters even in some of the major poets of our time. When I speak of consensus I'm not suggesting that people should write alike—only that it would be helpful if more poets would consider what typographical and other tools we do have at our disposal and what their *use* is. To point out that a carpenter's plane is not designed to be used as a knife sharpener or a can opener does not restrict how someone planes their piece of wood; and to indicate that objects specifically designed to whet knives or open cans do exist is not to dictate what shall be cut with the knife or whether the can to be opened should be of beer or beans.

Obviously the most important question and the one about which there's the most uncertainty is, what is the line? What makes a line be a line? How do you know where to end it if you don't have a predetermined metric structure to tell you? If it's just a matter of going by feel, by ear, are there any principles at all to help you evaluate your own choices? The way to find out, I believe, is to look at what it is a line *does*. Take a poem and type it up as a prose paragraph. Type it up again in lines, but not in its own lines—break it up differently. Read it aloud (observing the linebreak as roughly one-half a comma, of course—it is there to *use*, and if you simply run on, ignoring it, you may as well acknowledge that you want to write prose, and do so). As you perform this exercise or experiment you will inevitably begin to *experience* the things that linebreaks do—and this will be much more useful than being *told about* them. However, I'll list some of the things they do which you can listen for:

Unless a line happens to *consist* of a whole sentence, the linebreak *subtly interrupts* a sentence.

Unless a line happens to consist of a complete phrase or clause, it *subtly interrupts* a phrase or clause. (Though lines may also *contain* whole sentences, phrases, or clauses.)

What is the function of such interruptions? Their first function is to notate the tiny nonsyntactic pauses that constantly take place during the thinking/feeling process—pauses which can occur before any part of speech and which, not being a part of the logic of syntax, are not indicated by ordinary punctuation. The mind as it feels its way through a thought or an impression often stops with one foot in the air, its antennae waving, and its nose waffling. Linebreaks (though of course they may also happen to coincide with syntactic punctuation marks—commas or semi-colons or whatever) notate these infinitesimal hesitations. Watch cats, dogs, insects as they walk around: they behave a lot like the human mind. This is the reason why Valéry defines prose in terms of the purposeful (goal-oriented) walk, and poetry as the gratuitous dance. If linebreaks function as a form of nonsyntactic punctuation, for what purpose do they do so? In order to reveal the thinking/feeling *process*. What does that imply? I think it implies that the twentieth century impulse to move away from prescribed forms has not always been due to rebellion and a wish for more freedom, but rather to an awakened interest in the experience of journeying and not only in the destination. This statement doesn't mean to denigrate the great works of the past, which do, as a rule, focus on the achieved goal, not on the process of reaching it. All I mean is that just as a sentence is a complete thought, so a traditional form—the sonnet, the villanelle, etc., even blank verse—is a complete system; and though a great poet can bring about marvelous surprises within it, yet the expectations set up by our previous knowledge of the system are met, and we get a great deal of our gratification in reading such poems precisely from having our expectations met. And that's somewhat like receiving the fruit of the Hesperides without having travelled there—some other traveller has brought it back to us. But there's something in the twentieth century consciousness or sensibility that wants to share the travails of journeying; or we want at least to hear the tale of the journey. The poet-explorer heading for Mount Everest flew to Bombay or Delhi, what was it like? How did he or she get from there to Tibet? What were the Sherpas like? What about the foothills? Did you still want to get to Everest by the time you first saw the south face of the western peak? And so on. We are as interested in process and digression as in an ultimate goal.

At this point it strikes me that I seem to be making a statement about *content*, which was not my intention. I do not mean that I think we want every poem to be digressive. There can be poems, good poems, that meander (as long as each digression ultimately contributes to the needs of the composition), but I'm by no means holding any special brief for them, and it is not content that is in question, but structure. Perhaps I should switch metaphors: let's compare poems to paintings: the analogy would be that, if we choose open forms in which the movement of lines can record the movement of the mind in the act of feeling/thinking, thinking/feeling, we have, as it were, an interest in seeing the brushstrokes; we like to experience the curious double vision of the scene represented *and* the brushstrokes and palette knife smears and layers of impasto by which it is produced. In the process of giving us this experience by incorporating into the rhythmic structure of the poem those little halts or pauses which are not accounted for by the logic of syntax, a second essential effect is produced, and that is the change of pitch pattern inevitably brought about by observation of linebreaks. I've written elsewhere on this*—the way in

* See previous essay, "On the Function of the Line."

which *melody* is created not only by the interplay of vowels *within* lines but by the overall pattern of intonation scored by the breaking, or division, of the words *into* lines, and about how this melodic element is not merely an ornamental enhancement but, deriving as it does from the mimesis of mind process, is fundamentally expressive.

Let us look now at another "tool": indentation. Why do some poems seem to be all over the page? Indentations have several functions: one of them has to do with the fact that eye-ear-mouth coordination makes looking from the end of a line all the way back to the starting margin a different experience from that of looking from the end of a line to the beginning of an indented line—the latter is experienced as infinitesimally swifter. This registration of a degree of swiftness conveys, subliminally, a sense that the indented line is related to the preceding one with especial closeness. For example, I used indentation in these lines,

> up and up
> > into the tower of the tree

because if I had put all the words on one line I'd have lost the upstretching sound of the first half line—it would have dissipated. And if I'd gone back to the margin, I'd have lost the ongoing *into*-ness that stretches mimetically up into the tower of the tree. The other main function of indentations is to clearly denote lists or categories for the sake of clarity—but this too works not only *intellectually* (by way of the eye to the brain), but also *sensuously* (by way of the eye to the ear and the voice) and thus expressively. Through changes of tone and pitch elicited subliminally, the score provides a more subtle emotional graph than it could without them.

If you will take a look at this poem of mine, "A Son" (from *Life in the Forest*) you'll see a score that uses carefully consistent degrees of indentation: sub-categories of content within the whole syntactic composition are assigned specific degrees of indentation.

A *Son*

> A flamey monster—plumage and blossoms
> > fountaining forth
> > > > from her round head,
> > her feet
> > > squeezing mud between their toes,
> > a tail of sorts
> > > > wagging hopefully
> > and a heart of cinders and dreamstuff,
> > > flecked with forever molten gold,
> > drumrolling in her breast—
> bore a son.

> > > His father? A man
> not at ease with himself,
> half-monster too,
> half earnest earth,
> > > > fearful of monsterhood;
> > > > kindly, perplexed, a fire
> > > > smouldering.

> The son
> > took, from both monsters, feathers
> > of pure flame,

> > and from his mother,
> > > > alchemical gold,
> > and from his father,
> > > > > the salt of earth:

> > a triple goodness.

> If to be artist
> is to be monster,
> he too was monster. But from his self

uprose a new fountain,
        of wisdom, of in-seeing, of wingéd justice
        flying unswerving
        into the heart.   He and compassion
were not master and servant,
        servant and master,
but comrades in pilgrimage.

The first line presents the subject—flame-plumage-blossom-monster. The succeeding nine lines alternate between attributes and actions, and are enclosed by dashes which open in the middle of the first line. (The first line needed to be simple although interrupted by the dash which sets off the subsidiary clause, in order to link the monster firmly to her attributes.) The last line of the stanza goes back to the margin to complete the sentence: "a flamey monster/bore a son." The second stanza begins with an indented line because the subject of it is uncertain; a question opens the stanza and the person is described as half man and half monster. So the placing of the whole stanza on the page is somewhat wavering. Stanza three, beginning "The son," repeats the logic of stanza one, except that because it speaks of the son deriving characteristics from both parents—feathers of flame from both of them and also something magically transformational from the mother and something of basic human goodness from the father—the last line is centered: "a triple goodness." Stanza four is all on the margin side because it follows syntactically directly from the first skeletal, or scaffold sentence:

A monster
bore a son.
  ↓
If to be artist
is to be monster,
he too was monster.

But after the "But" statement there comes another indented passage—indented because it is descriptive, as the lines immediately preceding it are not. The last stanza starts with an indentation that is centered, because that centering on the page suggests (again, in a subliminal way, physiology conspiring with comprehension) a blending or meeting which is what the poem is talking about. The alternations of the concluding three lines echo those in stanzas one and three, but now I feel that this entire stanza should have been indented: that's to say centered, with its existing indentations intact; and it was a failure of craft-logic to leave it at the margin.

There is another matter about which there is a vague consensus but for which few people seem to know a *reason:* what do initial capital letters do and why have they been abandoned by so many twentieth century poets? Well, they stop the flow very slightly from line to line, and if one is using the kind of careful and detailed scoring devices I've been illustrating then their sheer unnecessariness is a distraction. Some people, however, like them for the very reason that they *do* stop the flow a tiny bit—so they can be *made* to function. What about using lower case initials throughout? Personally I dislike this practice because it looks mannered and therefore distracts the attention—especially lower case I (i); and I don't see any function in the absence of a capital letter to signal the beginning of a sentence—especially the very first sentence of a poem. But more important than whether you do or don't use capitals is consistency within any given poem. If you are not consistent in your use of any device, the reader will not know if something is merely a typographical error or is meant to contribute—as everything, down to the last hyphen, should—to the life of the poem.

These seem the principle technical points about which large numbers of people are confused. But I'd like to throw in a concept that doesn't have to do specifically with open forms—the idea of what I call *tune-up*. It involves diction. Obviously we all want to avoid clichés, except in dialogue or for irony; but sometimes even though we may be devoted to the search for maximum precision, we don't constantly check over our words to see if our diction is tuned-up to the maximum energy level consistent with the individual poem. Of course, our whole feeling about some poems may be that their tone should be relaxed. But how often a subject's inscape and our own experience of instress in confronting it (which then becomes an integral part of the poem's inscape) could really be sounded out more vibrantly! The technical or craft skill of tuning up is not the same as the process of revision. Major revision is undertaken when structure—whether of sequence, storyline, plot, of rhythm and melody, or of basic diction—has major ailments. But tune-up is something you do when you feel the poem is complete and in good health. It's sometimes a matter of dropping a few *a*'s or *the*'s or *and*'s to pull it all tighter—though beware you don't take out some necessary bolt or screw! But sometimes, more creatively, it's a matter of checking each word to see if, even though it has seemed precise, the correct word for the job, there is not—lurking in the wings of your mind's stage—another exotic, surprising, unpredictable, but even *more* precise word. Startle yourself. Before you leave the well-wrought, honest poem to set off on its own adventures through the world, see if with one final flick of the wrist you can shower it with a few diamond talismans that will give it powers you yourself—we ourselves—lack (poor helpless human creatures that we poets are) except at the moment of parting from the poems we have brought forth into daylight out of caverns we don't own but have at times been entrusted to guard and enter.

A "Craft Lecture" presented at Centrum, a writing conference at Port Townsend, Washington, Summer 1979.

Genre and Gender v.
Serving an Art

(1982)

THE TITLE "GENRE AND GENDER" suggests, and I suppose is meant to suggest, that genre may be determined by gender. That's an idea I find extremely foreign to my own experience. I don't believe I have ever made an aesthetic decision based on my gender. The genre a poem belongs to—lyric, narrative, meditative—is an aesthetic matter, a matter of the relation of form to content, like the decision to write not a poem but a story.

The content of a poem often reveals, or is naturally assumed to reveal, the sex of its author. Genre is determined by subject matter, and subject matter may on occasion emerge from experiences that are specifically male or female—but not more frequently than from such factors as a predominantly urban or predominantly rural life, from poverty or riches, from particular political convictions, or from individual temperamental or physical idiosyncracies. Clearly, many historical factors have affected what, how much, and *how* women write in various times and places, but none of these is essentially a matter of aesthetics. If in a particular period a woman is timid about her diction for fear of incurring hostility by using rough, harsh, or rude words, she is making a social (and psychological) decision rather than an aesthetic one. A true artist of either sex must necessarily be, *in relation to the art he or she serves*, even if shy and afraid about other things, a person of courage and energy who will not succumb to that kind of cultural pressure.

Artists have a reputation for ruthlessness. I don't think they are more ruthless as a class than any other; in fact I can think of many classes of person whose lack of empathic imagination makes them far more ruthless than a writer *can* be! But that reputation probably stems from the prime necessity, inherent in the vocation of the artist, of making aesthetic decisions even when they conflict with social expectations; of having, in other words, an intense awareness of artistic ethics. If a writer has that, his or her art will transcend gender. That is to say that if, for example, a woman poet writes poems on what her female body feels like to her, what it's like to menstruate, to be sexually entered by a man, to carry and bear a child and breast-feed it, her *subject* matter derives directly from her gender; but it will be the *structure* of the poem, its quality of images and diction, its details and its totality of sounds and rhythms, that determines whether or not it *is* a poem—a work of art. Her courage must be exercised not in relation to themes which once were considered impermissible (but are now almost demanded of her) but in refusing to let herself off any *aesthetic* hooks.

Without the sense of *serving an art*, of *serving* poetry and not utilizing it as a vehicle, like a bus, all the authenticity of content and all the best social intentions in the world, whether concilia-tory or militant, lofty or practical, will not help. A poem, like any other work of art, must have the potential of becoming wholly anonymous through accidents of history and yet retain-ing its numinous, mysterious energy and autonomy, its music, its magic. That is what I mean by the transcendence of any inessential factor—including gender.

In 1982 I took part in a symposium at the MLA on "Genre and Gender in Poetry by Women." *American Poetry* published my "statement" in its Fall 1983 issue (along with Ruth Stone's and with specially written companion state-ments by Diane Wakoski and Shirley Kaufman).

"News That Stays News"
(1978)

THINKING ABOUT THE SIGNIFICANCE of *periplum*, that word Pound often uses—

> periplum, not as land looks on a map
> but as sea bord seen by men sailing

—I see its applicability to the experiencing of numinous works of art from the mobile vantage point of one's own growth and change: the different angles and aspects of the work thus perceived, and the new alignments with its historical context, and also with the context of the perceiver's personal history.

As a coastal city might come, at a certain moment of sailing past it, into the most perfect, harmonious, and dramatic alignment with the mountains behind it and the sweep of its bay, so a supreme moment may be reached in one's own reception and appreciation of a novel, a poem, a string quartet. That does not mean all subsequent sightings of it will be a decline. The memory of that supreme vision will in some degree illuminate each subsequent look one takes.

There's an analogy to the *periplum* concept in a movie camera's slow panning across a scene. Indeed, one obtains a similar effect in a car or train, especially when viewing a downtown skyline from a bridge or elevated highway. But while these analogies may give to the reader who has never travelled by boat some physical sense of *periplum*'s literal meaning, their speed (in comparison to the slowness of a ship) does not allow for the kind of changes in the beholder that contribute to new perceptions. All the accrued life-experience which accompanies one on return visits to works of art is only sketchily symbolized even in the metaphoric description of time and change provided by the image of watching the coastal towers and mountains realign to the eye as the observer—perhaps going through changes of mood the while—moves past them in a half-becalmed sailboat from dawn to dusk, a whole long day, and finds them next morning still visible beyond the wake, as if floating between sky and sea.

A friend said to me, as we talked about the experience of discovering, in a supposedly familiar work, fresh and unexpected meanings, "So then one is reading a new book?" But no: if the work truly has the living complexity I term "numinous," it is rather that by one's own development, by moving along the road of one's own life, one becomes able to see a new aspect of the book. The newly seen aspect, facet, layer, was there all the time; it is our recognition of it that is new.

Sometimes an artist's technical consciousness directly, deliberately, contributes to the multi-aspected nature of a work; for example, in Henry James one finds, as well as projective references (back-and-forth cross references), certain "scenes"—in James's particular sense of pivotal, revealing moments—which work by means of the participation of the reader, who has previously been given enough knowledge of the characters to realize what must be passing through their minds at the moment of the "scene" itself. But there are works of a much simpler design which also provide different consecutive experiences to the reader, listener, or viewer who returns to them periodically, bringing new modifications of need or ability. The degree to which the originating artist was conscious of the manifold import of a work does not determine its actual multifariousness: the great work of art is always greater than the consciousness of its author.

Returning from that statement to the *periplum* metaphor, one may say, then, that although the architect of the city may have attempted to plan how it would look from all points of the compass as well as from among its streets and squares, he or she could not have foreseen every effect of light, of weather, or of exactly how, in time, certain trees would grow tall, hiding certain buildings, and others would fall, and small new ones be planted. Nor could the architect guess which surrounding hills would become bare from erosion, while others were terraced into new fields, or covered over with villas in a style wholly different from the style of the city; and even less predictable was the city's appearance to the eyes of strangers from distant places, who one day would look across the water from their passing ship and see the towers pass behind one another and emerge, and again pass and emerge, now in a mountain's shadow and now catching the light of the rising sun, as if dancing a pavane.

All this the architect cannot know. But if the city is beautiful and alive in its own logic (the logic of what the architect *could* know) then each perceived arrangement, each revelation of further correspondence between the parts of the city, and between the whole city and its site, is implicit *in* that logic.

Horses with Wings

(1984)

PEGASUS, A HORSE WITH wings: he flashes into sight of the inner eye with a silvery grace no poet ever possessed. And he is not a poet, not a poem. But to reflect upon him may tell us something new about both; or, more likely, will tell us something old but not recently remembered. For attributes, totems, symbolic images, not only possess their own identities but express something essential of the person or class of persons to which they are attached. And Pegasus is persistently linked to the idea of poetic inspiration.

Hawthorne's 19th century vision exquisitely saw him thus:

> Nearer and nearer came the aerial wonder, flying in great circles, as you may have seen a dove when about to alight. Downward came Pegasus, in those wide, sweeping circles, which grew narrower, and narrower still, as he gradually approached the earth. The higher the view of him, the more beautiful he was, and the more marvelous the sweep of his silvery wings. At last, with so light a pressure as hardly to bend the grass about the fountain, or imprint a hoof-tramp in the sand of its margin, he alighted, and, stooping his wild head, began to drink. He drew in the water, with long and pleasant sighs, and tranquil pauses of enjoyment . . ." Then, "Being long after sunset, it was now twilight on the mountain-top, and dusky evening over all the country round about. But Pegasus flew so high that he overtook the departed day, and was bathed in the upper radi-

ance of the sun. Ascending higher and higher, he looked like a
bright speck. . . .*

But scholarship reminds us that he was not all compact of
grace and charm. His antecedents are unpromising—dark and
violent—for one whose legend has come down to us as princi-
pally benevolent.

What analogies in the activity of poem-making or the nature
of poets and poetry may be illumined by his myth? What do his
own origins tell us?

HIS PARENTAGE

The father: Poseidon, god of the sea, above all represents the
undifferentiated power of the unconscious—a source of life but
also of terror. The individual who, admiring poetry, language,
Nature, attempts to make verses but is not impelled by some
trace at least of that power produces only mediocrity. Just as
Poseidon is associated with tempestuous seas rather than with
glassy calm, so poems rise up in the poet from intensity of
experience, even though they may evoke things calm, delicate,
or still, and even though composition, more often than not,
takes place when emotion is re-collected, its fragmented elements regathered by the imagination at a later, and *externally*
tranquil, time.

Poseidon causes earthquakes, though it might seem that
ocean, however stormy, is a remote source for inland cata-
clysms. Just so may poetry cause personal and social effects
distant from it in time or place, setting in motion a chain of
events beyond the poet's will or knowledge, although perhaps
consonant with his or her hopes. It is in this propensity that
Poseidon the earthshaker calls to mind Shelley's "legislators"
who in our own time are figured forth in a Bertolt Brecht, a
Pablo Neruda, a Yannis Ritsos, or a Nazim Hikmet, and also

* *Tanglewood Tales.*

in poets whose work affects the values and vision of their time less explicitly.

Poseidon as an embodiment of fecundity bespeaks the ramifications of such distant effects, wave upon wave into the distant horizon; and here his benign aspect appears, for in rocking, shaking, and opening out the static, passive, and finally receptive earth and making springs both hot and cold to jet from its caves, he causes it to bring forth nourishing plants. Thus does poetry rock and shake and open the mind and senses, moistening their aridity and enabling humans to bring forth their spiritual fruits.

The mother: Medusa. We may say Poseidon, god of the unconscious depths, is a powerful but morally neutral, dual, or ambiguous force; but what are we to make of Medusa? Is there any good to be known of her? Is there any trace of her in graceful Pegasus?

First we must note that Pegasus has an equine heritage on both sides of his family. The primordial force of water—at once nourishing and destructive, symbolic of impetuous desire—is associated very anciently with the horse of night and shadows, galloping out of the entrails of earth and the abyss of ocean. Similarly, Medusa's legends most anciently seem to place her as a manifestation of the Earth Mother's terrible and devouring aspects, taking on dragon forms and various other animal guises, including that of a mare. (Demeter herself, often depicted as horse-headed, and not unrelated to the Furies, and bore—to none other than Poseidon—the horse Arion, two of whose feet were human and who could speak like a man.) Medusa, then, although it is said that she was for a time, before Poseidon ravished her, a beautiful maiden—embodies the nightmare, the *cauchemar*.

Her equine connections are with the same unconscious animal force and fertility as these of Poseidon, who, if he took her in his equine form, as most accounts assert, came sweeping into Athene's temple with white mane flowing, a tidal wave with thundering hooves, his sperm the color of milky jade you may see as the breakers turn at the shoreline. The great oceanic horse is beautiful; but Medusa's horse aspect is part of her malignity.

This monstrous mother, whose hands were bronze, whose wings were brass, whose teeth were tusks, and her hair a writhing mass of snakes, was the only mortal among triplet sisters. Her serpentine hair is said to have been given her by Athene, furious at the desecration of her temple; but since all her siblings and half-siblings were monsters, it seems that her malign nature existed potentially even before her appearance became hideous. Her significance has been perceived as incarnating perverted impulses: a *refusal* of harmony, a *wilful* wickedness, rather than an incapacity for goodness. The word Gorgon is related to gargle, gurgle, and gargoyle: Medusa has been called "a shriek personified." All who gazed upon her were instantly petrified—paralyzed by the full, unveiled, unmediated vision of evil. The fact that Perseus managed to get close enough to sever her neck without himself being turned to stone, by the ruse of focussing on her mirror image—that mirror being indeed his shield—seems to suggest the way in which art provides a mode of perceiving evil and terror without being immobilized, but on the contrary enabled to come to grips with them. Frobenius saw in the Gorgon a symbol of the fusion of opposites; however, Medusa's refusal of internal harmony results in a stasis of conflict, not a positive synthesis. The components of her presence are utterly disparate and remain so. Her face, even though depicted as having elements of beauty, is contorted in a frightful snarl, as if she horrifies even herself. Contemplation of such "fusion," such simultaneity of warring elements, can kill—that is, it can defeat or explode the conscious rational mind, for it reveals a state beyond linear reach. But the experience of poetry provides, like the mirror of Perseus, a means for human consciousness to transcend the linear and by fitful glimpses, at least, to attain a vision of ultimate harmony, of reconciliation, not exclusion nor dilution. Thus the significance of the shielding mirror prefigures the reconciling aspect of Pegasus himself, as we shall see.

Erich Neumann, with a Jungian perspective, describes Perseus's mirror strategy as a *raising into consciousness* of an image which paralyzes only as long as it remains unconscious; and he makes a point of the pun of *reflection* inherent in the story. I would by no means dispute this; but his account is concerned with the universal psychological principles carried in the myth; whereas, for poets, the myth's particular significance is not the attainment of consciousness as such but the transformation and activating of conscious and unconscious experience brought about by the Imagination. And it is notable that when Neumann turns from Perseus and his mirror to Pegasus, he identifies the latter as the released "spiritual *libido* of the Gorgon," (my italics) who "combines the spirituality of the bird with the horse character of the Gorgon." (Here it is of interest to note that according to one account, it was as a bird that Poseidon came to the then fair Medusa, in that flowery meadow within the precincts of Athene's calm temple, and not as a wild horse. A sea bird, it would have been, with its hungry cry and fish-hook beak, fierce-eyed, as apt to dive under the tossing surface as to glide and hover on the salt breezes; symbolic, as bird, of spirit, but yet a wild spirit.)

HIS NATURE AND ASSOCIATIONS

Pegasus issues from the blood of Medusa (and specifically from her neck, that area of transition between two territories, mental and physical). Medusa, though able to embody opposites (the dual nature of the earth mother, fertile yet destructive; or, in later manifestations, her youthful beauty and subsequent ugliness) was not capable of so mingling them as to transform and transcend their conflict, for all her energy is expressed in wilful spite. But from the conjunction within her of Poseidon's un-

111

differentiated, everflowing energy and her own fixed intensity is born—or wrested out of her by a slash of the sickle—a new "fusion of opposites": one that is more truly a fusion: Pegasus. The earthy, physical horse is all complete—not, as in the centaur, the hippocampus, or the hippogriff, half horse and half man or fish or griffin, and not, as in his half-brother Arion, the horse with two human feet and the power of speech. Nor does Pegasus undergo periodic metamorphosis into a bird. He is at all times a horse (and a sexually potent one, for though no mate or offspring of his is ever mentioned, he is referred to as a stallion). He is a perfect horse; but a horse possessed of the superlative enhancement of wings. The development of horse symbolism from cthonic darkness and malign associations to the glorious team that draws the chariot of the sun is recapitulated in the development of the Pegasus legends, the earliest of which accord him no wings, and in his story itself, which depicts spiritual energy rising from such murky sources. In him contrasts are reconciled, and not by the disappearance of their characteristics but by their new and harmonious combination.

Poets—not, let it be emphasized, in their personal human aspect (or not in any greater degree than for any other individuals in whom the imagination is alive), but in the activity of poem-making—possess like Pegasus some inherent power of exaltation. But it is equally important to recognize that Pegasus was not constantly airborne. It was by striking his sharp hoof hard upon the rocky earth that Pegasus released the fountain of Hippocrene, the fountain of poetic inspiration henceforth sacred to the Muses. (Some say, too, that it was not until the moment that Medusa's blood, spurting from her neck, *touched earth* that he became manifest.) Poet and poem must strike hard and sink deep into the material to tap spiritual springs or give new birth to "the winged fountain."

In poetry we may observe traits of the parents as well as of Pegasus himself. There are poems vast, restless, almost formless, yet powerful, which evoke the character of Poseidon and the ocean's tidal rhythms. There are Medusan poems of rage and hatred, sharp-clawed with satire, writhing with serpentine humor and flashing forth venomous tongues of denunciation or despair.

And then there are those, far more numerous, which in various proportions combine, like Pegasus himself, earth and air; and it is these, not those in which the traits of Poseidon or Medusa dominate, that are most representatively poems. They may walk, trot, or gallop, but have the inherent power to soar aloft. Some poets hold this power in reserve, keeping Pegasus on a tight rein; others avail themselves of it with more or less frequency. Such flights are not to be equaled with abstraction, as may too easily be done if one assumes that the earthy horse represents the concrete and the wings the abstract. Pegasus as horse does indeed present the sensual, the sensuous, the concretely specific, but that physicality is itself related to the unconscious—and not only to the instinctive but to the intuitive as well. And his wings, which do not deform but increase and enhance his equine characteristics of speed and strength of motion, express not the abstractions of linear intellection but the transcendent and transformative power of Imagination itself.

But it would be no service to the understanding of poetry's essential nature and the poet's vocation to smooth over its stern or demonic aspects. Pegasus, sired by a ruthless god, born in violence of an abhorrent monstrosity, is himself a daimon, a force, an energy. He is, as Heine put it, not a virtuous utilitarian hack; nor is he a children's pet. Bellerophon only tames him with the help of a magical golden bridle, the gift of Athene. It is a beneficent act to help destroy the devastating Chimaera, whose three heads—of a goat, a snake, and a lion—embody licentiousness, insidious venom, and ruthless dominance; and the story reveals in parable that inspiration, not courage and strategy alone, overcomes these evils. Yet, not himself destructive, Pegasus, by lending to Bellerophon his indispensible swiftness and power to rise aloft, has become accessory to a killing. As a flying cloud, he may carry life-giving showers, but also can bring the devastation of flash floods. And after Bellerophon's hero-deed is done, it is the speed and levitational power of his steed that tempt him to hybris. Extreme speed is a way of referring to a kind of excessive eloquence, the words tumbling out too fast for coherence, and too many for each to be just and indispensible. A poet flying high and swiftly becomes a kind of bird, whose speech is not intelligible to humankind; or a breath of the storm-wind, which breaks what it sweeps over. Pegasus, anciently known as accursed as well as blessed, in latter days can perhaps be seen in this aspect as the steed of poets wilfully abstruse or brutally verbose. Finally, Bellerophon attempts to fly upon him to Olympus—and then Pegasus throws him. Whether Zeus sent a gadfly to sting him into this action, or he himself resented Bellerophon's presumption, the glorious familiar becomes instrumental in the hero's fall from grace, both by being that which (innocently) tempts and that which, misused, refuses further cooperation. Thereafter Pegasus is translated to the Olympian stables and becomes the bearer of thunder and lightning "at the behest of prudent Zeus": of those tremendous words from an apparent nowhere ("out of the sky," as we say) sounding within the mind or out in the bustling world, which come sometimes to strike us with terror or remorse, to illumine some obscure history or to reveal in a flash an abyss at our feet.

Eos, the dawn, sometimes rides Pegasus, bringing a saffron shimmer of first light. This daybreak appearance may bring to mind the astonishing poetry occasionally uttered (and occasionally written down) by young children, and also the poetic efflorescence that often takes place in adolescence. But like that of early morning sunshine, these promises are not always fulfilled. The poet of extraordinary gifts who early produces major work and dies very young is, or has become, a rarity; and the earliest work of those who live longer is seldom of more than historical interest. It is the pristine value of initial inspirations that Pegasus more aptly signifies when regarded as the horse of dawn. No matter what metamorphoses poem or stanza or image may have to pass through to become all that it can, its source and first appearance should not be despised.

Mantegna depicted Pegasus with Hermes. I have not found a source for this association, but since the painting shows the gods foregathered, one may suppose that after the downfall of Bellerophon, Zeus having summoned him to the Olympian heights, Pegasus and wingfooted Hermes would naturally be drawn to one another. Hermes is the god of fresh wind, who clears the skies; of travellers; of cunning wiles; of eloquence; guardian of flocks; messenger and psychopomp: a fit companion for one with the attributes of Pegasus. If Pegasus struck forth the fountain of inspiration, it was Hermes who invented the lyre. Indeed, the two share so much that one may take that list and apply much of it to the winged horse—swift as the wind, a potential benefactor of travellers, provider of the springs of eloquence. And though we don't find in Pegasus specific parallels for Hermes' cunning and trickery nor for his shepherd role, affinities with them are easily discernable in poets and poetry.

Jane Harrison, in *Themis*, speaks in passing of Pegasus "receiving" Dionysos at Eleutherae; being given, that is, in a powerful and unmistakable flash of recognition, the perception of a divinity. If it is indeed our Pegasus she refers to, I would interpret this event as emblematic of the way in which creative power has no upper limit; a sublime potential remains even when poetry has seemed to fly to the extremes of its own possibility.

HIS SIBLINGS

The offspring of Poseidon are many. There are a few who seem, however, to have a special relation to Pegasus. First of these is Chrysaor, his unidentical twin, formed like a man of great size and splendor and bearing, who stepped out of Medusa's spilt blood bearing a huge golden sword. Subsequently he united with "great Ocean's daughter," Callirhoe, whose name means Beautiful Stream, and fathered the monster Geryon whom Heracles later killed. Then we hear no more of him, as if he had sunk beneath the waves he wedded, carried by that river out into deep ocean. In him we may see figured the mind that never comes to consciousness. Born of the unconscious and the nightmare, it struggles as far as the beauty of one stream, plunges in, and is borne away, leaving behind only an aberrant production soon to vanish in its turn; just as an individual may produce one unfinished unshaped poem. The figure of Chrysaor also suggests wasted talent: mighty in appearance and with that attribute, the golden sword, yet he does no deeds and has no story.

Arion, with human speech and a trace of human form—two of his four feet—was one of the many half-brothers; his mother was Demeter, who had taken on the form of a mare when Poseidon, as a stallion, pursued her. Arion was dark and powerful and was ridden by Heracles and by Adrastus (survivor of the "Seven against Thebes"). Here is language without poetry, at the service of action; a plain prose. In contrast, Pegasus himself, not endowed with speech, yet acts as divining rod for the poetic fountain.

The third sibling relevant to my theme is Bellerophon. For though supposedly the son of Glaucus, Hesiod reveals that in fact Poseidon fathered him by the wife of Glaucus, and that it was he who provided Pegasus to help Bellerophon in his adventure. Bellerophon's ostensible father, Glaucus, was trampled and killed by his own horses, whom Aphrodite had driven mad in revenge for some offense. (It is the ghost of Glaucus that horses are seeing when some inexplicable terror makes them stall and rear.) But Bellerophon himself is a notable horseman. Though there is no identification of him as a poet, his close association with Pegasus, with springs and flying, as well as the inspired ingenuity with which he avails himself of his magical familiar in the strategy for slaying the Chimaera, suggest that he may stand for one. Or rather, if we look upon him and Pegasus together as forming a whole (as horse and rider do when, both superb, they are perfectly attuned to one another) then Bellerophon, to whom a golden bridle was given by Athene, goddess of vigilant and industrious intelligence, stands for the craft and skill necessary to the full activity of inspiration and creative imagination. Each needs the other for the fulfillment of his powers. Hawthorne, speaking as always in parables, tells that Bellerophon, after he first tamed him, offered Pegasus his freedom. Pegasus took flight, circled the skies, and once more spiralled down—returning voluntarily. And once again, when the Chimaera's bones and ashes lie strewn across the plain, the rider frees the steed, and is refused. Once craft and imagination have endured together the struggle to slay a monster or create a poem, imagination does not just fly off never to return. Pegasus was never really *tamed*, never *broken* like a common horse; it is only through the magic of special, goddess-given dream-intelligence that Bellerophon is able to exercise his regular equestrian skills upon him. He freely chooses to remain, as a comrade. Only when humility is lost and arrogant technique assumes it can assault heaven itself does the rider fall and the winged horse soar beyond reach.

CONCLUSION

In reviewing what Pegasus has to tell us about the poet, I find these correspondences:

The poet inherits a protean and unconscious power: fertile, amoral, capable of shaking mountains or of shaking dry seeds to life. The poet also inherits heterogeneities strange as Medusa's, whose distorted human face looked out from so anomalous a collection of bodily traits—snakes and claws, wings and

117

scales. These gorgonic features correspond to the quaking magma of emotion which, in poems of autobiographical confession or furious opinion, smothers response and turns to stone the minds over which it flows. The poet's inherent contradictions vary, in kind and in proportion, with the individual; but the archetypal poet, being also a representative Human Being, "Man (or Woman) the Analogist," contains the potential for many intensities, for all the passions and all the appetites; and—on a more differentiated level—for satire and sentiment, thundering prophecy and delicate nuance, comedy and the sublime. The poet has to be both a dreamy visionary and a meticulous and energetic worker, though often tormented by those conflicting needs.

The poet (always, I must reemphasize, in the work of poetry, and not in his or her mundane individuality) reconciles these disparities and incongruities. Here we see Pegasus as a metaphor for the poem rather than the poet. We must take his emergence from gorgon and sea-god as a given; the poem, correspondingly emerging from the poet, an autonomous third term, results from an alchemy scarcely less mysterious. Like Pegasus, the poet (and the poem too) is animal. Fully a horse, Pegasus is not particularly intellectual. His intelligence is intuitive. But a fine horse is alert in every rippling muscle; its ears, its nostrils, reflect complex awarenesses. And it is as consistent, as harmonious throughout its being, as Medusa was inharmonious. Even the excrement of a horse takes the form of neat spheres, like brown tennis-balls, full of grain for sparrows and pigeons. The poet as animal is human, and must accept and explore all that he or she incorporates—the gift of the senses, the gifts of memory and language and intellectual discernment, and, too, the burden or curse entailed in each of these gifts or blessings. Above all the poet must treasure the gift of intuition which transcends the limitations of deductive reasoning.

To say that the poem, as well as the poet, is animal means that it has its own flesh and blood and is not a rarified and insubstantial thing. It is compact of sounds, gutteral or sibilant, round or thin, lilting or abrupt, in all their play of pitch and rhythm, durations and varied pace, their dance in and with silence. Even its marriage to the Euclidean beauty of syntax is a passionate and very physical love affair; often it pulls the gravity and abstract elegance of grammar into that dance to whirl like a Maenad.

Pegasus has wings added unto his equine completeness. And the poet has, beyond even the penetrative gift of intuition, the power of imagination. The bridle of skill and craft may give Bellerophon power to direct the flight of the horse; but no skill, no effort, can produce wings where there are none. The imagination is the horse's wings, a form of grace, unmerited, unattainable, amazing, and freely given. It is with awe that any who receive it must respond.

Presented at the *What Is a Poet?* conference at the University of Alabama in 1984 and published with the other papers of this event in the volume of the same title, edited by Hank Lazer.

Great Possessions

"SONGS ARE THOUGHTS, SUNG out with the breath when people are moved by great forces and ordinary speech no longer suffices," said Orpingalik, the Eskimo poet, to Rasmussen (quoted in Sir Maurice Bowra's *Primitive Song*).

We are living in a time of dread and of awe, of wan hope and of wild hope; a time when joy has to the full its poignance of a mortal flower, and deep content is rare as some fabled Himalayan herb. Ordinary speech no longer suffices.

Yet much of what is currently acclaimed, in poetry as well as in prose, does not go beyond the most *devitalized* ordinary speech. Like the bleached dead wheat of which so much American bread is made (supposedly "enriched" by returning to the worthless flour a small fraction of the life that once was in it) such poems bloat us but do not nourish. Proust wrote in *Time Retrieved*,

> How could documentary realism have any value at all since it is *underneath* little details such as it notes down that reality is hidden—the grandeur in the distant sound of an airplane or in the lines of the spires of St.-Hilaire, the past contained in the savor of a madeleine, and so forth—and they have no meaning if one does not extract it from them. Stored up little by little in our memory, it is the chain of all the inaccurate impressions, in which there is nothing left of what we really experienced, which constitutes for us our thoughts, our life, reality, and a so-called "art taken from life" would simply reproduce that lie, an

art as thin and poor as life itself [as that superficial, lying life, that is to say] without any beauty, a repetition of what our eyes see and our intelligence notes [again I gloss this as meaning superficial intelligence as distinct from our *understanding*], so wearisome, so futile that one is at a loss to understand where the artist who devotes himself to that finds the joyous, energizing spark that can stimulate him to activity and enable him to go forward with his task. The grandeur of real art, on the contrary . . . is to rediscover, grasp again, and lay before us *that reality from which we become more and more separated as the formal knowledge which we substitute for it grows in thickness and inperviousness—that reality which there is grave danger we might die without having known and yet which is simply our life.*

Instead, we get too many mere notations. The lack of a unifying intelligence, of the implicit presence of an interpreting spirit behind such notations, is associated—and not accidentally—with a lack of music. By music I don't mean mere euphony, but the verbal music that consists of the consonance of sound and rhythm with the meaning of the words. These wizened offshoots of Williams's zeal for the recognition of the rhythmic structure of the American language demonstrate the mistake of supposing he was advocating a process of reproduction, of facile imitation—whereas what he was after was origins, springs of vitality: the rediscovery, wherever it might turn up (in language or incident), of that power of the imagination which first conceived and grasped *newness* in a new world, though the realization was ever and again nipped in the bud, blighted, covered over with old habits and strangling fears. Read him—the short early and later poems, and *Paterson*, and the longer poems of the great final flowering, from *The Desert Music* on; and the prose: *In the American Grain*, and essays like "The American Background," as well as the specifically "literary" essays such as those on Pound, Sandburg, or Stein, and the unclassifiable pieces such as "The Simplicity of Disorder." It is all there, said many ways, but clear and profound.

Williams emphasizes the necessity for the poet to deal with specifics, to locate himself in history—but never at the expense of the imagination. "They found," he wrote in "The American Background" of the first settlers, "that they had not only left England but that they had arrived somewhere else: at a place whose pressing reality demanded not only a tremendous bodily devotion but as well, and more importunately, great powers of adaptability, a complete reconstruction of their most intimate cultural make-up, to accord with the new conditions."

It is the failure, over and over, to make that adaptation—the timid clinging to forms created out of other circumstances—that he deplores, grieves over; the rare leap of imagination into the newly necessary, the necessary new, that he rejoices in. When he blasts Sandburg (in 1948, when Sandburg's *Complete Poems* came out), it is for formlessness, for lack of invention. If he underestimated Whitman (and sometimes he did), it was because he believed Whitman had failed to go far enough and to provide a structural model others after him could have used to go further—so that Whitman, by default, set American poetry back rather than advancing it (though surely this was equally due to the unreadiness of any young writers of Whitman's time to recognize what he was doing and pick up from it). While Williams criticizes Whitman and Sandburg, both of whom dealt with homespun "content" and whose diction was distinctively American, he praises Poe, Cummings, Pound, Marianne Moore, none of whom consistently, and some of whom never, wrote in simple imitation, reproduction, of the American idiom, as understood by some of those who today take Williams's name in vain in defense of their own banalities. Thoughts and impressions do not become songs, images do not flare, because the deep unconscious sources of song and image are battened under hatches. In reaction, there exists an equally prevalent and equally inadequate poetry that I think of as *mechanical surrealism*—the appearance of surrealism without its genuine content: poems strung together out of notebook jottings saved for a rainy day, poems that do not explore but contrive a fake, deliberate irrationality, works not of imagination, not of fancy—which has its genuine light charms—but of *spurious* imagination.

Underneath surface differences of content these two kinds of poetry are really very similar, and this underlying similarity is attested to in the lack of distinct formal differences between them. Whether the poet writes of beer cans, the Sunday funnies, and provincial malaise, or of strenuously strange and vague phantasmagoria, these competent jottings remain . . . competent jottings, rhythmically and sonically undistinguished, indistinguishable.

What then do we need? We need a new realization of *the artist as translator*. I am not talking about translation from one language to another, but of the translation of experience, and the translation of the reader into other worlds. To quote Proust again: "I perceived that, to describe these impressions, to write that essential book, the only true book, a great writer does not need to invent it, in the current sense of the term, since it already exists in each of us, but merely to translate it. The duty and task of a writer are those of a translator." What did he mean? The word comes from the past participle of the Latin *transferre*, "to transfer": to carry across, to ferry to the far shore. What Proust calls "documentary realism" only *relates;* that is, it carries us *back*, not forward; the process has that "photographic" fidelity he speaks of as insufficient for the complexity of our experience.* Since almost all experience goes by too fast, too superficially for our apperception, what we most need is not to *re*-taste it (just as superficially) but really to taste *for the first time* the gratuitous, the autonomous identity of its essence. My 1865 Webster's defines *translation* as "being conveyed from one place to another; removed to heaven without dying." We must have an art that translates, conveys us to the heaven of

---

*I'm using the term *photographic* idiomatically. For the art of photography I have every respect.

that deepest reality which otherwise "we may die without ever having known"; that *transmits* us there, not in the sense of bringing the information to the receiver but of putting the receiver in the place of the event—alive. *Transmit* (like *mission* and *missive*) comes from the same Latin root (*mittere*, "to send") as *mettre* and *mettere* in French and Italian, both meaning "to put." In English, *transmits* gives one the feeling of being at the sending end; the Italian *trasmettere* suggests being at the receiving end, as if it said "transput," and I am now using the English word with this latter feeling. If a poetic translation, or attempted act of translation, is weak or an operation of mere fancy, it does not "increase our sense of living, of being alive," which Wallace Stevens said was an essential function of poetry, but instead removes us from reality in a lapse of perception, taking us not deeper into but farther away from the world—a kind of dying. We must have poems that move away from the discursively confessional, merely descriptive, and from the fancies of inauthentic surrealism to the intense, wrought, bodied-forth and magical—poems that make us cry out with Carlyle, "Ah, but this sings!"

A poetry that merely describes, and that features the trivial egotism of the writer (an egotism that obstructs any profound self-explorations), is not liberated from contingency and does not fulfill what David Jones has called the *sine qua non* of art, "the gratuitous setting up of sacred objects to the unknown god." "By that sort of paradox," he says also, "man can act gratuitously only because he is dedicated to the gods. When he falls from dedication . . . the utile is all he knows and his works take on something of the nature of the works of the termite." (See David Jones's essay "Art and Democracy" in *Epoch and Artist*.) Poetry that is merely "self-expressive" in the current sense of the term is not even ultimately utile to the greatest degree, for while it temporarily "relieves feelings" or builds ego, it does not, cannot, give the writer—and certainly fails to give the reader—the deeper satisfaction of a work of autonomy and gratuitousness.

The distinction is between the temporarily therapeutic self-expression, which is equivalent to a gesture, expending its whole substance in the act—a letting off of steam—and the disinterested expression of being, which Walter F. Otto (as quoted by Kerenyi in his book *Asklepios*) describes in the following passage: "Wherever a creature emits even the simplest sequence of musical tones, it evinces a state of mind entirely different from that which occurs in the uncontrolled outcry. And this state of mind is the essential when we ask about the nature of the primordial musicality. It is often unmistakable that the song, even of animals, is sufficient unto itself, that is not intended to serve any purpose or produce any sort of effect. Such songs have aptly been characterized as *self*-expressions. *They arise from an intrinsic need of the creature to give expression to its being.*"* It is clear, I think, that here the emphasis must be on the word *self*—*self*-expression, the expression of the creature's very being, not self-*expression*, the blowing off of steam. As Otto continues, it becomes clear too how *self*-expression relates to the dynamic, kinetic concept of translation: "But self-expression demands a presence, for which it occurs. This presence is the environing world. No creature exists for itself alone; all are in the world, and this means: each one in its own world. Thus the singing creature expresses itself in and for its world. In expressing *itself** it becomes happily aware of the world, it cries out joyfully, it lays claim to the world." (And here I would add, "Or it becomes *un*happily aware of the world, but its cry of *self*-expression is still an affirmative act, for all awareness, all acknowledgment of self and world, is essentially affirmation." As Jane Harrison reminded us, "Aristotle said that poetry had two forms, praise which issued in hymns and heroic

*My italics.

poetry, blame which yielded . . . satire. . . . We analyze and distinguish but at bottom is the one double-edged impulse, the impulse toward life" (from *Prolegomena to the Study of Greek Religion*). "The lark rises," Otto goes on:

> to dizzy heights in the column of air that is its world; without other purpose, it is at the same time the language of the world's reality. A living knowledge rings in the song. When man makes music he doubtless has a much broader and richer environment. But the phenomenon is fundamentally the same. He too must express himself in tones, without purpose and regardless of whether or not he is heard by others. But here again *self-*expression and *revelation of the world* are one and the same. As he expresses himself the reality of the being that enfolds him speaks in his tones.

It may be objected that if the reality of an individual's being is indeed banal, then his banal expression of it should be accepted as valid. I disagree because I do not believe in the intrinsic banality of any existence. I believe with Carlyle that "no most gifted eye can exhaust the significance of any object" (*On Heroes, Hero-Worship and the Heroic in History*, 1841)—and if this inexhaustible significance is to be found in things, inanimate and animate, how can it not be true of man? But, says Rilke, "If a thing is to speak to you, you must for a certain time regard it as the only thing that exists, the unique phenomenon that your diligent and exclusive love has placed at the center of the universe, something the angels serve that very day upon that matchless spot" (*Selected Letters*). But that intensity of attention is rarely exercised—an attention which would lead the writer into a deeper, more vibrant language and so translate the reader into the heavens and hells that lie about us in all seemingly ordinary objects and experiences.

If we are to survive the disasters that threaten, and survive our own struggle to *make it new*—a struggle to which I believe we have no choice but to commit ourselves—we need tremendous transfusions of imaginative energy. We need life, and abundantly—we need poems of the spirit, to inform us of the essential, to help us *live* the great social changes that are necessary, and which must be internal if their external form is to succeed.

I had chosen the title "Great Possessions" from the *I Ching* hexagram without a clear sense of what I meant by it until I focussed on another sentence from Proust:

> That reality from which we become more and more separated as the formal knowledge which we substitute for it grows in thickness and imperviousness—that reality which there is grave danger we might die without having known and yet which is simply our life.

And in Thoreau's notebooks I found this entry:

> Thurs. Dec. 10 1840. I discover a strange track in the snow, and learn that some migrating otter has made across from the river to the wood, by my yard and the smith's shop, in the silence of the night.—I cannot but smile at my own wealth, when I am thus reminded that every chink and cranny of nature is full to overflowing.—That each instant is crowded full of great events.

Artists must go more deeply into their dormant, unused, idle "great possessions."

All authentic art shows up the vagueness and slackness of ninety per cent of our lives—so that art is in its nature revolutionary, a factor instigating radical change, even while (giving "the shock of recognition," and naming and praising *what is*) it is conservative in a real sense.

The poet in our time, "moved by great forces," must live in the body as actively as he lives in his head; he must learn to extend himself into whatever actions he can perform, in order to be "part of the solution and not part of the problem," and not to negate, by passivity and hypocrisy, the force of his own words.

But personal commitment, along with a close *attention* to things and people, to the passing moments filled to the brim with past, present, and future, to the Great Possessions that are our real life, is inseparable from attention to language and form. Poetry is intrinsically revolutionary, that is, a dynamic force, but it is not so by virtue of talking *about* any one subject rather than another (though if the poet has political concerns they will not be excluded, and *not* to have political concerns—in the broad and deep sense of the term—is surely impossible to the aware adult in the last quarter of the twentieth century). Broad or narrow in focus, sad, angry, or joyful, "song that suffices our need" does so by way of its very substance of sound and vision.

The Poet in the World
(1967)

THE POET IS IN labor. She has been told that it will not hurt but it has hurt so much that pain and struggle seem, just now, the only reality. But at the very moment when she feels she will die, or that she is already in hell, she hears the doctor saying, "Those are the shoulders you are feeling now"—and she knows the head is out then, and the child is pushing and sliding out of her, insistent, a poem.

The poet is a father. Into the air, into the fictional landscape of the delivery room, wholly man-made, cluttered with shining hard surfaces, steel and glass—ruthlessly illuminated, dominated by brilliant whitenesses—into this alien human scene emerges, slime-covered, skinny-legged, with a head of fine black hair, the remote consequence of a dream of his, acted out nine months before, the rhythm that became words, the words that were spoken, written down.

The poet is being born. Blind, he nevertheless is aware of a new world around him, the walls of the womb are gone, something harsh enters his nose and mouth and lungs, and he uses it to call out to the world with what he finds in his voice, in a cry of anger, pathos, or is it pure announcement?—he has no tears as yet, much less laughter. And some other harshness teases his eyes, premonition of sight, a promise that begins at once to be fulfilled. A sharp smell of disinfectant is assaulting his new nostrils; flat, hard, rattling sounds multiply, objects being placed on glass surfaces, a wheeled table pushes out of the way, several voices speaking; hands are holding him, moving on his skin, doing things to his body—wetness, dry softness, and then up-ness, down-ness, moving-along-ness: to stillness in some kind of container, and the extraordinary experience, lasting an eternity, of lying upon a permanently flat surface—and finally closeness to something vaguely familiar, something warm that interposes a soothing voice between him and all else until he sleeps.

It is two years later. The poet is in a vast open space covered by rectangular gray cobblestones. In some of the crevices between them there is bright green moss. If he pokes it with a finger it feels cold, it gives under pressure but is slightly prickly. His attention is whirled away from it by a great beating of wings around him and a loud roucouing. People with long legs who surround him are afraid he will take fright at the flock of pigeons, but he laughs in wild pleasure as they put lumps of bread into his hands for him to throw to the birds. He throws with both hands, and the pigeons vanish over his head and someone says, Cathedral. See the big building, it's a Cathedral. But he sees only an enormous door, a mouth, darkness inside it. There is a feather on his coat. And then he is indoors under a table in the darkish room, among the legs of the table and of the people, the people's feet in shoes, one pair without shoes, empty shoes kicked off nearby. Emerging unseen he steps hard on something, a toy train belonging to another child, and it breaks, and there is a great commotion and beating of wings again and loud voices, and he alone is silent in the midst of it, quite silent and alone, and the birds flying and the other child crying over its broken train and the word cathedral, yes, it is ten years later and the twin towers of it share the gray of the cobblestones in the back of a large space in his mind where flying buttresses and flying pigeons mean cathedral and the silence he knows is inside the great door's darkness is the same silence he maintained down among the feet and legs of adults who beat their wings up above him in the dark air and vanished into the sky.

It is Time that pushed them into the sky, and he has been living ten, twenty, thirty years; he has read and forgotten thousands of books, and thousands of books have entered him with their scenes and people, their sounds, ideas, logics, irrationalities, are singing and dancing and walking and crawling and shouting and keeping still in his mind, not only in his mind but in his way of moving his body and in his actions and decisions and in his dreams by night and by day and in the way he puts one word before another to pass from the gate of an avenue and into the cathedral that looms at the far end of it holding silence and darkness in its inner space as a finger's-breadth of moss is held between two stones.

All the books he has read are in the poet's mind (having arrived there by way of his eyes and ears, his apperceptive brain-centers, his heartbeat, his arteries, his bones) as it grasps a pen with which to sign yes or no. Life or death? Peace or war?

He has read what Rilke wrote:

> . . . verses are not, as people imagine, simply feelings (we have those soon enough); they are experiences. In order to write a single poem, one must see many cities, and people, and things; one must get to know animals and the flight of birds, and the gestures that flowers make when they open to the morning. One must be able to return to roads in unknown regions, to unexpected encounters, to partings long foreseen; to days of childhood that are still unexplained, and to parents whom one had to hurt when they brought one some joy and one did not grasp it (it was a joy for somebody else); to childhood illnesses that begin so strangely with such a number of profound and grave transformations, to days spent in rooms withdrawn and quiet and to mornings by the sea, to the sea itself, to oceans, to nights of travel that rushed along loftily and flew with all the stars—and still it is not enough to be able to think of all this. There must be memories of many nights of love, each one

unlike the others, of the screams of women in labor, and of women in childbed, light and blanched and sleeping, shutting themselves in. But one must also have been beside the dying, must have sat beside the dead in a room with open windows and with fitful noises. And still it is not yet enough, to have memories. One must be able to forget them when they are many and one must have the immense patience to wait till they are come again. For the memories themselves are still nothing. Not till they have turned to blood within us, to glance and gesture, nameless and no longer to be distinguished from ourselves—not till then can it happen that in a most rare hour the first word of a poem arises in their midst and goes forth from them. (From *The Notebook of Malte Laurids Brigge* 1908.)

This the poet has known, and he has known in his own flesh equivalent things. He has seen suddenly coming round a corner the deep-lined, jowled faces and uncertain, unfocusing eyes, never meeting his for more than an unwilling second, of men of power. All the machines of his life have directed upon him *their* power, whether of speed or flickering information or disembodied music. He has seen enormous mountains from above, from higher than eagles ever fly; and skimmed upstream over the strong flow of rivers; and crossed in a day the great oceans his ancestors labored across in many months. He has sat in a bathtub listening to Bach's *St. Matthew Passion*, he has looked up from the death of Socrates, disturbed by some extra noise amid the jarring and lurching of the subway train and the many rhythmic rattlings of its parts, and seen one man stab another and a third spring from his seat to assist the wounded one. He has seen the lifted fork pause in the air laden with its morsel of TV dinner as the eyes of the woman holding it paused for a moment at the image on the screen that showed a bamboo hut go up in flames and a Vietnamese child run screaming toward the camera—and he has seen the fork move on toward its waiting mouth, and the jaws continue their halted movement of mastication as the next image glided across the screen.

He has breathed in dust and poetry, he has breathed out dust and poetry, he has written:

> Slowly men and women move in life,
> cumbered.
> The passing of sorrow, the passing
> of joy. All awareness
>
> is the awareness of time.
> Passion,
> however it seems to leap and pounce,
> is a slow thing.
> It blunders,
> cracking twigs in the woods of the world.

He has read E. M. Forster's words, "Only connect," and typed them out and pasted them on the wall over his desk along with other sayings:

> The task of the poet is to make clear to himself, and thereby to others, the temporal and eternal questions which are astir in the age and community to which he belongs.
>
> —Ibsen

> We have the daily struggle, inescapable and deadly serious, to seize upon the word and bring it into the directest possible contact with all that is felt, seen, thought, imagined, experienced.
>
> —Goethe

> The task of the church is to keep open communication between man and God.
>
> —Swedenborg

And below this the poet has written, "For *church* read *poet*. For *God* read *man and his imagination, man and his senses, man and man, man and nature—well, maybe 'god,' then, or 'the gods'* . . ."

What am I saying?

I am saying that for the poet, for the man who *makes* literature, there is no such thing as an isolated study of literature. And for those who desire to know what the poet has made, there is therefore no purely literary study either. Why "therefore"? Because the understanding of a result is incomplete if there is ignorance of its process. The literary critic or the teacher of literature is merely scratching a section of surface if he does not live out in his own life some experience of the multitudinous interactions in time, space, memory, dream, and instinct that at every word tremble into synthesis in the work of a poet, or if he keeps his reading separate from his actions in a box labeled "aesthetic experiences." The interaction of life on art and of art on life is continuous. Poetry is necessary to a whole man, and that poetry be not divided from the rest of life is necessary to *it*. Both life and poetry fade, wilt, shrink, when they are divorced.

Literature—the writing of it, the study of it, the teaching of it—is a part of your lives. It *sustains* you, in one way or another. Do not allow that fatal divorce to take place between it and your actions.

It was Rilke, the most devoted of poets, the one who gave himself most wholly to the service of his art, who wrote:

> . . . art does not ultimately tend to produce more artists. It does not mean to call anyone over to it, indeed it has always been my guess that it is not concerned at all with any effect. But while its creations, having issued irresistibly from an inexhaustible source, stand there strangely quiet and surpassable among things, it may be that involuntarily they become somehow exemplary for *every* human activity by reason of their innate disinterestedness, freedom and intensity. . . .*

*From a letter to Rudolf Bödlander, *Letters of Rainer Maria Rilke*, Vol. II.

> For as much as the artist in us is concerned with *work*, the realization of it, its existence and duration quite apart from ourselves—we shall only be wholly in the right when we understand that even this most urgent realization of a higher reality appears, from some last and extreme vantage point, only as a means to win something once more invisible, something inward and unspectacular—a saner state in the midst of our being.*

He is saying, in these two passages from letters, that though the work of art does not aim at effect but is a thing imbued with life, that *lives* that life for its own sake, it nevertheless *has* effect; and that that effect is ultimately moral. And morality, at certain points in history, of which I believe this is one—this year, even if not this day—demands of us that we sometimes leave our desks, our classrooms, our libraries, and manifest in the streets, and by radical political actions, that love of the good and beautiful, that love of life and its arts, to which otherwise we pay only lip service. Last spring (1966) at a Danforth Conference, Tom Bradley, one of the speakers, said (I quote from my notes): "Literature is dynamite because it asks—proposes— moral questions and seeks to define the nature and worth of man's life." (And this is as true of the most "unengaged" lyric poem, intrinsically, as of the most didactic or discursive or contentious). Bradley continued, "The vision of man we get from art conditions our vision of society and therefore our political behavior. . . . Art and social life are in a dialectical relationship to each other that is synthesized by political action."

The obligation of the poet (and, by extension, of others committed to the love of literature, as critics and teachers or simply as readers) is not necessarily to write "political" poems (or to focus attention primarily on such poems as more "relevant" than other poems or fictions). The obligation of the writer is: *to*

*From a letter to Gertrude Oukama Knoop in Rilke, *Selected Letters*.

take personal and active responsibility for his words, whatever they are, and to acknowledge their potential influence on the lives of others. The obligation of teachers and critics is: *not to block the dynamic consequences of the words they try to bring close to students and readers.* And the obligation of readers is: *not to indulge in the hypocrisy of merely vicarious experience, thereby reducing literature to the concept of "just words," ultimately a frivolity, an irrelevance when the chips are down.* . . . When words penetrate deep into us they change the chemistry of the soul, of the imagination. We have no right to do that to people if we don't share the consequences.

People are always asking me how I can reconcile poetry and political action, poetry and talk of revolution. Don't you feel, they say to me, that you and other poets are betraying your work as poets when you spend time participating in sit-ins, marching in the streets, helping to write leaflets, etc. My answer is no; precisely because I am a poet, I know, and those other poets who do likewise know, that we must fulfill the poet's total involvement in life in this aspect also. "But is not the task of the poet essentially one of conservation?" the question comes. Yes, and if I speak of revolution it is because I believe that only revolution* can now save that earthly life, that miracle of being, which poetry conserves and celebrates. "But history shows us that poets—even great poets—more often fulfill their lives as observers than as participants in political action—when they do become embroiled in politics they usually write bad poems." I answer, good poets write bad political poems only if they let themselves write deliberate, opinionated

---

*In the late 1960s the word "revolution" was in common use among peace activists of almost all kinds. Although we might disagree about the exact form revolution should take and how it was to come about, there was consensus about the need for radical changes in the way human society organized itself. Most people who were infants then or not yet born—today's generation—have no positive associations with the word; and though many of us who are older see no less need for such changes, we are hesitant to use a term which unfortunately more often conveys the idea of bloody violence and civil war than a vision of a just and peaceful community. Yet "radical change" is a phrase vitiated by being meaninglessly repeated by politicians as they seek election. One has no recourse but to beg the reader's cooperation in attempting to comprehend the intention of words which have lost their efficacy but for which at this time (1992) there seem to be no alternatives.

136

rhetoric, misusing their art as propaganda. The poet does not *use* poetry, but is at the service of poetry. To *use* it is to *mis*use it. A poet driven to speak to himself, to maintain a dialogue with himself, concerning politics, can expect to write as well upon that theme as upon any other. He can not separate it from everything else in his life. But it is not whether or not good "political" poems are a possibility that is in question. What is in question is the role of the poet as observer or as participant in the life of his time. And if history is invoked to prove that more poets have stood aside, have watched or ignored the events of their moment in history, than have spent time and energy in bodily participation in those events, I must answer that a sense of history must involve a sense of the present, a vivid awareness of change, a response to crisis, a realization that what was appropriate in this or that situation in the past is inadequate to the demands of the present, that we are living our whole lives *in a state of emergency* which is—for reasons I'm sure I don't have to spell out for you by discussing nuclear and chemical weapons or ecological disasters and threats—unparalleled in all history.

When I was seven or eight and my sister sixteen or seventeen, she described the mind to me as a room full of boxes, in aisles like the shelves of a library, each box with its label. I had heard the term "gray matter," and so I visualized room and boxes as gray, dust-gray. Her confident description impressed me, but I am glad to say I felt an immediate doubt of its authenticity. Yet I have since seen lovers of poetry, lovers of literature, behave as if it were indeed so, and allow no fruitful reciprocity between poem and action.*

"No ideas but in things," said William Carlos Williams. This does not mean "no ideas." It means (and here I quote Wordsworth) that "language is not the dress but the incarnation of thoughts." "No ideas but in things," means, essentially, "Only connect." And it is therefore not only a craft-statement,

---

* At this point in the talk as originally given, I inserted the poem, "O Taste and See," from my book of the same title.

not only an aesthetic statement (though it is these things also, and importantly), but a moral statement. *Only connect. No ideas but in things.* The words reverberate through the poet's life, through *my* life, and I hope through your lives, joining with other knowledge in the mind, that place that is not a gray room full of little boxes. . . .

Written for a symposium on the question, "Is There a Purely Literary Study?" held at Geneseo, New York, in April 1967.

Paradox and Equilibrium
(1988)

TO SUPPOSE THAT ART (of any kind—literary, visual, theatrical, etc.) can be politically and socially "engaged" and still possess its aesthetic integrity is to concede to art an unrestricted, multifarious nature that includes hortatory, and consequently even the (morally) utile. Pure poetry, diatribe, and passionate exhortation meet in the prophets. But the modern artist who wants at once to show truth and urge action must confront the fact that violent and horrific images are commonplace in the age of "live coverage" and instant replays. How can it serve to record, in words or pictures, "man's inhumanity to man"—and to the earth and all that is in it—when people have developed such protective shells of numbness? There is only one way—the way of aesthetic power.

The Japanese painters Iri and Toshi Maruki, with unexampled single-mindedness and stamina (both emotional and aesthetic) have devoted their lives' best energies to documenting and evoking the bleakest and most dread realities of their—of our—time. The double paradox of their achievement is that they have made beauty from horror, yet have not, in doing so, softened or diluted the horror.

Though I have long defended the possibility of writing "engaged" poetry that is as fully poetry, with all its artistic values intact, as any other, I cannot think of a body of poetic work one might cite as equivalent in this paradoxical intensity, with the

139

exception of Dante's *Inferno*. I am not claiming that what is beautiful in the Marukis' work is equal (or similar) in beauty to that in Dante's poetry, but that their attainment of an extraordinarily sustained synthesis of irreconcilable elements is one to which I can think of no other parallel.

Literature is full of moments of such synthesis, but provides no comparable unrelenting lifetime engagement. In visual art, one recalls Goya; but the *Disasters of War* form only one part of his large oeuvre (even if many would feel it is the most essential part). Kollwitz maintained a consistent focus, but on a far smaller range of images; besides, hers is a world not only of poverty and oppression but of struggle, maternal protectiveness, heroism, and thus of hope—like the worlds of Brecht, Hikmet, or Neruda. And Dante knows that Purgatory and Paradise lie ahead, no less real than Hell. But in an interview Toshi Maruki admits to despair, "because we have not the strength to stop war," and Iri Makuri says that "we don't paint this reality so that people will rethink things or so that we can create a world that is not so hellish. It wouldn't do to paint with such a sense of self-importance. . . . The point is that all of us, all living beings, are living in that reality. We paint that reality."

Another paradox: such commitment to the theme, such a profound sense of creating from within the hell they depict—and such detachment or nonattachment. Toshi Maruki accepts despair, and at the same time says, "If we all must live in hell, perhaps in time people will begin to understand this reality . . . and if each person understands, we will be able to stop war." And Iri Maruki: "If people happen to learn something from the painting, that is wonderful; if they don't, that is all right too." Perhaps no Western artist is sincerely capable of such disclaimers. Yet part of the secret of any engaged work that has depth and lasting power resides in something not altogether dissimilar: not a detachment exactly, but an intense concern for the formal properties of the work which is not diminished or overshadowed by passionate commitment to content.

A few years ago I saw an exhibition of antinuclear paintings. Some had an obscure or an oblique relation to the theme; some mimicked the ugliness of their subject with a kind of frenzy, and from these it was easy to turn away unmoved. But one stood out: a medium-sized circular painting that showed the stone framework of what had been a stained glass window. Through the aperture, the glass all gone, was visible a sunset sky, deeply flushed—and below it a desolate, empty, ravaged stretch of ground, extending to the horizon, where no living thing remained. An evocation of tragic, utter silence. The power of its beauty, the power of its message, were indissoluble. I believe I shall never forget it.

Like that painting, the Marukis' lifework demonstrates that the engaged art which can effectively fulfill its didactic potential is art which sacrifices no aesthetic values to make its point.

To maintain an equilibrium between the unflinching memorialization of what human beings are capable of doing, in all its terrifying ghastliness, and the beauty of line, form, and color, is not to subvert a didactic engagement with something alien to its purpose, even though I have called it a paradoxical achievement; nor is such beauty a mere sugar coating to help us down the vile pill, for it is impotent unless fused with its content. It is not a sugar coating—yet without it no one would consent, or indeed be able, to look for long or repeatedly at images that rub our noses in such content.

We humans cannot absorb the bitter truths of our own history, the revelation of our destructive potential, *except* through the mediation of art (the manifestation of our other, our constructive, potential). Presented raw, the facts are rejected: perhaps not by the intellect, which accommodates them as statistics, but by the emotions—which hold the key to conscience and resolve. We numb ourselves, evading the vile taste, the stench. But whether neutralized into statistics or encountered head-on without an artist-guide (as if Dante wandered through Hell without a Vergil), the facts poison us unless we can find a way both to acknowledge their reality with our whole selves and, accepting it, muster the will to transcend it.

Only such an acknowledgement of our past, our complicit present, our possible (many say probable) future, such a coming to consciousness, can further the assumption of responsibility that could (that must) prevent that unthinkable/ thinkable future, and instead, swerve us off and away from our doom-bound road.

In 1988 the Massachussetts College of Art gave Honorary Degrees to the Marukis, who created the Hiroshima and Nagasaki Murals and have gone on to depict a number of other outstanding crimes of our lifetime. A number of writers and visual artists were honored by an opportunity to contribute to an ilustrated catalogue for the exhibition which accompanied their visit.

Poetry, Prophecy, Survival

(early 1980s)

IF A WRITER'S SUBJECT matter frequently includes issues that are prominent in the history of his or her own time—if he or she engages, as is virtually inevitable once such issues enter the work at all, on one side or the other of a controversy—the English-speaking public will demand that that writer account for so doing, and justify the presence of the political in the literary. I said English-speaking because this is much less true in some other cultures—the Hispanic or the Slavic for example. And I should also qualify *writer* by saying especially one whose main work is in poetry.

Political subject matter is looked upon either as an intruder into the realm of poetry, or as a matter that requires special discussion every time it occurs, and can't just be taken for granted like any other subject. So the poet is challenged to respond to many questions, ranging from the hostile (which may elicit defense or a shrug of disregard) to the genuinely, and sometimes profoundly, enquiring; and these last reach the artistic conscience and cause the poet to search for authentic personal responses. One such stimulating question I received in the mail was this one:

What relation has the poetry of joy, proclamation, affirmation, to politics?

I would answer:

A poetry of anguish, a poetry of anger, of rage, a poetry that, from literal or deeply imagined experience, depicts and denounces perennial injustice and cruelty in their current forms, and in our peculiar time warns of the unprecedented perils that confront us, can be truly a high poetry, as well wrought as any other. It has the obvious functions of raising consciousness and articulating emotions for people who have not the gift of expression. But we need also the poetry of praise, of love for the world, the vision of the potential for good even in our species which has so messed up the rest of creation, so fouled its own nest. If we lose the sense of contrast, of the opposites to all the grime and gore, the torture, the banality of the computerized apocalypse, we lose the reason for trying to work for redemptive change. Not as an escape—not instead of but as well as developing our consciousness of what Man is doing to the world and how we as individuals are implicated—we need more than ever before to contemplate daily (and to make, if we are so fortunate as to be capable of it) works of praise, works that by power of imagination put us in mind—re-mind us—of all that makes the earth's survival, and our own lives, worth struggling for. To imagine goodness and beauty, to point them out as we perceive them in art, nature, or our fellows, and to create works that celebrate them—are essential incentives to finding a route out of our apparent impasse. A passionate love of life must be quickened if we are to find the energy to stop the accelerating tumble (like a fallen man rolling over and over down a mountain) towards annihilation. To sing awe—to breathe out praise and celebration—is as fundamental an impulse as to lament.

Yet, while nature (albeit defiled and threatened) and art, past and present, *inspire* us (put fresh air in our lungs to keep us alive), we must demand of ourselves and our contemporaries an acknowledgement of the political iniquities among which we, nevertheless, at times sing out in joy; and then we must *do* what each of us finds possible in behalf of justice, mercy, survival and change. As William Morris said, "I am tired of the fine art of unhappiness."

The same correspondent asked,

What is the relation between affliction and imagination?

And I answered that:

Affliction is more apt to suffocate the imagination than to stimulate it. The action of imagination, if unsmothered, is to lift the crushed mind out from under the weight of affliction. The intellect by itself may point out the source of suffering; but the imagination illuminates it; by that light it becomes more comprehensible. It becomes a discrete entity, separate from the self. This is what I meant when I wrote that

> To speak of sorrow*
> works upon it
>   moves it from its
> crouched place barring
> the way to and from the soul's hall—

Crass, complacent obliviousness to suffering obviously does not coexist with imagination—the insensitively cheerful are uncreative. But that does not mean that neurosis is the *sine qua non* for the operation of creative imagination. Neurosis saps energy while the creative imagination, itself not languid, demands energy in those it inhabits. Imagination is not anesthetic.

But is it all a cop-out, a facile hugging of the personal life? my correspondent said.

No, I replied. Though imagination's wings can lift the individual out of private pits of gloom, it is a *creative* function, producing new forms and transforming existing ones; and these come into being *in the world*, autonomous objects avail-

*That is, to speak of sorrow in the light of imagination: from "To Speak," *The Sorrow Dance*, New Directions, 1966.

145

able to others, and capable of transforming *them*. It is when that transformative power is denied by a certain evasive and deliberate detachment that a cop-out occurs. There is a kind of wilful ignorance not so much of the *facts* of history but of their moral and physical implications. And sometimes there is a kind of contempt for action, an attitude that attributes superiority to detached observation or deliberate disregard as contrasted with political participation, especially other than verbal participation.

More and more, in this time of ultimate choices, ultimate *choice*, the spectacle of poets blithely detached from concern with anything so mundane as day to day political action (and even in individuals prone to private gloom, such unconcern appears blithe!) is one which detracts from the validity and impact of their poems. It is a detachment which trivializes their own work.

A poetry articulating the dreads and horrors of our time is necessary in order to make readers understand what is happening, really understand it, not just know *about* it but feel it: and should be accompanied by a willingness on the part of those who write it to take additional action towards stopping the great miseries which they record. The extent and nature of action to be undertaken by artists and intellectuals (or anyone else) is, of course, a matter for the individual conscience; it can't be prescribed. But just to tell the tale and walk away isn't enough.

And a poetry of praise is equally necessary, that we not be overcome by despair but have the constant incentive of envisioned positive possibility—and because praise is an irresistible impulse of the soul. But again, that profound impulse—the radiant joy, the awe of gratitude—is trivialized if its manifestations do not in some way acknowledge their context of icy shadows. It is not (I believe) a question of any poet being morally obliged to write politically engaged poems. A sense of moral obligation has never and can never be the *source* of art even though it may be one of its factors. It is a question of that *context* being palpable in the work although perhaps never named, never made explicit.

But, came the next question, still wanting a fuller justification:

What of the facts of genocide, oppression, conflict? Is creativity in the arts a way out of history?—A collective cop-out, if not a personal one—an evasion?

On the contrary, I think the arts are—among other things—a way *into* history. Intellect informs, but emotion—feeling—will not respond (especially to facts about events too distant or too vast to be experienced directly through the senses) unless imagination gives us the vision of them, presents (makes present) the unwitnessed, gives flesh to the abstract.

The responses this series of questions evoked in me have sometimes been paralleled by being asked to speak on the subject of poetry and prophecy. Prophecy is a word often associated with poetry, and there was a time when I felt the association was hyperbolic, because I was thinking too exclusively of the *predictive* sense of the word *prophecy*.

However, if we look at the Old Testament prophets—and certainly in western culture they are the basic model—we see that whether or not we take them to be gifted with foreknowledge (foreknowledge either taken to be intuitive, ecstatic and visionary, or to be the conclusions of rational ethical observations), they have without question other roles too: they *warn* of the effects and consequences of evildoing and foolishness; they *upbraid* the people for wrong or stupid behavior; and they take a powerful stand against corrupt and oppressive rulers. A Catholic Biblical scholar has listed four types of prophetic utterance—*Threat, Promise, Reproach*, and *Admonition*. Promise and admonition would include, no doubt, both the ecstatic vision of a desirable future and the less reproachful, more pleading voice that urges the people toward virtue. Above all, I would add, the prophets provide words of *witness*.

It seems to me that poetry is rarely if ever the expression of psychic precognition of events, but frequently partakes of those five types of utterance. *Threat* often takes the form of imprecation and bitter satire if directed towards a power structure, or, if directed towards the people, of warning—while *reproach* also takes the form of *lament* (in fact lamentation is an additional prophetic mode of utterance). So it can be said that poets often share the prophet's stance in these ways, though not all poets are prophets, and probably *no* poets, *as poets*, have occult knowledge of future events.

And what about prophets, are they necessarily poets? Perhaps not, strictly speaking: yet it is clear that whatever their messages—admonitions, reproaches, warnings, or promises and visions of a better life, "a new heaven and a new earth"— what they had to say had to be said *powerfully*, with imagination and linguistic resourcefulness, if it were to get across to the people. So to some extent they *had* to be poets, or at least persons whose eloquence and oratory could survive being written down, so that it could reach further and be pondered. The deepest listening, the ear of imagination, rejects all that merely *says*, that fails to *sing* in some way. And this brings one to a very important factor which is shared by poets and prophets: prophetic utterance, like poetic utterance, transforms experience and moves the receiver to new attitudes. The kinds of experience—the recognitions or revelations—out of which both prophecy and poetry emerge, are such as to stir the prophet or poet to speech that may exceed their own known capacities: they are "inspired," they breathe in revelation and breathe out new words; and by so doing they transfer over to the listener or reader a parallel experience, a parallel intensity, which impels that person into new attitudes and new actions. Of course, this doesn't necessarily happen instantly. Some listeners are impervious, others are changed so subtly by a poem or by a prophet's words that a long time elapses between cause and effect. But fast or slow, if the prophecy or the poem is the mysterious genuine article and the receiver's sensibility is open to it, some change does take place, I am convinced. It is for this reason that I've always felt poetry and the other arts had a potential for contributing to social change no matter how remote from political, social, current or ethical issues they may seem to be. They don't bring about change in themselves, but they can contribute to it simply by stimulating the imagination and thus making empathy and compassion more *possible*, at least.

But we live in an unprecedented time, a time when as we all know the fate of the Earth itself lies in the balance as never before; when day by day powerful forces all over the globe are tipping that balance further towards extinction. And this country, the USA, is playing a major part in that suicidal and globicidal insanity. In this dangerous, extraordinary time we can't, I feel, rely solely on the subtle and delicate possibilities of change implicit in the giving and receiving of *all* art; we also need direct images in our art that will waken, warn, stir their hearers to action; images that will both appall and empower. All of us feel sometimes that it is already too late; but this feeling alternates with the powerful creative energy, the will to live and to preserve life, we all carry in us somewhere. Just because—prophets, poets, or listeners, readers—we are *not* (or are very seldom and then unreliably) oracular, we *do not* know that the worst is bound to happen; and that suspension in not-knowing, bleak though it is, is the source of hope. And hope *also* calls for witness, for the articulation poetic art (call it prophecy if you will) can give it. We make poems, as the Inuit poet Orpingalik said, "when ordinary speech no longer suffices." And William Carlos Williams wrote that

> It is difficult
> to get the news from poems
> yet men die miserably every day
> for lack
> of what is found there.

Hugh Kenner, in a lecture, beautifully defined what poets seek (if they really *are* poets) as "the power to make things as moving as the things they have been moved by." That is to say, they don't *necessarily* seek to describe or evoke what they've been moved by, though sometimes they may; but do necessarily seek to make, out of language, things that will embody equivalent or similar *qualities*. Such things will elicit related responses in others.

What many people don't recognize is that poets write poems from the same impulse that others read them. People turn to poems (if they are aware poetry exists) for some kind of illumination, for revelations that help them to survive, to survive in spirit not only in body. These revelations are usually not of the unheard-of but of what lies around us unseen or forgotten. Or they illuminate what we feel but don't *know* we feel until it is articulated. It has been said that the personal is political. I'm not always sure what that means, but I know that to me the obverse is often true, and it is when I feel the political/social issues personally that I'm moved to write of them, in just the same spirit of quest, of talking to myself in quest of revelation or illumination, that is a motivating force for more obviously "personal" poems.

It is when this impulse of personal necessity informs the political that the poems—once they have come into autonomous aesthetic being—become stepping-stones in one's slow pilgrimage, or small Virgils leading the soul's Dante around the spiral of hell and paradise. And if they can so function for the writer, then they have a chance of doing so for the reader. The writer is given a voice to articulate what many others feel but can't say (yet he or she would only be pompous and patronizing if at the time of writing the work did not seem entirely personal).

The separation between poetry of political content and all other poetry is an artificial one. Poets who are conscious and concerned about the world around them may quite naturally sometimes write poems arising from that awareness, just as they may write about anything else that impinges upon and affects their being. It is rare that a writer will consistently confine him- or herself to a single topic. While it is quite true that a great deal of verse written on political themes is not truly poetry, or, if it is poetry, is flawed in comparison with poems on other themes by the same writers, this in no way implies that those themes are beyond the proper reach of poetic art. There is, in fact, an underlying arrogance in the condemnation of "engaged" poetry as an illegitimate, essentially anti-literary endeavor: who dare fix the limits of any art? To have devised the dome was difficult, to paint the Sistine Chapel's ceiling might have appeared impossible until it was done. Great difficulties do not invalidate any endeavor. In the case of "political poetry," the more it is shoved into confinement as a special, separate category, the harder it is to create—for it must have all the virtues, including all the lyricism, of any other poetry, and this is often forgotten when writers themselves accept that artificial isolation and exclude the political from the lyrical and the lyrical from the political. But the greatest impediment of all to the creation of truly poetic poetry dealing with political themes is a lack of what I will call "full internalization of need." Robert Frost knew what he was talking about when he said, "No tears for the writer, no tears for the reader; no surprise for the writer, no surprise for the reader."

Critics and general readers would often better understand poetry if they did not habitually assume in the poet a more didactic intent than is in fact the case. Even in poems whose content is social and political, whose tone is one of protest or denunciation, the poet has not had designs upon the reader in the manner often attributed to him or her; that spirit of strategy proper to rhetoricians and demagogues is remote from the spirit of poetry. (It has a rightful place in the work of dramatists because of their different relationship to audience.)

The compositional sense which adjusts, refines, adds or

eliminates is strategic, yes: but in relation to an intuited whole work, not to an audience. There must be faith in the capacity of people to receive (eventually, if not at once) works that are good. To coax and woo the public is an expression of disdain, and corrupts the work itself. And the exploration of content and medium which activates the compositional sense, but is distinct from it, is a personal quest as uncertain and as open to shocks and epiphanies for the poet as for the defenseless, trusting, courageous reader.

The need for "songs—thoughts sung out with the breath when people are moved by great forces"—for the poetry lacking which "men die miserably every day," metaphorically or literally, often because their lives have not even recognized that need, much less satisfied it—is felt by poets themselves, and they seek to satisfy it as *readers*, just like anyone else. But if they are to make poems sufficient to *others'* needs, they must seek for survival and revelation *in their own poems* too—in the voyage of exploration and discovery that writing is. For an authentic poetry (or any other art) the one who demands must become the one who supplies. Poets must seek in their own poems the news found nowhere else, or die for the want of it. Those who are moved to create political poetry are as much in need of it as anyone else, and only an intuitive recognition of that fact (in addition to being gifted with the poet's special relationship to language, the *sine qua non* of any achievement in the art) will enable them to make poems that give to others what they seek themselves.

Perhaps that assertion itself implies a philosophy, which is to say, a political belief (for every philosophy is also a politics). The philosophy implied here is founded in a sense of the interdependence of all things, a sense of belonging to, rather than dominating, an ecosystem; and of the osmosis, the reciprocal nature, of the sustaining relationship between the parts of an ecosystem.

152

One of the political things poetry, whether or not overtly political in its content, can do is to reveal that unity, that trembling web of being.

Variants of this piece were orally presented on two or three different occasions.

Poetry and Peace:
Some Broader Dimensions

(1989)

Is THERE A POETRY of peace? A few years ago I participated in a panel at Stanford, on the theme of Women, War and Peace. During the question period, someone in the audience, whom I could not see—we speakers were on a stage, and the house lights were down—but whom I afterwards learned was the distinguished psychologist Virginia Satir, said that poets should present to the world images of peace, not only of war; everyone needed to be able to *imagine* peace if we were going to achieve it. Since I was the only poet on the panel, this challenge was mine to respond to—but I had only a lame and confused response to make. Afterwards I thought about it, and I remember discussing the problem—the problem of the lack of peace poems—with some poet friends, Robert Hass and David Shaddock, a few days later. What was said I've forgotten, but out of that talk and my own ponderings a poem emerged which was in fact my delayed response. In it, I wrote,

> . . . But peace, like a poem,
> is not there ahead of itself,
> can't be imagined before it is made,
> can't be known except
> in the words of its making,
> grammar of justice,
> syntax of mutual aid.

>   A feeling towards it,
> dimly sensing a rhythm, is all we have
> until we begin to utter its metaphors,
> learning them as we speak.
>   A line of peace might appear
> if we restructured the sentence our lives are making,
> revoked its reaffirmation of profit and power,
> questioned our needs, allowed
> long pauses . . .
>   A cadence of peace might balance its weight
> on that different fulcrum; peace, a presence,
> an energy field more intense than war,
> might pulse then,
> stanza by stanza into the world, . . .*

This analogy still holds good for me. Peace as a positive condition of society, not merely as an interim between wars, is something so unknown that it casts no images on the mind's screen. Of course, one could seek out Utopian projections, attempts to evoke the Golden Age; but these are not the psychologically dynamic images Ms. Satir was hoping for, and I can think of none from our own century, even of the nostalgic or fantastic variety, unless one were to cite works of prose in the science fiction category. (And these, particularly if one compares them with the great novels of life as it is—with *War and Peace* and *The Brothers Karamazov*, with *Middlemarch* or *Madame Bovary* or *Remembrance of Things Past*—are entertainments rather than illuminating visions, because they tend to be works of fancy rather than imagination, at least in so far as they deal with human emotions and behavior.) Credible, psychologically dynamic poetic images of peace exist only on the most personal level. None of us knows what a truly peaceful world society might feel like. Since peace is indivisible, one society, or one culture, or one country alone could not give its members a full experience of it, however much it evolved in its own justice and

*From "Making Peace," *Breathing the Water*, New Directions, 1987.

positive peace-making: the full experience of peace could only come in a *world* at peace. It's like the old song,

> *I* want / *to* be happy,
> *but* I / can't be happy
> *un*less / you are
> happy too!

Meanwhile, as Catherine de Vinck (a Catholic writer all of whose work expresses her deep faith) says in her *Book of Peace*, "Right Now":

Right Now

> Right now, in this house we share
>   —earth the name of it
>   planet of no account
>   in the vast ranges of the sky—
> children are dying
>   lambs with cracked heads
>   their blood dripping on the stones.
>
> Right now, messengers reach us
>   handing out leaflets
>   printed with a single word:
>   death
> misspelled, no longer a dusky angel
> death in the shape of a vulture
>   landing on broken bodies
>   torn flesh.
>
>   .   .   .
>
> How can we mix this knowledge
>   with the bread we eat
>   with the cup we drink?
> Is it enough to fill these words
>   these hollow flutes of bones
>   with aching songs?

And terror is what we know most intimately—that terror and the ache of chronic anxiety Yarrow Cleaves articulates in "One Day."

One Day

When you were thirteen, thoughtful,
you said, "When
the bomb falls, I won't run, I won't
try to get out of the city like
everyone else, in the panic."

When I was a child,
younger than you, I had to
crouch on the floor
at school, under my desk.
How fast could I do it?
The thin bones of my arms
crossed my skull,
for practice. My forehead
went against my knees. I felt
the blinding light of the
windows behind me.
I knew what the bombs did.

"I'll find a tree," you said,
"and the tree will protect me."

Then I turned away, because
I was crying and because you are my child.

What if you stood on the wrong side?

What if the tree, like me, had
only its ashes to give?

What if you have to stand one day
in blasted silence,
screaming, and I can never,
never reach you?

Meanwhile, what we do have is poems of protest, of denouncement, of struggle, and sometimes of comradeship. Little glimpses of what peace means or might mean come through in such poems as Margaret Randall's "The Gloves."

The Gloves

Yes we did march around somewhere and yes it was cold,
we shared our gloves because we had a pair between us
and a New York city cop also shared his big gloves
with me—strange,
he was there to keep our order
and he could do that
and I could take that
back then.
We were marching for the Santa Maria, Rhoda,
a Portuguese ship whose crew had mutinied.
They demanded asylum in Goulart's Brazil
and we marched in support of that demand,
in winter, in New York City,
back and forth before the Portuguese Consulate,
Rockefeller Center, 1961.
I gauge the date by my first child
—Gregory was born late in 1960—as I gauge
so many dates by the first, the second, the third, the fourth,
and I feel his body now, again, close to my breast,
held against cold to our strong steps of dignity.
That was my first public protest, Rhoda,
strange you should retrieve it now
in a letter out of this love of ours
alive these many years.
How many protests since that one, how many
marches and rallies
for greater causes, larger wars, deeper wounds
cleansed or untouched by our rage.
Today a cop would never unbuckle his gloves
and press them around my blue-red hands.

158

Today a baby held to breast
would be a child of my child, a generation removed.
The world is older and I in it
am older,
burning, slower, with the same passions.
The passions are older and so I am also younger
for knowing them more deeply and moving in them
pregnant with fear and fighting.
The gloves are still there, in the cold,
passing from hand to hand.

In that poem (focussed on a small intimate detail—gloves to keep hands warm—and raying out from it to the *sharing* of that minor comfort, and so to the passing from hand to hand, from generation to generation, of a concern and a resolve) peace as such is very far off-stage, a distant unnamed hope which cannot even be considered until issues of justice and freedom have been addressed and cleared. Yet a kind of peace is present in the poem, too, the peace of mutual aid, of love and communion.

The very fine Welsh poet R. S. Thomas, who, though an Anglican priest, often seems more profoundly skeptical and pessimistic than many secular poets, offers in "The Kingdom" a remote and somewhat abstract view of the possibility and nature of peace and a basic prescription for getting there:

It's a long way off but inside it
There are quite different things going on:
Festivals at which the poor man
Is king and the consumptive is
Healed; mirrors in which the blind look
At themselves and love looks at them
Back; and industry is for mending
The bent bones and the minds fractured
By life. It's a long way off, but to get
There takes no time and admission

Is free, if you will purge yourself
Of desire, and present yourself with
Your need only and the simple offering
Of your faith, green as a leaf.

But faith is not complacency; and is grossly distorted if it
leads to passivity, to a belief that God will pull our chestnuts
out of the fire or fix everything with celestial bandaids. Catherine de Vinck corrects any such mistake: we must *act* our faith,
she says, at the end of the last poem in her *Book of Peace*, by
practical communion with others, offering up and sharing our
bodily nourishment, the light of our belief, the living-space we
occupy. The time for *making* peace, for constructing or evolving it, the title of this poem makes us recognize, is now:

A Time for Peace

We can still make it
        gather the threads, the pieces
        each of different size and shade
        to match and sew into a pattern:
                Rose of Sharon
                wedding ring
                circles and crowns.

We can still listen:
        children at play, their voices
        mingling in the present tense
        of a time that can be extended.

Peace, we say
        looking through our pockets
to find the golden word
        the coin to buy that ease
                that place sheltered
                from bullets and bombs.

But what we seek lies elsewhere
 beyond the course of lethargic blood
 beyond the narrow dream
  of resting safe and warm.

If we adjust our lenses
 we see far in the distance
figures of marching people
 homeless, hungry, going nowhere.
Why not call them
 to our mornings of milk and bread?
The coming night will be darker
 than the heart of stones
unless we strike the match
 light the guiding candle
 say yes, there is room after all
  at the inn.

That prescription is for a beginning, a change of attitude, a change of heart; but while it is true that if millions of people acted on it it would revolutionize society, it is *only* a beginning.

What about testimonies of peace on a personal level? Yes, I do believe that poems which record individual epiphanies, moments of tranquillity or bliss, tell us something about what peace might be like. Yet because there *is* not peace they have, always, an undertone of poignancy. We snatch our happiness from the teeth of violence, from the shadow of oppression. And on the whole we do not connect such poems with the idea of *peace as a goal*, but, reading them, experience a momentary relief from the tensions of life lived in a chronic state of emergency.

Muriel Rukeyser, in a poem begun on the trip to Hanoi she and I and Jane Hart made together in 1972, shortly before Nixon's Christmas "carpet-bombing" of the North, wrote of the paradoxical *presence* of peace we felt there in the midst of war:

161

It Is There

Yes, it is there, the city full of music,
Flute music, sounds of children, voices of poets,
The unknown bird in his long call. The bells of peace.

Essential peace, it sounds across the water
In the long parks where the lovers are walking,
Along the lake with its island and pagoda,
And a boy learning to fish. His father threads the line.
Essential peace, it sounds and it stills. Cockcrow.
It is there, the human place.

On what does it depend, this music, the children's games?
A long tradition of rest? Meditation? What peace is so profound
That it can reach all habitants, all children,
The eyes at worship, the shattered in hospitals?
All voyagers?
                    Meditation, yes; but within a tension
Of long resistance to all invasion, all seduction of hate.
Generations of holding to resistance; and within this resistance
Fluid change that can respond, that can show the children
A long future of finding, of responsibility; change within
Change and tension of sharing consciousness
Village to city, city to village, person to person entire
With unchanging cockcrow and unchanging endurance
Under the
                    skies of war.

On that journey I had felt the same thing—the still center, the
eye of the storm: "Peace within the / long war" I called it, in a
poem called "In Peace Province."

Yes, though I have said we cannot write about peace because
we've never experienced it, we do have these glimpses of it, and
we have them most intensely when they are brought into relief
by the chaos and violence surrounding them. The longing for
peace, however, is a longing to get beyond not only the mo-
mentariness of such glimpses but also the ominous dualism that

162

too often seems our only way of obtaining these moments. Experienced only through the power of contrast, a peace in any larger sense would be as false as any other artificial Paradise, or as the hectic flush of prosperity periodically induced in ailing economies by injections of war and arms-industry jobs and profits.

An important understanding we have belatedly begun to gain is that the issue of peace (in the sense of freedom from military conflict) and the issue of social justice (with its economic, racial, and educational dimensions, and its outstanding deficits such as hunger, homelessness, crime, violence, abuse, and lack of medical care) not only cannot be separated from each other but cannot be rationally considered without an equal focus on ecology. The poetry of ecology (and the related prose of a number of current writers too) is not a poetry *of peace*, in the depictive sense which I maintain is not possible "ahead of itself," but it is as important to the *cause* of peace as anything now being written.

John Daniel, in his book *Common Ground*, writes of the mystery of there being anything at all, and of love for the earth:

Of Earth

Swallows looping and diving
by the darkening oaks, the flash
of their white bellies,
the tall grasses gathering last light,
glowing pale gold, silence
overflowing in a shimmer of breeze—
these could have happened
a different way. The heavy-trunked oaks
might not have branched and branched
and finely re-branched
as if to weave themselves into air.
There is no necessity
that any creature should fly,

that last light should turn
the grasses gold, that grasses
should exist at all,
or light.

        But a mind thinking so
is a mind wandering from home.
It is not thought that answers
each step of my feet, to be walking here
in the cool stir of dusk
is no mere possibility,
and I am so stained with the sweet
peculiar loveliness of things
that given God's power to dream worlds
from the dark, I know
I could only dream Earth—
birds, trees, this field of light
where I and each of us walk once.

This is a clear example of the kind of poem, the kind of perception, which must for our time *stand in* for a poetry of peace. It is
an epiphany both personal and universal, common to all conscious humans, surely, in kind if not in degree. Whether they
remember it or not, surely everyone at least once in a lifetime is
filled for a moment with a sense of wonder and exhilaration.
But the poem's poignancy is peculiar to the late twentieth century. In the past, the dark side of such a poem would have been
the sense of the brevity of our own lives, of mortality within a
monumentally enduring Nature. Eschatology, whether theological or geological, was too remote in its considerations to
have much direct impact on a poetic sensibility illumined by
the intense presentness of a moment of being. But today the
shadow is deeper and more chilling, for it is the reasonable fear
that the earth itself, to all intents and purposes, is so threatened
by our actions that its hold on life is as tenuous as our own, its
fate as precarious. Poets who direct our attention to injustice,
oppression, the suffering of the innocent and the heroism of

those who struggle for change, serve the possibility of peace by stimulating others to support that struggle. Yesterday it was Vietnam, today it is El Salvador or Lebanon or Ireland. Closer to home, the Ku Klux Klan rides again, the Skinheads multiply. Hunger and homelessness, AIDS, crack and child abuse. There are poems—good, bad, or indifferent—written every day somewhere about all of these, and they are a poetry of war. Yet one may say that they are a proto-peace poetry; for they testify to a rejection which, though it cannot in itself create a state of peace, is one of its indispensable preconditions. For war is no longer (if it ever was) a matter of armed conflict only. As we become more aware of the inseparability of justice from peace, we perceive that hunger and homelessness and our failure to stop them are forms of warfare, and that no one is a civilian. And we perceive that our degradation of the biosphere is the most devastating war of all. The threat of nuclear holocaust simply proposes a more sudden variation in a continuum of violence we are already engaged in. Oil spills are events in that ongoing war. Deforestation is a kind of protracted trench-warfare.

Our consciousness lags so far behind our actions. W. S. Merwin has written about this time-lag:

Chord

While Keats wrote they were cutting down the sandalwood forests
while he listened to the nightingale they heard their own axes echoing through the forests . . .
while he thought of the Grecian woods, they bled under red flowers
while he dreamed of wine the trees were falling from the trees . . .
while the song broke over him they were in a secret place and they were cutting it forever . . .
when he lay with the odes behind him the wood was sold for cannons
when he lay watching the window they came home and lay down
and an age arrived when everything was explained in another language

165

The tree has become a great symbol of what we need, what we destroy, what we must revere and protect and learn from if life on earth is to continue and that mysterious hope, *life at peace*, is to be attained. The tree's deep and wide root-system, its broad embrace and lofty reach from earth into air, its relation to fire and to human structures, as fuel and as material, and especially to water which it not only needs but gives (drought ensuing when the forests are destroyed) just as it gives us purer air—all these make it a powerful archetype. The Swedish poet Reidar Ekner has written in "Horologium" as follows:

> Where the tree germinates, it takes root
> there it stretches up its thin spire
> there it sends down the fine threads
> gyroscopically it takes its position
> In the seed the genes whisper: stretch out for the light
> > and seek the dark
> And the tree seeks the light, it stretches out
> > for the dark
> And the more darkness it finds, the more light
> > it discovers
> the higher towards the light it reaches, the further down
> > towards darkness
> it is groping
>
> Where the tree germinates, it widens
> it drinks in from the dark, it sips from the light
> intoxicated by the green blood, spirally it turns
> the sun drives it, the sap rushes through the fine pipes
> > towards the light
> the pressure from the dark drives it out
> > to the points, one
> golden morning the big crown of the tree
> > turns green, from all directions insects, and birds
> It is a giddiness, one cone
> > driving the other

Inch after inch the tree takes possession of its place
it transforms the dark into tree
it transforms the light into tree
it transforms the place into tree
It incorporates the revolutions of the planet, one after the other
the bright semicircle, the dark semicircle
Inside the bark, it converts time into tree

The tree has four dimensions, the fourth one
      memory
far back its memory goes, further back than that of Man,
      than the heart of any living beings
for a long time the corpse of the captured highwayman hung
      from its branches
The oldest ones, they remember the hunting people, the shell
  mounds,
      the neolithic dwellings
They will remember our time, too; our breathing out,
      they will breathe it in
Hiroshima's time, they breathe it in, cryptomeria
also this orbit of the planet, they add it to their growth
Time, they are measuring it; time pieces they are, seventy centuries
      the oldest ones carry in their wood

Ekner causes us to perceive the tree as witness; and when we
are stopped in our tracks by a witness to our foolishness, the
effect is, at least for a moment, that which A. E. Housman
described when he wrote,

> But man at whiles is sober,
>   And thinks, by fits and starts;
> And when he thinks, he fastens
>   His hand upon his heart.

No; if there begins to be a poetry of peace, it is still, as it has
long been, a poetry of struggle. Much of it is not by the fa-

mous, much of it is almost certainly still unpublished. And much of it is likely to be by women, because so many women are actively engaged in nonviolent action, and through their work they have been gathering practical experience in ways of peaceful community. Ann Snitow, writing in 1985 about the Greenham Common Peace Camp in England, said that,

> . . . In a piece in the *Times Literary Supplement* . . . "Why the Peace Movement Is Wrong," the Russian émigré poet Joseph Brodsky [has] charged the peace movement with being a bunch of millenarians waiting for the apocalypse. Certainly there are fascinating parallels between the thinking of the peace women and that of the radical millenarian Protestant sects of the 17th century. Both believe that the soul is the only court that matters, the self the only guide, and that paradise is a humble and realizable goal in England's green and pleasant land. The millenarians offered free food just like the caravans now on the Common: Food, says one sign. Eat till You're Full.
>
> But the women are not sitting in the mud waiting for the end, nor are they—as Brodsky and many others claim—trying to come to terms with their own deaths by imagining that soon the whole world will die. On the contrary . . . the women believe that the dreadful sound [of the last trump] can be avoided, if only we will stop believing in it. . . . They, too, have imagined the end, and their own deaths, and have decided that they prefer to die without taking the world with them. Nothing makes them more furious than the apathy in the town of Newbury, where they are often told, "Look, you've got to die anyway. So what difference does it make how you go?" These are the real millenarians, blithely accepting that the end is near.
>
> In contrast, the women look very hardheaded, very pragmatic. . . . They refuse to be awed or silenced by the war machine. Instead they say calmly that what was built by human beings can be dismantled by them, too.
>
> . . . Where is it written, they ask, that we must destroy ourselves?

A poetry of struggle and vision must be informed by an equally passionate refusal to accept the worst scenario as inevitable—but only after facing the fact that we have come very close to the brink. And it is sobering to reflect that it may be harder by far to halt the ecological catastrophe we have brought about than to dismantle our arsenals.

There can be, then, a poetry which may help us, before it is too late, to attain peace. Poems of protest, documentaries of the state of war, can waken or reinforce a necessary recognition of urgency. Poems of praise for life and the living earth can stimulate us to protect it. (The work of Gary Snyder, of Wendell Berry, comes to mind among others.) Poems of comradeship in struggle can help us—like the thought of those shared gloves in the Margaret Randall poem—to know the dimension of community, so often absent from modern life. And there is beginning to be a new awareness, articulated most specifically in the writings of Father Thomas Berry, the talks and workshops of people like Miriam McGillis or Joanna Macy, that we humans are not just walking around *on* this planet but that we and all things are truly, physically, biologically, part of one living organism; and that our human role on earth is as the consciousness and self-awareness of that organism. A poem by John Daniel, who almost certainly had not read Thomas Berry, shows how this realization is beginning to appear spontaneously in many minds (perhaps rather on the lines of the story of the hundredth monkey):

> . . . a voice is finding its tongue
> in the slop and squall of birth.
>
> It sounds,
>
> and we, in whom Earth happened to light
> a clear flame of consciousness,
> are only beginning to learn the language—

who are made of the ash of stars,
who carry the sea we were born in,
who spent millions of years learning to breathe,
who shivered in fur at the reptiles' feet,
who trained our hands on the limbs of trees
and came down, slowly straightening
to look over the grasses, to see
that the world not only is

                but is beautiful—

we are Earth learning to see itself . . .

If this consciousness (with its corollary awareness that when we exploit and mutilate the earth we are exploiting and mutilating the body of which we are the brain cells) increases and proliferates while there is still time, it could be the key to survival. A vision of peace cannot be a vision of a world in which *natural* disasters are miraculously eliminated: but it must be of a society in which companionship and fellowship would so characterize the tone of daily life that unavoidable disasters would be differently met. Earthquakes and floods do, anyway, elicit neighborliness, briefly at least; a peaceful society would have to be one capable of *maintaining* that love and care for the afflicted. Only lovingkindness could sustain a lasting peace.

How can poetry relate to that idea? Certainly not by preaching. But as more and more poets know and acknowledge (as I believe they are already starting to do) that we are indeed "made of the ash of stars," their art, stirring the imagination of those who read them (few, perhaps, but always a dynamic few, a thin edge of the wedge) can have an oblique influence which cannot be measured. We cannot long survive at all unless we *do* move towards peace. If a poetry of peace is ever to be written, there must first be this stage we are just entering—the poetry of *preparation* for peace, a poetry of protest, of lament, of praise for the living earth; a poetry that demands justice, renounces violence, reveres mystery. We need to incorporate into our daily lives this psalm from the Hako (Pawnee, Osage, Omaha) tradition:

Invoking the Powers

> Remember, remember the circle of the sky
> the stars and the brown eagle
> the supernatural winds
> breathing night and day
> from the four directions
>
> Remember, remember the great life of the sun
> breathing on the earth
> it lies upon the earth
> to bring out life upon the earth
> life covering the earth
>
> Remember, remember the sacredness of things
> running streams and dwellings
> the young within the nest
> a hearth for sacred fire
> the holy flame of fire

From a lecture given in the 1989 Boston University "Celebrating Peace" series. A version of the text is included in Volume II of the *Boston University Studies in Philosophy & Religion*, published by Notre Dame University Press in 1990.

Biography and the Poet

(1992)

I WANT TO TALK about the relationship of certain kinds of poems to a current trend in literary biography, and to pose some questions I think readers and writers should be asking about this relationship, its causes and its implications. The kind of biographies I'm thinking of are those which explore and reveal whatever in the subject's life was dubious, scandalous, sensational. Such accounts of the lives of poets are popular, and are read by thousands of people who are not habitual readers of poetry: the skeletons dragged out of the poet's closet (in one case with the collusion of her heirs and psychiatrist) are apparently far more compelling to them than poems, and if they do go on to read the poems too it is often with the same prurient curiosity stimulated by the biography.

Writers of what is called "confessional" poetry—poetry which voluntarily makes public, often in startling, emphatic imagery, experiences and perceptions which once were considered private—are not the only poets whose lives are investigated in this manner, but "confessional" poems do seem to give tacit encouragement in the trend. If the author was willing to disclose intimacies, has not the biographer thereby been given license to do so? This question leads to others, and indicates, I believe, that we need to learn to discriminate better between works of art, which though sometimes openly self-revealing attain aesthetic integrity, and works which, wholly or in part, are manifestations of exhibitionism. (When the latter happen to concern experiences similar to the reader's own, the distinction may be hard to make, for the content will be undeniably emotive; in readers who have not had analogous experiences, that content may elicit pity or empathic compassion.) Before we look further into this matter, however, let us turn to that of biography.

In considering the nature of biography (and I'll restrict this to biographies of poets, though it obviously applies to others as well) we need to reflect on its function or functions. First, we must suppose the subject's creative opus is of such quality that a biography is called for at all; or else that his or her relation to a movement, to other more important writers, or some similar historical or sociological reason, merits such study. Second, we must ask if the book is intended as a work of reference, in which, by consulting the all-important index and chronology, we can find dates and facts relating to the subject's work. Whether the subject exchanged ideas with X, Y, or Z, or was influenced by them; or at what date a certain poem was composed and whether an earlier version of it exists—information of this kind may expand our understanding of the poems themselves. And third, if the biography is one which attempts, through the use of letters, diaries, interviews, and the biographer's own impressions and opinions, to describe the poet's states of mind, physical presence, personality, medical history, and sexual experiences, we must ask whether this "inside" information, like the "bare facts" of the well-indexed reference book, adds valuably to what we receive from the subject's own creative opus. It is natural that if we enjoy the work, or think it important, we feel some interest in the person who made it. But we know virtually nothing of Shakespeare's life, and that little is held to be unverifiable; would the millions who have been affected by the plays be even more deeply enriched if every episode of his life were to be found documented in some antique hoard of papers? I think not. Yet there are biographies that truly instruct and delight.

An example of an excellent biography which combines two functions is Walter Jackson Bate's *Life of Keats*. Together with all its well-indexed factual data, Bate suggests what less cut-and-dried factors may have entered into the composition of this or that poem; but he refrains from psychologizing for the sake of psychologizing. The work itself is always the central focus of his attention. The people, places, books, conversations, and impressions of Keats' life are discussed because of their bearing on his poems, the raison d'être of the biography, and not in order to satisfy any mere inquisitiveness. In contrast, the biographies I deplore focus on any scandalous or dramatic peculiarities of the poet, and whether they are relevant to the poems as works of art is not seriously questioned.

If biographies like Bate's and others of its caliber constitute personal critiques and tributes without straying into the over-subjective, much less into mere sensationalism and gossip, they are helped in this by the time elapsed since their subjects lived and died. One problem with modern biography is that "lives" get written before their subjects are cold in their graves. (If they go a step further and biographize living persons, authorization or vigorous denial can at least take place!) But with or without a decent interval, there should be a recognition that although our understanding of cultural history is increased by a certain range of factual information, yet all that is most interesting about an artist's life must be in the work itself. There the autobiographical is often completely transformed, or, if undisguisedly recounted, is selected, and invested with a significance which transcends the ephemeral and narrowly personal. When this transcendence does not take place, autobiographical material lacks the resonance we find in poems pervaded by a larger context. Yeats' Maude Gonne is not just Maude Gonne, and the poet is not just Willy Yeats who was in love with her. She is Cathleen Ni Houlihan, she is Ireland herself, and he the Irish people in love with their country. In our own time, Milosz only writes explicitly of his own life-story as much as is demanded by his major theme, the human intellect and the human soul within the turmoil of twentieth century history. No one could extract a biography from his *Collected Poems*. William Carlos Williams, who so strongly emphasized the virtue of the concrete image and of "finding the universal in the local," was equally discreet and selective in his poems. They come directly out of his experience, yes, yet we can learn from them precious little in the way of biography: that he was a doctor, most of whose patients were poor immigrants; that his wife's name was Floss; that he lived in New Jersey, in sight of the New York skyline across the Hudson—that's about it. Even when, in old age, he obliquely confesses to Floss the infidelities which accompanied his love for her, he does not even verge on making public the physical details of events intrinsically intimate. Biographically speaking, Williams reveals almost as little as Wallace Stevens or T. S. Eliot. As A. N. Wilson wrote in a review of a life of Arthur Ransome, the author of *Swallows and Amazons* and other first-rate children's books, "the money, the illnesses, the marriages . . . are just the chaff which the imagination has discarded." In other words, the lives of poets and other artists are not usually more interesting than anyone else's. Conversely, great novels make us realize that the most uneventful of lives can have deep interest. Those subtle currents of feeling and perception a great writer of fiction can reveal beneath the surface of "ordinary" lives are far more interesting than the scandals and dramas some biographers bring to the fore. If a poet's life is more interesting than his or her poetry, it doesn't say much for the poems. It is in these, if they are good, that one can trace those essential hidden streams of inner life.

Perhaps in the kind of poem from which it seems as if not enough chaff has been discarded, the real problem is not so much a lack of selectivity as an insistent inclusion of material once thought of as private, and which can dominate a poem to the detriment of its intended focus and its artistic integrity.

When this happens, the relation between poet and reader—or *poem* and reader—changes. Just as alcoholism, mental breakdowns, violence, and turbulent sexual histories of celebrities in any field makes them magnets for popular curiosity, so the inclusion in poems of certain kinds of intimate data lays them open to a *prying* kind of reading even before a biographer embarks on any investigation of the author.

There is a restraint in, for instance, the enduringly moving elegies of the past—whether we think, in our own century, of Rexroth's poem to his first wife, Andrée Rexroth, or back to Ben Jonson's farewell to his seven-year-old first-born son, or the *Exequy* of Henry King—a restraint rarely found in more contemporary poems of bereavement. (A notable exception seems to me to be David Ray's *Sam's Book*, because what emerges most strongly from this group of poems is not so much the father's inconsolable grief slowly modulating from initial shock to full integration with his ongoing life—though that is strongly and memorably conveyed—as the vivid spirit of the boy Sam himself, individual, yet archetypal.)

As much as lack of restraint, perhaps what troubles me in many comparable contemporary poems is their egotism. Elegies which are self-centered or excessively confessional often make us feel guilty of unkindness and insensitivity if we dare to think for a moment that the recently dead beloved is, in effect, being exploited. It is not that we doubt the reality of the anguish itself; yet we feel manipulated by its instant and repeated public display. When the protagonists of a particular real-life love-story broken by death are spotlighted in the survivor's poems (which one by one may be beautiful) these poems as a set cannot convey archetypal grief but remain exclusively attached to a specific life-history. The same is true of love poems: a sensuality evoked by anecdotally restricted means is less erotic than that which is less explicit, more stylized, more mysterious.

What motivates poets to give away information which makes them more than normally vulnerable to vulgar curiosity? We need to couple this question with a similar enquiry into the public appetite for scandal, shock, and any kind of intimate revelation—which in some degree all of us share, as we all breathe the same cultural air. I cannot pretend to unravel the social psychology involved; but I think I see some historical factors that have affected certain poetic practices and their acceptance by readers.

One of these was that during the 1950s or early '60s William Carlos Williams' emphasis on the concrete local particulars of daily life as a poet's vital source quietly began to be diluted and distorted. The result was thousands of banal poems, poems in which a description (possibly of intrinsic interest) of something the writer had seen was prefaced by the entirely superfluous information that he *had* seen it and was on his way to a tavern at the time as he needed a beer. The setting had gobbled up the gemstone, since at least as much time was given to the preface as to the point. Poems of this type became so prevalent that they were accepted as the norm (and they have certainly not disappeared from the scene). This norm, with its gratuitous reiteration of the first person singular, paved the way for the further narcissism which ensued as the confessional school came to the fore. (I should mention here that though Robert Lowell is cited as that school's chief instigator, his own work in the confessional vein is sharply differentiated by his overriding historical sense, which places all that stems from his individual history into a larger objective configuration.) Then, later in the '60s, a number of concepts began to be voiced in American society which, as they filtered slowly into some degree of general acceptance and into the minds of poets too, underwent distortion just as Williams' ideas had done. One of these concepts was encapsulated in the slogan, "Let it all hang out." Whether this expression originated with one of the Beat poets or elsewhere, its primary significance was political, and its aesthetic adoption was a secondary effect, dependent on individual artistic judgment and choice.

As people awoke to the hypocrisy of the state's claim to be defending democracy rather than admitting that the war in Vietnam, like other wars, was being fought for a whole complex of economic and geopolitical reasons, a lot of other hypocrisies came to light at the same time. A whole generation became aware of the disparity between their parents' way of living and their stated values. "Let it all hang out" emerged as a cry for truthfulness, for an end to lying in politics and the whole social fabric; a call to proclaim that the Emperor (in this case, what in those days we called The War Machine, and by extension the social system supporting it) had no clothes of truth and justice. Naturally the arts could not but be affected; however, instead of the ever-greater concern for artistic precision and integrity which should have been the logical translation into creative works of this underlying meaning, the slogan was interpreted as a justification for an aesthetic of exhibitionism.

There is a difference between dragging a skeleton out of a cupboard into daylight and keeping the skeleton on permanent display. The "group grope" (does anyone remember that expression?) may be the opposite of prudery but is not its only alternative. In a D.C. jail after a big demonstration and mass arrest in the early '70s I recall seeing a young woman masturbating in the midst of a crowd of other women. No one made even a whispered comment. That a private act was being made utterly public was apparently considered acceptable—or at least no one dared to remonstrate for fear of being thought puritanical. Modesty was taken for prudery, an attachment to privacy was mistaken for elitism and a lack of open-hearted frankness.

The slogan "the personal is political" came into use around the same time. What this should mean, I think, is that how you act in daily life should reflect your political convictions. For example, it is hypocritical and also ineffective to work for peace and justice if you are belligerent to family and friends. But by many people it was used as an excuse to retreat from political action of any kind; and to some poets, it seems to have meant that the "particular and local" were enough in themselves without any concern for finding the universal. Of course, it is fatal to go in deliberate search of universality—that way only pomposity lies; yet a poet does need to know and acknowledge a larger frame of reference than his or her own accidental particulars; and without some longing to reach out to such a context, little of poetic substance will result.

Linked to this theme of "the personal is political" is the journal-writing movement of the '70s and '80s, an outgrowth of "human potential," "personal growth," and other holistic programs, and closely associated with feminism though it is not exclusive to women's groups. Keeping a journal or diary can be really valuable to anyone—though one has to beware that one doesn't start to make it the goal of living. But for poets it can create a problem. Journals or diaries are in essence private. Poems, too, deal with intimate experience, but they select and transform it, if they are good poems. Too often, the measure of candor appropriate to a free-standing work of art is superseded by the much larger measure that may serve a cathartic purpose in the psychological development of the diarist, whose pages are to be read by no one but their writer—and perhaps only once by him or her, since the act of writing has itself fulfilled the need. The widespread encouragement of journal-writing and its discussion as an art genre, along with the publication of selections from the journals of living writers, has tended to blur the distinctions between "private" and "public." It seems that some poets lose a sense of where diary ends and poem begins. Journal entries which consist of philosophical or other reflections, record observations of nature, and so forth, are a fascinating kind of informal essay; and from those in which a writer or other artist talks about craft and creative process, or edges up on a work about to begin, there is often much more to be learned than from formal essays. One is grateful to the

179

author for granting a glimpse into the alchemist's kitchen. But I've seen other published diary excerpts of such a confidential nature that, once again, one questions motivation.

Is there perhaps, in every act of artistic communication, something questionable? We poets are strangely willing to read in public, thus baring our souls with more immediacy than when paper and print intervene, and exposing them, after the reading, to impertinent questions from total strangers. I wonder about this willingness every time I read! The justification, of course, is the belief that one has *made a work*. All makers of art must believe that they are contributing a thing to the sum of things, and that it has some value and a life of its own to live. Without such belief they would not be able to serve the art they practice; however modest, however self-critical, without that grain of faith an artist is paralyzed. But that justification cannot extend to genuine journals. Isn't there something kinky about voluntarily "sharing," as they say, something the very nature of which is destroyed by so doing? A compulsive need, like a Dostoyevsky character, to turn the reader into a voyeur? It is the same phenomenon I have remarked on in regard to some poems. And again, audience compliance involves us all in some measure.

A blurring of the boundary between private and public leads to the gradual loss of the very idea of privacy—a loss which, like the increasing attrition of certain grammatical nuances, and a vocabulary shrinking except in technological words, is a form of erosion affecting the whole human ecology. Television and the development of communications technology are generally, and I think correctly, held responsible for some of this erosion. As everyone knows, extreme violence, actual and fictive, has long since erupted into people's livingrooms, interspersed with advertisements, comedy, and scenes of explicit sexual intercourse, in such a way that all these things run together—equally vivid, equally meaningless. The telephone has intruded into our lives at unwelcome moments for over a century now. Data banks contain, we are told, all manner of information about us which we were not aware of having imparted to anyone. Marked trails, garbage cans, and garbage (not always in the cans) make a sense of solitude hard to find for those who seek it in what is supposed to be wilderness. One might think privacy and intimacy would be all the more valued in such an environment, but instead their very nature is obscured. When external factors invade what we possess of them, they meet little resistance. How many people, for example, take any steps to prevent telemarketing calls, calls which not only interrupt them at the dinner table or whatever else they happen to be doing, but in which the caller immediately addresses them by their first name?

Yet another factor, deeper than these, is contemporary embarrassment at formalities, at anything recognized as ritual (though unrecognized rituals exist in daily life). This is clear in religious ceremonies, where something parallel to excessive naturalism in the dramatic theater is often substituted for the powerful distancing inherent in the traditional liturgical practices of any religion—practices from which theater itself evolved. Yet there is a deep human need for ritual. Old forms of it, like old prosodic forms, may not accommodate, unchanged, the changing needs of the people, but the new forms that evolve lose their power if they lose the very character of ritual or ceremony, just as new formal explorations in poetry must retain their intrinsically poetic character and not become a form of journalism.

The embarrassment at formality which (along with a lack of imagination) results in unsatisfactory alternatives to rituals that have ceased to be emotionally effective, seems to be related to that same blurring of boundaries. When everything is made personal (as in a priest greeting the people at the beginning of Mass with "Good morning," to which they reply, "Good morning, Father," instead of saying "Peace be with you" and receiving the response, "And with thy spirit"), then the personal is indistinguishable from the public: the priest is greeted as an individual, and this obscures the nature of his office as priest, which transcends the personal. In the same way, a certain distancing which the great poets of the past demonstrate—the assumption of the bard's mantle, like the vestments of the priest—has been forgone in our time, less for the sake of relevancy than out of some feeling that ceremony is absurd (as indeed it can be when it is undertaken self-consciously and without conviction).

The publication of poems which like diaries (though sometimes with an undeniable beauty or force of language) present unmediated, untransformed, accounts of the most intimate experience, represent a kind of self-invasion. And one of the most troubling aspects of this is its disregard for others.

> My love's manners in bed
> are not to be discussed by me

wrote Robert Creeley in 1959. I've read many a poem that made me feel the author would have done well to profit by this maxim. But adults can object and defend themselves if they feel exposed and exploited as characters in someone's drama of self-revelation; children can not. Yet there are many poems in which a parent—and I have to acknowledge that, in my observation, it is most often a mother—writes of a child in ways liable to cause acute, even traumatic embarrassment when that child sooner or later reads that poem. These are poems—or images in poems—which focus on the child's body, and in particular its genitalia. Imagine a shy adolescent finding in print a graphic description of his little penis at age five, its color and shape! Worse, imagine his schoolmates reading the poem and teasing him about it! Was the description vital to the poem? Often, I would say it was not. But in some instances it may be. In that case, the writer should have recognized, I think, that though tone and intent were tender, the poem should remain unpublished—at least until the child is an adult and his consent can be requested.*

It is important to note a type of autobiographical poem which does not partake of the gratuitous and self-important, but which brings to light acts of oppression and cruelty. Victims of racism, rape, torture, incest, and other abuses and crimes who dare to tell their stories speak for others who have been stifled and silenced by their own sufferings and who too often have felt, in some confused way, complicit. Some degree of liberation may come to them in knowing that they are not unique in what happened to them. Whether a more general knowledge of, for example, child abuse, actually helps to make a society less prone to it I doubt, however; it almost seems, depressingly, as if the more instances that are uncovered the more it proliferates. This seems true of rape also. But this can only be a matter of conjecture, whereas the breaking of silence in such instances is of clear personal benefit, and if it results in poems of high integrity these should, of course, be published.

Highly evolved, compassionate individuals who have come to perceive, over time, the oppressions in the lives of their own oppressors (which, in some instances, were the cause of their warping) and who have seen remorse, growth, and change take place in such individuals, will still face an ethical dilemma in deciding whether to publish poems which retrospectively explore past misdeeds. But the right decision might be to set aside these scruples, for such objective revelations, unlike the work of narcissistic poets who exploit themselves and their intimates, are not exclusively self-serving although they may free their authors from the paralysis of shame and concealment.

The principle of consideration for the privacy of others could of course be carried to absurdity, and prevent the publication of virtually everything; its application calls for common sense

*A friend pointed out to me that such poems manifest the all too common unconscious assumption among parents that their children "belong" to them, like extensions of their own bodies.

as well as sensitivity. But a corrective is certainly needed—not from without, in the form of censorship, but from within the poet as a scrupulous avoidance of exploitively or hurtfully utilizing the lives of others: a form of *self*-censorship exercised with a balance of aesthetic and ethical awareness.

This leads one to ask, if catharsis is one of the functions of art, can it co-exist with such compunction? It's a serious question. But one has to follow it with another: catharsis for whom? For the writer, the writing has already provided it, and publication is inessential. For the reader, what is cathartic is not necessarily what was so for the writer; and cannot catharsis for the reader happen except at the expense of the writer's intimates? Is loss of intimacy for the writer the sacrifice without which no redemption can occur? Nothing in the Greek dramatists, whose work first consciously attempted that "purification by pity and fear," leads one to suppose so, nor is there later evidence of such a necessity.

If poets and readers undertook to ponder these questions it might, perhaps, have an effect on the market for sensational biography. The poet's own idea of what constitutes a "Life" may have to change before the biographies do. How different in its assumptions from those of our time is the bare list of facts, more of them about his brother than himself, with which the seventeenth-century poet Henry Vaughan modestly, albeit with eager courtesy replied to John Aubrey's request for particulars of his life! How that modesty contrasts with the egotism of writers who assume the reader wants to know that they have smelly feet or that a sibling once deliberately pissed on them . . . .

Iris Origo, the admirable historian, wrote that the two great virtues of the biographer are enthusiasm and veracity, and that three "insidious temptations . . . assail" him or her: "to suppress, to invent, or to sit in judgement." But she speaks also, in the same essay on the art of biography, of "a new age of journalism, which is too curious about the great" and which Henry

James described as emanating from "the cunning and ferocity of . . . inquisitive hunters whose quarry is all that calls for privacy and silence." Origo's own work demonstrates how a biographer, like a poet, can maintain veracity and avoid the suppression which would falsify, yet can judiciously discard chaff, just as a poet must (though much of what is chaff to poems is vital grain to biography, e.g., historical minutiae of genuine relevance).

Proust's criticism of "the method of Sainte Beuve" was essentially that the information it collected did not throw light on an author's work but was concerned with the irrelevant. An argument can be made for the relevancy of much biographical information, but not for all of it. As long as poets publish with a disregard for their own and other's privacy, they contribute to the trashing of that very realm of inwardness which is the source of their art. The deepest communication, the lasting communion of which poetry is capable, always flows from that inner center outward to meet the other inward depth that receives it. I will close with a quotation that beautifully articulates that reality: "The reason for this correcting and rewriting was his search for strength and exactness of expression," Pasternak wrote, in Dr. Zhivago:

> but it also corresponded to the promptings of an inward reticence which forbade him to expose his personal experiences and the real events of his past with too much freedom, lest he should offend or wound those who had directly taken part in them. As a result, the steaming and pulsing of his feelings was gradually driven out of his poems, and so far from their becoming morbid and devitalized, there appeared in them a broad peace and reconciliation which lifted the particular to the level of the universal, accessible to all.

Anne Sexton:
Light Up the Cave
(1974)

ANNE SEXTON'S DEATH SOME weeks ago saddened a great many people. In addition, it startled those who had assumed that, despite all the troubles of which her poetry told, she had come to the long stretch of middle age with some reserves of strength. I am told, though, that the friends who knew her best were confirmed in their fear that her determination towards suicide had not really been deflected. My own sadness at the death of a fellow poet is compounded by the sense of how likely it is that Anne Sexton's tragedy will not be without influence in the tragedies of other lives.

She herself was, obviously, too intensely troubled to be fully aware of her influence or to take on its responsibility. Therefore it seems to me that we who are alive must make clear, as she could not, the distinction between creativity and self-destruction. The tendency to confuse the two has claimed too many victims. Anne Sexton herself seems to have suffered deeply from this confusion, and I surmise that her friendship with Sylvia Plath had in it an element of identification which added powerfully to her malaise. Across the country, at different colleges, I have heard many stories of attempted—and sometimes successful—suicides by young students who loved the poetry of Plath and who supposed that somehow, in order to become poets themselves, they had to act out in their own lives the events of hers. I don't want to see a new epidemic of the same syndrome occurring as a response to Anne Sexton's death.

The problem is not, however, related only to suicide *per se*. When Robert Lowell was at the height of his fame among student readers (his audience nowadays is largely an older one) many of them seemed to think a nervous breakdown was, if not imperative, at least an invaluable shortcut to artistry. When W. D. Snodgrass's *Heart's Needle* won the Pulitzer Prize, young couples married and divorced, it seemed, especially in order to have the correct material to write about.

I am not being flippant. Innumerable young poets have drunk themselves into stupidity and cirrhosis because they admired John Berryman or Dylan Thomas and came to think they must drink like them to write like them. At the very least it is assumed that creativity and hangups are inevitably insepa-rable. One student (male) said to me recently, "I was amazed when the first poet I met seemed to be a cheerful person and not any more fucked up than anyone else. When I was in high school I got the idea you *had* to be fucked up to be a real artist!" And a young English teacher in a community college told me she had given up writing poetry because she believed there were unavoidable links between depression and anxiety and the making of art. "Don't you feel terrible when you write poems?"

What exactly is the nature of the confusion, and how has it come about? The mistake itself lies in taking what may possi-bly be an occupational hazard as a prescriptive stimulus to artistic activity. Whether artists as a class are in fact more vulnerable than other people, or whether their problems merely have more visibility, a serious and intelligent statistical study might perhaps tell us. It makes no difference: the point is that while the creative impulse and the self-destructive impulse can, and often do, coexist, their relationship is distinctly acausal; self-destructiveness is a handicap to the life of art, not the reverse.

Yet it is the handicaps themselves that so often allure the young and untried. The long lives of so many of the greatest artists, sometimes apparently uneventful, sometimes full of passion and suffering, but full too of endurance, and always dominated by love of their work, seem not to attract as models. Picasso, Matisse, Monet, Cezanne, Pissarro, Corot, Rembrandt, Titian, Tintoretto, J. S. Bach, Stravinsky, Goethe, William Carlos Williams, Stevens, Pound, Neruda, Machado, Yeats, Shakespeare, Whitman, Tolstoi. . . . There is romance in their tenacity, their devotion, but it is overlooked. Why is this? There are topical reasons, but their roots are in the past, their nature historical and political.

In summary, western culture began, during the Renaissance—only recently, that is to say, in the calendar of human history—to emphasize individuality to a degree merely foreshadowed in Greece and Rome or in the theological dramas of the Old Testament. Geographical and scientific discoveries spurred the sense of what humanity on its own could do. The "Elizabethan world picture" had wholeness and consistency; but it held the seeds of an expanded view of things. And as feudal social systems underwent economic changes with the rise of the merchant class and the growth of banking procedures, so, too, the social and economic circumstances in which art was produced underwent changes that heightened the new sense of individuality.

The relationship of the artist to other people rapidly altered. The people began to become "the public," "the audience" and the poet, set aside from that "public," began to become more private, more introspective. When his work (or hers—but it was a long time before there were women poets in any numbers) was printed it was increasingly a revelation to the public of the highly personal, rather than being to a large degree the voice of the people itself which it had been the bard's task, in earlier times, to sound forth. The value put on individual expression, the concept of "originality," and ultimately even upon individualism as a creed, had been pushed further by the time we reach the period of Romanticism, which developed alongside the Industrial Revolution and was in part reactive to the prospect of facelessness presented to the prophetic eye by that phenomenon.

Twentieth-century alienation is another phase of the reaction. What began as a realization of human potential, a growth of *individuated* consciousness (to use Jung's useful term) out of the unconscious collective, became first a glorification of willful, essentially optimistic individualism, echoing the ambitious, optimistic individualism of its capitalist context, and then, as that turned sour and revealed more and more of greed in its operations, led to the setting of a high esthetic and moral value upon alienation itself.

But alienation is of ethical value, is life-affirmative and conducive to creativity only when it is accompanied by a political consciousness that imagines and affirms (and works toward) an alternative to the society from which it turns away in disgust. Lacking this, the alienated person, if he or she is gifted, becomes especially a prey to the exploitation that characterizes capitalism and is its underlying principle. The manifestations—in words, music, paint, or what have you—of private anguish are exploited by a greedy public, a public greedy for emotion at second hand because starved of the experience of community. Concurrently, for the same reasons, a creative person—whether a pop star or a Sylvia Plath, a John Berryman, or an Anne Sexton—internalizes the exploitive, unwittingly becoming *self*-exploitive.

And if the public is greedy, the critics, at their worst, are positively ghoulish, or at the least, irresponsible. I feel, for instance, that it is irresponsible for a columnist, in a memorial eulogy, to have written of Anne Sexton, "The manner of her death is at once frightening and fascinating to those who responded to her poetry, sharing as they do many of the same fears and insecurities she articulated so well. Her death awakens those fears and insecurities, the way some of her poems did, it raises them up from where they hide, buried by ordinary, everyday things." It is irresponsible because it is a statement made without qualification or development in a context of praise, and without, therefore, helping readers to see (as I suppose the writer herself does now see) that to raise our fears and insecurities into consciousness in order to confront them, to deal with them, is good; but that if the pain is confused with art itself, then people at the receiving end of a poem describing a pain and insecurity they share are not really brought to confront and deal with their problems, but are instead led into a false acceptance of them as signs or precursors of art, marks of kinship with the admired artist, symptoms of what used to be called "the artistic temperament."

Again, when I read the blurbs on the back of the late John Berryman's prizewinning *Delusions, etc.*, and see what A. Alvarez wrote of Berryman's work and death, I feel that a poisonous misapprehension of the nature of poetry is being furthered. "For years," Alvarez says, "I have been extolling the virtues of what I call extremist poetry, in which the artists deliberately push their perceptions to the very edge of the tolerable. Both Berryman and Plath were masters of the style. But knowing now how they both died I no longer believe that any art—even that as fine as they produced at their best is worth the terrible cost."

At first glance this statement might be taken as being in accord with my own viewpoint; but its effect (since it is obvious that Alvarez believes their art to have been of the highest possible quality, perhaps the best poetry of their time) is still to extol the pursuit of the almost intolerable, the deliberate driving of the self to extremes which are not the unavoidable, universal extremes imposed by the human condition, but— insofar as they are deliberately sought—are luxuries, or which, if part and parcel of individual mental illness, should rather be *resisted* than encouraged in the name of art. In assuming that the disasters of those writers' lives were a form of payment for the virtues of their art, Alvarez, even while he says he has come to feel it is not worth the cost, perpetuates the myth that confounds a love affair with death with a love affair with art.

Thus it is that long lives devoted to the practice of art seem lacking in allure, and young would-be artists, encouraged by people older than themselves but equally confused, equally apt to mistake handicap for power, model their lives on the lives of those who, however gifted, were vanquished by their sorrows. It is not understood that the greatest heroes and heroines are truly those who hold out the longest, or, if they do die young, do so unwillingly, resisting to the last.

An instance would be the young guerilla poets of Latin America, so many of whom have been killed so young. (At least one of them, Javier Heraud, of Peru, would surely have been a major poet. He was shot down at the age of 23.) They were not flirting with death, any more than Victor Jara, the extraordinary and beloved Chilean musician and poet who was murdered in the stadium in Santiago during the CIA coup (1972). They died politically conscious deaths, struggling for a better life, not just for themselves but for their people, for The People. Their tragedy is very different from the tragedy of suicide; they were conscious actors in dramas of revolutionary effort, not helpless victims.

Anne Sexton's struggle has its political dimensions too—but hers is the story of a victim, not a conscious participant. Anne Sexton the well-to-do suburban housewife, Anne Sexton in Bedlam, Anne Sexton "halfway back," Anne Sexton the glamorous performer, Anne Sexton timid and insecure, Anne Sexton saying she had always hoped to publish a posthumous volume, Anne Sexton in her garage breathing in the deadly fumes, was—whatever the clinical description of her depression—"caught in history's crossfire." Not because she was a woman—the problem is not essentially related to gender or to sexual stance. Not because she didn't have radical politics—

god knows they are not a recipe for great art or for long life (though I can't help feeling that a little more comprehension of the relation of politics to her own life might have helped her). But because she herself was unable to separate her depression and her obsession with death from poetry itself, and because precisely her most enthusiastic readers and critics encouraged that inability.

The artist, the poet (like Hokusai, who called himself "the old man mad about painting" and felt that at seventy he had begun to learn, at ninety would have some command of his powers, and at a hundred would begin to do justice to what he saw in Nature) needs the stamina of an astronaut and the energy derived only from being passionately in love with life and with art. "This is this world, the kingdom I was looking for!" wrote John Holmes. And "You must love the crust of the earth on which you dwell. You must be able to extract nutriment out of a sand heap. Else you will have lived in vain," wrote Thoreau.

Such purity, integrity, love, and energy—rarely fully attained but surely to be striven for—are undermined by our exploitive society, which romanticizes its victims when they are of a certain kind (thus distracting us from the unromanticizable lives of the suffering multitude). It romanticizes gifted individuals who have been distorted into an alienated individualism, a self-preoccupation that is *not* individuation, *not* maturation.

Anne Sexton wrote in *Wanting to Die*,

> Suicides have already betrayed the body.
> Stillborn, they don't always die,
> but dazzled, they can't forget a drug so sweet . . .
> To thrust all that life under your tongue!—
> that, all by itself, becomes a passion.

Too many readers, with a perversity that, yes, really does seem to me to be bound up with white middle-class privilege and all its moral disadvantages, would sooner remember and identify with lines like those than with these, which (in *The Death Notebooks*) she also wrote:

> Depression is boring, I think
> and I would do better to make
> some soup and light up the cave.

To recognize that for a few years of her life Anne Sexton was an artist *even though* she had so hard a struggle against her desire of death is to fittingly honor her memory. To identify her love of death with her love of poetry is to insult that struggle.

Originally published in the *Real Paper*, Boston, Massachusetts, 1974, and reprinted in *Ramparts*.

Some Duncan Letters–
A Memoir and a Critical Tribute

(1975)

IN THE EARLY SPRING of 1948 I was living in Florence, a
bride of a few months, having married American literature, it
seemed, as well as an American husband. Both of us haunted
the U.S.I.S. library on the via Tornabuoni—Mitch to begin
rereading at leisure the classics of fiction he had been obliged to
gallop through meaninglessly at Harvard, I to discover, as a
young writer of the British "New Romantic" phase of the
1940s, the poetry of what was to be my adopted country. I had
read at that time a minimal amount of Pound (anthologized in a
Faber anthology) and Stevens ("discovered" in Paris a few
months before when Lynne Baker lent me a copy of *The Blue
Guitar*). William Carlos Williams I had found for myself in the
American bookstore on the Rue Soufflot, near the Sorbonne,
but though I knew with mysterious certainty that his work
would become an essential part of my life, I had not yet heard
enough American speech to be able to hear his rhythms properly; his poems were a part of the future, recognized but held in
reserve. The rest of American poetry was *terra incognita*, except
for Whitman (in the William Michael Rossetti edition of 1868)
and a few poems by Emily Dickinson, Robert Frost, and Carl
Sandburg—again, anthology pieces only. I had read Eliot; but
like most English readers at that time, I thought of him as an
English poet (and of course, the fact that it was possible to do so
was precisely what made Williams so angry with him, as I later

understood). Also I had read and loved, at George Woodcock's house in London a year or so before, a few poems from Rexroth's *Signature of All Things*.* Those were the limits of my acquaintance with U.S. poetry.

The American library was not, to my recollection, rich in poetry; but among my findings were some issues of *Poetry*, Chicago; and in one of these, a review by Muriel Rukeyser of Robert Duncan's *Heavenly City, Earthly City*. Both these people, then just names to me, were to become, in varying ways, close friends who influenced my history—as did Dr. Williams. Thinking back from the present (1975) I realize how destiny was sounding the first notes, in that cold Florentine spring, of motifs that would recur as dominant themes in the fifties and sixties (and in the case of Muriel Rukeyser, with whom I visited Hanoi in 1972, into the seventies) and which, indeed, are so interwoven in my life that whatever changes befall me they must be forever a part of its essential music.

In Muriel's review of *Heavenly City, Earthly City*, she quoted:

> There is an innocence in women
> that asks me, asks me;
> it is some hidden thing they are
> before which I am innocent.
> It is some knowledge of innocence.
> Their breasts lie undercover.
> Like deer in the shade of foliage,
> they breathe deeply and wait;
> and the hunter, innocent and terrible,
> enters love's forest.

These lines, and the whole review, so stirred me that I convinced myself no one in Florence needed that particular issue of *Poetry* more than I did, and I not only kept it out for

*Rexroth had struck up a correspondence with me at that time, for he was editing *New British Poets*. He was the first American writer I knew personally—but I had not met him except through letters.

months but, when we left for Paris, took it with me. . . .

Retrospectively, I see that I was drawn to Duncan's poems of that period not only by their intrinsic beauty but because they must have formed for me a kind of transatlantic stepping stone. The poems of my own first book (*The Double Image*, 1946) and those that Rexroth included in *The New British Poets* (New Directions, 1949) belonged to that wave of Romanticism which Rexroth documented, an episode of English poetry that was no doubt in part a reaction against the fear, the drabness, and the constant danger of death in the daily experience of civilians as well as of soldiers in WWII. While the subject matter of the poems of the "New Romantic" movement may often have been melancholy and indeed morbid, the formal impulse was towards a richly sensuous, image-filled music. When the war ended, English poetry quickly changed again and became reactively dry, as if embarrassed by the lush, juicy emotionalism of the forties. But though not many individual poems of the New Romantics stand up very well to time and scrutiny, they still seem preferable to the dull and constipated attempts at a poetry of wit and intellect that immediately succeeded them, for their dynamic connected them with a deeper, older tradition, the tradition of magic and prophecy and song, rather than of ironic statement. And it was to that old, incantatory tradition that Duncan, then and always, emphatically (and, as I did not then know, consciously) belonged. So here, I must have intuited, was an *American* poet whose musical line, and whose diction, were accessible to me. It must have made my emigration, which I knew was not far distant, seem more possible, more real.

In a 1964 letter, after talking about a then new poem of mine called "Earth Psalm," Duncan says it caused him to re-read "To Death," a poem in my 1946 volume (now in *Collected Earlier Poems*). "I began to conjure," he said, "the Tudor, no Stuart (something between King James's Bible and Bunyan) dimension (a fourth dimensional of you) with figures from a masque. . . . Haven't we, where we have found a source, or some expression of what we love in human kind, to give it a place to live today, in our own gesture (which may then speak of nobility or ardour)—Well, if Orpheus can come forward, so, by the work of the poem, Death and His Bride in brocade—"

"How many correspondences there are," he goes on to say, "between your *Double Image*, 1946, and my *Medieval Scenes* written in 1947. In this poem 'To Death'—'brocade of fantasy': in 'The Banners' where the 'bright jerkins of a rich brocade' is part of the fabric of the spell; or in 'The Conquerors' compare 'The Kingdom of Jerusalem'. . . ." And after a few more lines of comment he begins, right *in* the letter, the poem "Bending the Bow":

> We've our business to attend Day's
> duties, bend back the bow in dreams as we may,
> til the end rimes in the taut string
> with the sending . . .
>
> I'd been
>
> in the course of a letter—I am still
> in the course of a letter—to a friend,
> who comes close in to my thought so that
> the day is hers. My hand writing here
> there shakes in the currents of . . . of air?
> of an inner anticipation of . . . ? reaching to touch
> ghostly exhilarations in the thought of her.

But here, noting the life-loom caught in the very act of its weaving, I anticipate. In 1948 I had nothing of Duncan's but those quotations in *Poetry*, fragments congenial and yet mysterious; and when I arrived in New York for the first time in the fall of that year I was too passive, disorganized, and overwhelmed by unrecognized "culture shock" (the term had not yet been invented) to do anything so methodical as to try and find his book or books: so that when I did happen upon *Heav-*

enly City, Earthly City on the sale table outside the Phoenix Bookshop on Cornelia St., just a few blocks from where I was living, it seemed an astonishing, fateful coincidence—as in a sense it was.

The book enlarged and confirmed my sense of affinity and brought me, too, a further dim sense of the California of fog, ocean, seals, and cliffs I was by then reading about in Robinson Jeffers.

> Turbulent Pacific! the sea-lions bark
> in ghostly conversations and sun themselves
> upon the sea-conditiond rocks.
> Insistent questioner of our shores!
> Somnambulist, old comforter!

Duncan wrote in the title poem; and:

> Sea leopards cough in the halls of our sleep.
> swim in the wastes of salt and wreck of ships,

and:

> The sea reflects, reflects in her evening tides
> upon a lavender recall of some past glory,
> some dazzle of a noon magnificence.

Much, much later—in 1966, it must have been, when I visited Carmel and Monterey—there was possibly some recall of those lines in a poem of mine, "Liebestodt": "Where there is violet in the green of the sea . . ."

But the impact of Duncan's rich romanticism was perhaps less powerful by the time I found the book, for I was also beginning to get a grip on William Carlos Williams' sound by then, able to "scan" it better now that I was surrounded by American speech, no longer baffled by details like "R.R." (railroad—in England it is railway) or obstructed in reading by the difference in stresses (e.g., the first American menu I saw announced "Hot Cakes" which I ordered as "hot *cakes*").*

Now I was quickly, eagerly, adapting to the new mode of speaking, because instinct told me that to survive and develop as a poet I had to. Williams showed me the way, made me listen, made me begin to appreciate the vivid and figurative language sometimes heard from ordinary present-day people, and the fact that even when vocabulary was impoverished there was some energy to be found in the here and now. What I connected to, originally, in Duncan, was a music based in dream and legend and literature; and though my love of that music has proved to be enduring, it was not uppermost in my needs and pleasures just then when I was seeking a foothold in the realities of marriage, of keeping house in a tenement flat, raising a strenuous baby, buying groceries at the Bleecker Street Safeway.

Meanwhile Duncan, unknown to me still, was changing too, on the other side of the continent. There was of course this big difference in us, a thread of another texture in among those that we held in common: he had a sophistication I lacked, which gave to his romanticism an edge, not of the type of wit academics of the period cultivated anxiously—like a young man's first whiskers—but of an *erotic irony* such as Thomas Mann adumbrates in his essays on Goethe and elsewhere. He was not only a few years older than I: he had already an almost encyclopedic range of knowledge, had studied history with Kantorowitz, had read Freud; and he lived in a literary and sexual ambience I didn't even know existed. Whatever he wrote was bound to include an element of complex consciousness; indeed, I can see now that while my task was to develop a greater degree of conscious intelligence to balance my instincts and intuitions, *his* was, necessarily, to keep his consciousness, his diamond needle intellect, from becoming overweening, violat-

---

* And, as in this instance, the different perception of parts of speech, the English retaining *hot* as an adjective, and Americans creating a compound noun, hotcakes.

ing the delicate feelings-out of the Imagination. It was just because his awareness of every nuance of style, of every double meaning, was so keen, that he has, through the years, been almost obsessively protective of the gifts of chance, of whatever the unconscious casts upon his shore, of "mistakes" which he has cherished like love-children.

My first direct contact with Duncan came in the early fifties and was almost a disaster. By this time I had become friends with Bob Creeley and *Origin* had begun to appear. Mitch and I had gone back to Europe on the G.I. Bill in 1950, when our son was just over a year old, and in 1951 the Creeleys came to live a mile or two away from us in the Provençal countryside. Sitting on the ground near our cottage, by the edge of a closely pruned vineyard under the slope of the Alpilles, Creeley and Mitch would talk about prose, and Creeley and I about poetry: Williams, Pound, Olson's "Projective Verse" which had just come out; how to cut down a poem to its sinewy essence— pruning it like the vines. I learned a lot; and am not sure what, if anything, I gave in exchange, though I know I was not merely a silent listener. Duncan had not yet met or been acknowledged by either Olson (with whom Creeley was corresponding) or Creeley,* and though he had not been dislodged from my mind I don't recall mentioning him. After I was back in New York, and just before Cid Corman included some poems of Duncan's in *Origin* (1952) I received a communication from a San Francisco address signed only "R.D." It was a poem-letter that (I thought) attacked my work, apparently accusing it of brewing poems like "stinking coffee" in a "staind pot." When the letter spoke of "a great effort, straining, breaking up all the melodic line," I supposed the writer was complaining. How I could have misread what was, as Duncan readers will recognize, "Letters for Denise Levertov: an A muse ment"—how I could have so misinterpreted his tribute, it is difficult now to imagine. I've never been given to paranoia;

*Robert Duncan had, however, sent *Medieval Scenes* to Olson as early as 1948.

perhaps it was simply that the mode of the poem, with its puns, lists, juxtapositions (more Cubist than Surreal) was too sophisticated for me to comprehend without initiation. I had at the time not even read half the people he mentions in the poem as sources, or at any rate as forming an eclectic tradition from which I thought he was saying I had unwarrantably borrowed (but to which, in fact, he was joyfully proclaiming that I belonged): Marianne Moore, Pound, Williams, H.D., Stein, Zukofsky, Bunting, St.-J. Perse. Of these, I had by then read only Williams, Marianne Moore and Perse in any quantity; I knew Pound's *ABC of Reading* pretty well but had not tackled the *Cantos*. Of H.D. I knew only the anthologized Imagist poems of her youth, and of Stein only "Melanctha"; of Zukofsky and Bunting, nothing. Duncan also speaks in the poem of Surrealism and Dada: and I was at least somewhat acquainted with French Surrealism (and the English poet, David Gascoyne's book about it) but with Dada not at all. So much of the corresponding intellectual background, in the simplest sense, was lacking in me as a recipient of the letter.

I wrote to "R.D." enquiring plaintively why he had seen fit to attack me for a lack of originality, for I took phrases like

> Better to stumb–
> ll to it,

and

> better awake to it. For one
> eyes-wide-open vision
> or fotograph
> than ritual,

as stern admonitions, when, of all the names he cited, only Williams was to me a master, and from him I believed myself to

201

be learning to discover my own voice. I concluded my letter by saying, in all innocence, "Is it possible that the initials you signed with, R.D., stand for Robert Duncan? You don't sound like him!—But in case that's who you are, I'd like to tell you I loved *Heavenly City, Earthly City*, and therefore hope it's not Robert Duncan who dislikes my poems so much." I quote from memory, but that's a pretty close approximation. It is a wonder that Duncan was not furious at my stupidity; especially at my saying he did not sound like himself. If he had been, I wonder if our friendship would ever have begun? Certainly if it had not, my life would have been different. But luckily he responded not with anger (or worse, not at all) but with a patient explanation (on the envelope he added the words, "It is as it was in admiration") of his intent, including his sense—central to an understanding of his own poetry—that "borrowings" and "imitations" were in no way to be deplored, but were on the contrary tributes, acts of faith, and the building stones of a living tradition of "the communion of poets." This concept runs through all of Duncan's books. It is most obvious in the Stein imitations, or in his titling books *Derivations*, or *A Book of Resemblances*, but is implicit in every collection, though not in every poem; and it is closely tied to his recognition of poetry (and of all true art) as being a "power, not a set of counters" as he put it in a section of "The H.D. Book" that deals with H.D.'s detractors, the smart, "bright" critics. If Poetry, the Art of Poetry, is a Mystery, and poets the servers of that Mystery, they are bound together in fellowship under its laws, obedient to its power. Those who do not recognize the Mystery suppose themselves Masters, not servants, and manipulate Poetry's power, splitting it into little counters, as gold is split into coins, and gaming with it; each must accumulate his own little heap of manipulative power-counters—thus so-called originality is at a premium. But within the Fellowship of the Mystery there is no hoarding of that Power of Poetry—and so-called borrowings are simply sharings of what poetry gives to

202

its faithful servants.* By the light of this concept we can also understand Duncan's often criticized "literariness," his frequent allusions to works of literary and other art and his many poems that not only take poetry itself as theme but overtly incorporate the "languaging" process into their essential structure—as he does even in this very first "Letter" in the sections subtitled "Song of the Languagers," and later in such poems as "Keeping the Rhyme," "Proofs," "Poetry, A Natural Thing" or "The Structure of Rime" series, and so many others.

Some readers—even deep and subtle ones—object to poems about poems (or about the experiencing of any works of art) and about writing and language, on the grounds that they are too inverted. I have never agreed (except in regard to conventional set pieces which seem written in fulfillment of commissions or in the bankrupt manner of British poets laureate celebrating Royal weddings). If much of a poet's most passionate and affective experiences are of poetry itself (or literature more generally, or painting, etc.) why should it not be considered wholly natural and right for him to celebrate those experiences on an equal basis with those given him by nature, people, animals, history, philosophy, or current events? Poetry also is a current event. The poet whose range is confined to any single theme for most of a working life may give off less energy than one who follows many themes, it is true—and if any single thing characterizes those whom we think of as world poets, those of the rank of Homer, Shakespeare, Dante, it is surely breadth of range. But Duncan, although in tribute to the Mystery he is avowedly and proudly "literary," cannot be accused of narrow range, of writing *nothing but* poems about poetry.

---

*This does not necessarily imply that the poet should erase his signature from his works nor that poetry or other art work is best undertaken communally. To me the sense of chronology, the cumulative power of a lifetime's work, is of profound importance; and it can only be experienced if authorship and sequence are known. As for "group poems," I find them superficial: each individual needs solitude in order to bring his or her experience in life and language to fruition in the poem, and it is through communion with ourselves that we attain communion with others. Duncan's own practice seems sufficient evidence that he would agree.

It was in 1955 that I first met Duncan. He spent a few days in New York on his way, with Jess, to spend a year in Europe—chiefly in Majorca, near to Robert Creeley with whom he had by this time entered into correspondence but still not met. I am not able to locate the letters that preceded this joyful meeting, nor do I remember our conversation. But the tentative friendship that had begun so awkwardly was cemented by his visit, and I recall with what a pang I watched him go down the stairs, he looking back up the stairwell to wave farewell, I leaning over the banister.* I gave him a notebook for his journey; he used it as a drawing book and gave it back to me full of pictures a year later; and still later I wrote captions for them.

Whatever had passed between us before that time—and Duncan years later claimed that "we must have been in full correspondence by fall of '54"—it was now that the exchange of letters which continued into the early seventies began in earnest. Somehow, in the course of a busy life and many changes of dwelling, a few of the letters Duncan wrote to me have been mislaid, though I am confident that they are not irretrievably lost, for I always treasured them. I have a stack of letters for every year from 1955 to 1972. The written word was not the only dimension of our friendship: from time to time Duncan would come East; in 1963 he and I were both at the Vancouver Poetry Conference; and three times I was in the San Francisco Bay Area (in 1969 for six months). At these times we would have the opportunity to "talk out loud" rather than on paper and I have happy memories of visits to museums and galleries, to the Bronx Zoo and the Washington Zoo, and of walks in the Berkeley Hills. Over the years we acquired many mutual friends; and during my son's childhood Duncan and Jess befriended him too, sending him wonderful old Oz books they

---

*It is possible Duncan had some half-conscious memory of this moment when years later he spoke of his special feeling for a poem called "Shalom." The "man/going down the dark stairs" in that poem was not he, but it has come to seem to be as much about him as anyone, in the way poems do, with time, come to admit more than their first inhabitants.

would find in thrift shops. But it was the correspondence, with its accompaniment of poems, newly finished or in progress, that sustained the friendship most constantly and importantly.

Looking through these letters from Robert I am confirmed in my sense of their having been for me, especially in the first ten years, an extremely important factor in the development of my consciousness as a poet. Pondering what I gave Duncan in exchange, besides responding in kind to his admiration and love, I recall his speaking of how writing to me and to Creeley gave him "a field to range in," and in a 1958 letter he writes of me as serving as a "kind of artistic conscience" (not that he needed one). I had, certainly, the great advantage of not being connected to any "literary world" in particular, and being quite free from the factionalism so prevalent in San Francisco.

Both Duncan and I are essentially autodidacts, though he did have a high school and some college education while I had no instruction after the age of twelve, and the education I received before that was unconventional. I had a good background in English literature, a strong sense of the European past, and had read widely but unmethodically. Duncan read deeply in many fields I was ignorant of—the occult, psychoanalysis, certain areas of science. He did not teach me about these matters, which were not what I was really interested in— but he did give me at least some awareness of them as fields of energy. Because of my family background I knew a little about Jewish and Christian mysticism, so that when Duncan mentioned the Shekinah or Vladimir Solovyóv I recognized what he was talking about. The Andrew Lang *Fairy Books* and the fairytales of George MacDonald (and some of his grown-up stories too) were common ground, along with much, much else—many loves in literature and art. It was in those areas of twentieth-century literature, American poetry in particular, of which at the time of that first "Letter" I had been ignorant, and—more importantly—in the formation of what I think of as "aesthetic ethics," that Duncan became my mentor. Throughout the correspondence there run certain threads of fundamental disagreement; but a mentor is not necessarily an absolute authority, and though Duncan's erudition, his being older than I, his often authoritative manner, and an element of awe in my affection for him combined to make me take, much of the time, a pupil role, he was all the more a mentor when my own convictions were clarified for me by some conflict with his. Perhaps there was but one essential conflict—and it had to do with the role of a cluster of sources and impulses for which I will use "convictions" as a convenient collective term (though no such term can be quite satisfactory). Although, having written poetry since childhood (beginning, in fact, several years before Duncan wrote *his* first poems), I had experienced "lucky accidents" and the coming of poems "out of nowhere," yet I needed, and was glad to get from him, an aesthetic rationale for such occurrences—reassurances to counter the "Protestant ethic" that makes one afraid to admit, even to oneself, the value of anything one accomplishes without labor. Nevertheless, then and now (and I fully expect to so continue) my deepest personal commitment was to what I believed Rilke (whose letters I'd been reading and rereading since 1946) meant in his famous admonition to Herr Kappus, the "Young Poet," when he told him to search his heart for its *need*. The "need to write" does not provide academic poem-blueprints, so there was no conflict on that level; but such "inner need" *is* related to "having something" (at heart) "to say," and so to a high valuation of "honesty." Our argument would arise over Duncan's sense that what I called honesty, he (as a passionate anarchist or "libertarian") sometimes regarded as a form of self-coercion, resulting in a misuse of the art we served. He saw a cluster, or alignment, that linked *convictions* with *preconceptions* and *honesty* with *"ought,"* while the cluster I saw linked *convictions* with *integrity* and *honesty* with *precision*. Related to this was my distrust of Robert's habit of attributing (deeply influenced as he was by Freud) to every slip of the tongue or unconscious pun not merely the relevation of some hidden attitude but, it appeared to me—and it seemed and still seems perverse of him—*more validity* than what the speaker meant to say, thought he or she said, and indeed (in the case of puns and homonyms noticed only by Duncan) *did* say. To discount the earnest intention because of some hinted, unrecognized, contradictory coexisting factor has never seemed to me just; and to automatically suppose that the unrecognized is necessarily *more* authentic than what has been brought into consciousness strikes me as absurd. Jung (whom I was reading throughout the sixties—Duncan disliked his style and for a long time refused to read him)* had made the existence of the "dark side," and the imperative need to respect it, very clear to me. It was Duncan's apparent belief that the dark side was "more equal," as the jest puts it, that I could not stomach.

However, the first time I find this matter touched upon in one of Robert's letters it was not in a way that affronted or antagonized me but one which, on the contrary, belongs with the many ways in which he opened my mind to new realizations. I had been puzzled by some ballads of his, inspired, in part, by Helen Adam (to whose fascinating work he soon introduced me). I found them, I suppose, a curious retrogression from the exciting pioneering into the "open field" in which we and a few others were engaged. What was the Duncan of *Letters*, the Duncan who in a letter of that same summer (1955) was excited by my poem "The Way Through" (printed in *Origin*) and who shared my love of Williams, what was he doing being so "literary"?—I must have asked. For I myself was engaged in "de-literarifying" myself, in developing a base in common speech, contemporary speech rhythms. "I don't really understand your ballads," I wrote (I quote now from Duncan's tran-

*By the summer of '63 he had somewhat relented, however; "Oh yes, it's true I'm most likely to bridle at the mention of 'Jung.' But, while there is an argumentative cast always in Jung that I find exasperating and dislike finally (the having the answer to things in a schema), there is always much and often so much else that I find revelatory. I look forward with the usual mixture of prejudice and expectation to reading the *Autobiography*." It is amusing to see Duncan claim to dislike argumentativeness, given his own contentiousness!

scription of part of my letter in his preface for a projected volume to be called *Homage to Coleridge*), "why you are writing that way. It seems wasteful both to yourself and in general . . . when I remember what else you have written, even long since, as well as of late especially, I can't quite believe they aren't like something you might have written very long ago." My hesitations about questioning anything he did are evident in the circuitous syntax and its qualifiers—"I don't really"—"I can't quite"—"it seems". . . . And in his reply he wrote,

> . . . it is the interest in, not the faith, that I wld take as my clue. Ideally that we might be as readers or spectators of poetry like botanists—who need not tell themselves they will accept no matter what a plant is or becomes; or biologists—who must pursue the evidence of what life is, haunted by the spectre of what it ought to be [though] they might be. As *makaris* we make as we are, o.k., and how else? it all however poor must smack of our very poorness or if fine of our very fineness. Well, let me sweep out the old validities: and readdress them. They are inventions of an order within and out of nonorders. And it's as much our life not to become warriors of these orders as it is our life to realize what belongs to our order in its when and who we are and what does not. I can well remember the day when Chagall and Max Ernst seemed bad to me, I was so the protagonist of the formal (like Arp or Mondrian) against the Illusionary. The paintings have not changed. Nor is it that I have *progressed*, or gone in a direction. But my spiritual appetite has been deranged from old convictions.

This openness was something I was happy in; and indeed, in such passages Duncan often sounded for me a note of "permission" to my native eclecticism that some shyness in me, some lack of self-confidence, longed for. Yet even this liberation was in some degree a source of conflict—not between us, but within me. For years no praise and approval from anyone else, however pleasant, could have reassured me until I had Robert's approval of a poem; and if I had that—as I almost always did—no blame from others could bother me. "The permission liberates," wrote Duncan in 1963 (about a procedure of his own, relating to a habit of "reading too much the way some people eat too much" as he put it elsewhere) "but then how the newly freed possibility can insidiously take over and tyrannize over our alternatives."

Duncan's wit is not a dominant note in the letters but it does flash forth, whether in jest or in epigram. In September 1959 for example, he complains that Solovyóv had been, alas, "a Professor of Philosophy—that hints or sparks of a life of Wonder can show up in such a ground is a miracle in itself. What if Christ's disciples had not been simple fishermen and a whore, and he the son of a carpenter, but the whole lot been the faculty of some college?" Of a highly cultured friend he wrote in 1957, "he has enthusiasms but not passions. . . . He collects experience [but he doesn't] undergo the world." He described San Francisco audiences for poetry readings (preparing me for my first public reading anywhere, in December 1957, which he had gone to considerable trouble to arrange): "The audiences here are avid and toughened—they've survived top poetry read badly; ghastly poetry read ghastly; the mediocre read with theatrical flourish; poets in advanced stages of discomfort, ego-mania, mumbling, grand style, relentless insistence, professorial down-the-nosism, charm, calm, schizophrenic disorder, pious agony, auto-erotic hypnosis, bellowing, hatred, pity, snarl and snub."

Among recurring topics are friendships and feuds among fellow writers: his publishing difficulties (due in part to his very high standards of what a book should look like and in what spirit its printing and publication should be undertaken); and—more importantly—his current reading and its relationship to his work; as well as his work itself. Sometimes poems would have their first beginnings right there on the page, as "Bending the Bow" did; or if not their beginning, the origins of poems

209

enclosed are often recounted. (These, however, I do not feel inclined to quote; they are a part of the intimacy of communion, not to be broadcast—not because they say anything Robert might not say to someone else or to the world in general, but because in their context they are said in an expectation of privacy.)

It is not easy to isolate from the fabric some threads of the essential, the truly dominant theme I have already named—clumsily but not inaccurately—the "ethics of aesthetics"; for the pattern of the whole is complex: negatives and positives entwined and knotted. Everywhere I discover, or rediscover, traces both of the riches Duncan's friendship gave me and of the flaws in mutual confidence which by the 1970s impoverished that friendship.

Perhaps a point at which to begin this drawing-out of one thread is what he says about revision. I had read the notebook excerpts, printed in a S.F. broadside, in which the beautiful phrase occurs, "My revisions are my re-visions." In the beginning I supposed it to mean it was best never to work-over a poem, but instead to move on to the next poem—the renewed vision. But taking it to myself as the years passed, I have come to know its meaning as being the necessity of constant re-visioning *in the very act* of refining: i.e., that changes made from outside the poem, applied as a reader would apply (supply) them, cannot partake of the poem's vitality; the valid, viable *re*working of a poem* must be as much from within, as seamlessly internal to the process, as the primary working. Duncan himself in May 1959 explicated:

> I revise (*a*) when there is an inaccuracy, then I must re-see, as e.g. in the Pindar poem—now that I found the reproduction we had someplace of the Goya painting, I find Cupid is not wingd: in the poem I saw wings. I've to summon up my attention and go at it. (*b*) when I see an adjustment—it's not polishing for me,

---

*I.e., whether or not it takes place on the same day as a first draft or over a span of months or even years.

but a "correction" of tone, etc., as in the same poem "hear the anvils of human misery clanging" in the Whitman section bothered me, it was at once the measure of the language and the content—Blake! not Whitman (with them *anvils*) and I wanted a long line pushed to the unwieldly with (Spicer and I had been talking about returning to Marx to find certain correctives—as, the ideas of *work*) Marxist flicker of *commodities*. (*c*) and even upon what I'd call decorative impulse: I changed

> follow
> ~~obey~~ to the letter
> freakish instructions

to gain the pleasurable transition of l to l-r and f to f-r.

The idea in back of no revisions as doctrine was that I must force myself to abandon all fillers, to come to correct focus *in the original act;* in part there's the veracity of experience (. . . the poem "comes" as I write it; I seem—that is—to follow a dictate), but it's exactly in respect to that veracity that I don't find myself sufficient. . . . I had nothing like "I write as I please" in mind, certainly not carelessness but the extreme of care kept in the moment of a passionate feeling. . . . My "no revisions" was never divorced from a concept of the work. Concentration. . . . I've got to have the roots of words, the way the language works, at my fingertips, learned in the nerves from whatever studies, in addition to the thing drawn from—the sea, a painting, the face of Marianne Moore—before there's even the beginning of discipline. And decide, on the instant, that's the excitement, between the word that's surrounded by possible meanings, and the word that limits direction.

Copying this out in December 1975 I find the dialogue continuing, for I feel I want to respond to that last sentence: ah, yes, and here I see a source of the difference in tendency between your poetry and mine (though there is a large area in which our practices overlap): you *most often* choose the word that is "surrounded by possible meanings," and willingly drift

211

upon the currents of those possibilities (as you had spoken in "The Venice Poem" of wishing to drift) and I *most often* choose the word that "limits direction"—because to me such "zeroing in" is not limiting but revelatory.

In August of the same year (1958) Duncan resumes the theme:

> I've found myself sweating over extensive rehaulings of the opening poem of the field and right now am at the 12th poem of the book which I want to keep but have almost to reimagine in order to establish it. . . . It's a job of eliminating what doesn't belong to the course of the book, and in the first poem of reshaping so that the course of the book is anticipated. I mistrust the rationalizing mind that comes to the fore, and must suffer through—like I did when I was just beginning twenty years ago—draft after draft to exhaust the likely and reach the tone in myself where intuition begins to move. It comes sure enuf then, the hand's feel that "this" is what must be done. . . .

He quotes Ezra Pound saying in a 1948 manifesto, "You must understand what is happening"; and makes it clear the significant emphasis is on "what is happening," the presentness, the process. "Most verse," Duncan comments, "is something being made up to communicate a thing already present in the mind—or a lot of it is. And don't pay the attention it shld to what the poet don't know—and won't [know] until the process speaks." He quotes the passage from T. S. Eliot's *Three Voices of Poetry* in which Eliot, alluding to a line from Beddoes, "bodiless childful of life in the gloom / crying with frog voice, 'What shall I be?'" noted that there is "first . . . an inert embryo or 'creative germ' and, on the other hand, the language . . . [The poet] cannot identify this embryo until it has been transformed into an arrangement of the right words in the right order." And from Eliot he passes directly to a recent poem by Ebbe Borregard—

What Ebbe's got to do is to trust and obey the voice of *The Wapitis*. Where obedience means certainly your "not to pretend to know more than he does." But the poem is not a pretention to knowing; it is not, damn it, to be held back to our knowing, as if we could take credit for the poem as if it were a self-assertion. We have in order to obey the inspired voice to come to understand, to let the directives of the poem govern our life and to give our minds over entirely to know[ing] what is happening.

Most of this rang out for me in confirmation of what I believed and practiced. But I question one phrase—that in which he *opposes*, to the trusting of a poem's own directives, the communication of "a thing already present in the mind"; for unless one qualifies the phrase to specify a fully formed, intellectualized, *conscious* "presence in the mind" I see no true opposition here. The "veracity of experience" does not come into being only in the course of the poem, but provides the ground from which the poem grows, or from which it leaps (and to which it fails to return at its peril). "The sea, a painting, the face of Marianne Moore," *are* indeed the "things drawn from." What the writing of the poem, the process of poetry, the following-through of the *radiant gists* (in W. C. Williams' phrase) of language itself, does for the writer (and so for the reader, by a process of transference which is indeed communication, communion) is to *reveal the potential* of what is "present in the mind" so that writer and reader *come to know what it is they know*, explore it and realize, real-ize, it. In the fall of 1965, commenting anew on my "Notes on Organic Form" which he had read in an earlier, "lecture" form, he quotes with enthusiasm: "whether an experience is a linear sequence or a constellation raying out from and in to a central focus or axis . . . discoverable only in the work, not before it." In that phrase, however, I meant "discoverable" quite precisely—not "that which *comes into being* only in the work" but that which, though present in a dim unrecognized or *ungrasped* way, is only *experi-*

213

enced in any degree of fullness in art's concreteness: The Word made Flesh, Concept given body in Language. One cannot "discover" what is not there. Yet the poem is not merely a representation of the thing discovered—a depiction of an inscape seen; it is itself a new inscape, the seen and the seer conjoined. And it is in the action of synthesizing, of process in language, that the poet is voyager, sailing far beyond that lesser communication, the conveyance of information, to explore the unknown. Duncan seems always on the brink of saying one does not even *start off* from the known.

At times it seems as if it were his own brilliant intellect he is struggling to keep from domination of his art—beating not a dead horse but a horse that does not exist in me, or in others about whose poetry he wrote. In 1956, writing from a small village in Majorca, wondering if he and Jess can afford to travel to London at Christmas time (their budget was $100 a month) he spoke of:

> . . . craving the society of English speech. My notebooks are becoming deformed by the "ideas" which ordinarily I throw away into talk, invaluable talk for a head like mine that no waste basket could keep clean for a poem. I can more than understand dear old Coleridge who grew up to be a boring machine of talk; I can fear for my own poor soul. And, isolated from the city of idle chatter, here my head fills up, painfully, with insistent IMPORTANT things-to-say. I toss at night, spring out of bed to sit for hours, crouched over a candle, writing out—ideas, ideas, ideas. Solutions for the universe, or metaphysics of poetry, or poetics of living. Nor does my reading matter help—I have deserted Cocteau for a while because his ratiocination was perhaps the contagion; and the Zohar which irritates the cerebral automatism. Calling up, too, conflicts of poetry's—impulses toward extravagant fantasy, my attempt to reawaken the "romantic" allegiances in myself, to Poe, or Coleridge, or Blake, are inhibited by a "modern" consciousness; I grow appalled at the diffusion of the concrete. . . .

And in 1958:

> Sometimes when I am most disconsolate about what I am work-
> ing at, and most uneasy about the particular "exaltations" that
> may not be free outflowings of imagination and desire but ex-
> cited compulsions instead . . . I feel guilty before the ever-
> *present* substantial mode of your work.

But of course, it was more than an overactive intellect that he
had to contend with; the struggle was often with the sheer
complexity of vision. His cross-eyes saw deep and far—and it
is part of the artist's honor not to reduce the intricate, the
multitudinous, multifarious, to a neat simplicity. In 1961 he
wrote:

> It's the most disheartening thing I find myself doing in this
> H.D. study, trying to win her her just literary place—and what
> I find (when I reflect on it) is that I lose heart (I mean I get that
> sinking feeling in my heart and lungs, I guess it is, as if I had
> played it false). I know I can't just avoid this playing it false—
> you know, direct sentences like sound bridges from good solid
> island to good solid island; and contrive thought lines like pipe
> lines to conduct those few clear streams—because the bog is the
> bog [he has previously written of "the bog I get into with prose"]
> *and I really want to discover it on its own terms,* [my italics] which
> must be the naturalist's terms. . . . That damned bog would
> have to be drained and filled in to be worth a thing, but it is a
> paradise for the happy frog-lover, or swamp-grass enthusiast—
> and in its most rank and treacherous backwaters a teeming
> world of life for the biologist. . . .

Instances of particular changes made in poems in progress
(and here I return to the interwoven theme of revision) occur in
many letters, following poems sent earlier. The mind's bog was
fully inhabited by very exact, green, jewel-eyed frogs. Here
are two typical examples:

Nov. 29, 1960

Dear Denny, That *Risk!*—how hard it seems for me to come down to cases there. This time it is not the wording (tho I did alter "simple" to "domestic" in "turning the mind from domestic pleasure") but what necessitated my redoing the whole 3 pages was just the annoying fact that I had phrased certain lines wrong—against my ear. I never did read it "not luck but the way it falls choose / for her, lots" etc., which would mean either an odd stress of the phrase on "for" or a stress I didn't mean on "her." I was reading it from the first "choose for her" with the stress of the phrase on "choose"; and that terminal pitch heightening "falls" in the line before. And again: What did I think I was hearing when I divided "I had not the means / to buy the vase" or whatever—was it?—worse! "I had not the means to buy / the vase" etc.? Anyway, here I was going on like any hack academic of the automatic line-breaking school . . . not listening to the cadence of the thing. My cadence, my care, is changing perhaps too—and I was notating this from old habits contrary to the actual music.

Or in March 1963 he gives the following revisions for "Structure of Rime XXI":

"solitude" for "loneliness" . . . "A depresst key" for "a touched string"—a depresst key is what it actually is (when the sympathetic sound rings) and also because both "depresst" and "key" refer to the substrata of the poem.

"steps of wood" = notes of the scale on a xylophone . . .

There are also the occasional suggestions for revision—or for more comprehensive change—of my own work (for until the late sixties we probably exchanged manuscripts of most of what we wrote). Sometimes his criticism was deeply instructive; of this the most telling instance concerns a 1962 poem in which I had *overextended my feelings*. Hearing that a painter we both knew (but who was not a close friend of mine, rather a friendly acquaintance whose work had given me great pleasure) had leukemia or some form of cancer, I plunged, as it were, into an ode that was almost a premature elegy. An image from one of his paintings had already appeared in another poem of mine—"Clouds"—which Duncan particularly liked. In his criticism of this new poem he showed me how the emotional measure of the first (which dealt with matters "proved upon my pulses," among which the remembrance of clouds he had painted ". . . as I see them—/ rising / urgently, roseate in the / mounting of somber power"—"surging / in evening haste over hermetic grim walls" entered naturally, although the painter as a person played no part in the poem) was just. Whereas in the new poem, focussing with emotional intensity upon an individual who was not in fact anywhere close to the center of my life, however much his paintings had moved me, the measure was false. Although I thought (and looking it over now, still think) the poem has some good parts, I was thoroughly convinced, and shall never publish it. It was a lesson which, like all valuable lessons, had applicability not only to the particular occasion; and one which has intimately to do with the ideogram Ezra Pound has made familiar to us—the concept of integrity embodied in the sign-picture of "a man standing by his word."

There were other occasions, though, when I paid no attention to Robert's criticism because he was misreading. For example, reading my prose "Note on the Imagination" in 1959, he speaks of,

> distrusting its discrimination (that just this is imagination and that—"the feared Hoffmanesque blank—the possible monster or stranger"—was Fancy), but wholly going along with the heart of the matter: the seed pearls of summer fog in Tess's hair, and the network of mist diamonds in your hair. But the actual distinction between the expected and the surprising real thing here (and taking as another term the factor of your "usual face-

in-the-mirror") is the contrived (the work of Fancy) the remembered (how you rightly [say] "at no time is it hard to call up scenes to the mind's eye"—where I take it these are remembered) and the presented. But you see, if the horrible, the ugly, the very feard commonplace of Hoffman and Poe had been the "presented thing" it would have been "of the imagination" as much as the delightful image. . . .

. . . The evaluation of Fancy and Imagination gets mixed up with the description. All these terms of seeing: vision, insight, phantasm, epiphany, it "looks-like," image, perception, sight, "second-sight," illusion, appearance, it "appears-to-be," mere show, showing forth . . . where trust and mistrust of our eyes varies. However we trust or mistrust the truth, necessity, intent etc. of what is seen (and what manifests itself out of the depths through us): we can't make the choice between monster as fancy and the crown-of-dew as imagination.

Here the disagreement is substantial, for the very point I was trying to make concerned the way in which the active imagination illuminates common experience, and not by mere memory but by supplying new detail we recognize as authentic. By common experience I mean that which conforms to or expresses what we share as "laws of Nature." Hoffman's fantasies, known to me since childhood, had given me pleasure because they were "romantic" in the vernacular sense (and my edition had attractive illustrations) but they did not illumine experience, did not "increase the sense of living, of being alive," to use Wallace Stevens's phrase. In the "Adagia" Stevens says that "To be at the end of reality is not to be at the beginning of imagination, but to be at the end of both." To me—then and now—any kind of "sci fi," any presentation of what does not partake of natural laws we all experience, such as gravity and mortality, is only a work of imagination if it is dealing symbolically with psychic truth, with soul-story, as myth, fairytales, and sometimes allegory, do. Duncan continues:

Jess suggests it's not a matter of either/or (in which Fancy represented a lesser order and Imagination a higher order . . .) but
of two operations or faculties. Shakespeare is rich in both imagination and fancy . . . where Ezra Pound totally excludes or
lacks fancy. . . . George MacDonald [spoke] of "works of
Fancy and Imagination." But I think he means playful and
serious. Sometimes we use the word "fancy" to mean trivial;
but that surely does injustice to Shelley's landscapes or Beddoes' Skeleton's Songs or the description of Cleopatra's barge
that gives speech to Shakespeare's sensual fancy.

And here I think the difference of views is semantic. For I
indeed would attach the words "playful" and sometimes "trivial" and frequently "contrived" or "thought-up," to the term
fancy, and for the instances cited in Shelley or Beddoes, would
employ the term *fantasy*. The description of Cleopatra's barge
is neither fancy nor fantasy but the rhetoric of enthusiasm
accurately evolving intense sensuous experience: an act of
imagination. Fantasy does seem to me one of the functions of
the imagination, subordinate to the greater faculty's deeper
needs—so that "In a cowslip's bell I lie" and other evocations of
faery in the *Midsummer Night's Dream*, for example, are delicate
specifics, supplied by the power of fantasizing, for the more
precise presentation of an *imagined*, not fancied or fantasied,
world that we can apprehend as "serious"—having symbolic
reality—even while we are entertained by its delightfulness
and fun. The more significant divergence of opinion concerns
"the presented thing," as Duncan called it—for there he seems
to claim a value for the very fact of presentation, as if every
image summoned up into some form of art had thereby its
justification; a point of view he certainly did not, does not,
adhere to, and yet—perhaps, again, just because he has had
always so to contend with his own contentiousness and tendency to be extremely judgmental—which he does seem sometimes to propound, almost reflexively. "What I do," he wrote
in January '61:

—in that letter regarding your essay on Imagination, or yesterday in response to your letter and the reply to ———'s piece . . . is to contend. And it obscures perhaps just the fact that I am contending my own agreements often. . . . Aie! . . . I shall never be without and must work from those "irritable reachings after fact and reason" that must have haunted Keats too—

What Duncan says here seems, unfortunately, to be manifested in this very statement, which assumes without due warrant that just because Keats saw in Coleridge that restless, irritable reaching, he was himself subject to it. Yet, however contentious, Duncan is often self-critical in these letters—as above, or as when he speaks (Sept. 1964) of "my . . . 'moralizing,' which makes writing critically such a chore, for I must vomit up my strong puritanical attacking drive. . . . this attacking in others what one fears to attack in oneself. . . ." And in the midst of arguments he was often generous enough to combine self-criticism, or at least an objective self-definition, with beautiful examples of his opponent's point of view—for instance, in the Oct. 1959 letter already referred to, discussing Fancy and Imagination, he says,

> Jess said an image he particularly remembers from Tess is stars reflected in puddles of water where cows have left hoof tracks—But, you know, I think I am so eager for "concept" that I lose those details. Or, more exactly—that my "concept" lacks details often. For, where you or Jess bring my attention back to the "little fog" intenser "amid the prevailing one" or the star in the cowtracked puddle: the presence of Tess and Angel leaps up. . . . But for me it's not the perceived verity (your seed pearls of summer fog from Tess; or Madeline Gleason years ago to demonstrate the genius of imagination chose a perceived verity from Dante where the eyes of the sodomites turn and:
>
>> e si ver noi aguzzavan le ciglia,
>> come vecchio sartor fa nella cruna.

"towards us sharpened their vision, as an aged tailor does at the eye of his needle") I am drawn by the conceptual imagination rather than by the perceptual imagination. . . .

There were other times when Robert objected to some particular word in a poem of mine not in a way that instructed me but rather seemed due to his having *missed* a meaning. He himself was aware of that. In October 1966 he writes:

> And especially with you, I have made free to worry poems when there would arise some feeling of a possible form wanted as I read. Sometimes, as in your questionings of the pendent of Passages 2, such queries are most pertinent to the actual intent of the poem. And I think that even seemingly pointless dissents from the realized poem arise because along the line of reasoning a formal apprehension, vague but demanding, has arisen that differs from the author's form. In a mistaken reading, this will arise because I want to use the matter of the poem to write my own "Denise Levertov" poem. Crucially astray.

He wanted me to change an image of grief denied, dismissed, and ignored, in which I spoke of "Always denial. Grief in the morning, washed away / in coffee, crumbled to a dozen errands between / busy fingers" to "dunked" or "soaked" in coffee, not understanding that I meant it was washed *away*, obliterated; the "errands," the "busy fingers," and whatever other images of the poem all being manifestations of a turning away, a refusal to confront grief.*

The attribution to others of his own intentions, concerns, or hauntings, an unfortunate spin-off of his inner contentions, occasioned another type of misreading—a reading-into, a suspicion of nonexistent complex motives that obstructs his full comprehension of what *does* exist. "What is going on," he writes in July 1966, "in your:

*My error, I see now (1992) was that I did not make it clear that "crumbled" was not in an appositive relation to "washed away," but an alternative one—the word "or" should have preceded "crumbled."

still turns without surprise, with mere regret
to the scheduled breaking open of breasts whose milk
runs out over the entrails of still-alive babies,
transformation of witnessing eyes to pulp-fragments,
implosion of skinned penises into carcass-gulleys*

—the words in their lines are the clotted mass of some operation . . . having what root in you I wonder? Striving to find
place in a story beyond the immediate.

In this comment of his I find, sadly, that the "irritable reaching" stretches beyond "fact and reason" to search out complications for which there is no evidence. He misses the obvious. Having listed the lovely attributes of humankind, I proceeded, anguished at the thought of the war, to list the destruction of those very attributes—the violence perpetrated by humans upon each other. Because I believed that "we are members one of another" I considered myself morally obliged to attempt to contemplate, however much it hurt to do so, just what that violence can be. I forced myself to envision, in the process of writing, instances of it (drawing in part on material supplied by the Medical Committee for Human Rights or simi-lar accounts; and elaborating from that into harsh language-sounds). There was no need to look for "what was going on" in me, "from what root" such images came—one had only to look at the violation of Vietnam. And from the misreading of this very poem stemmed, ultimately, the loss of mutual confidence that caused our correspondence to end—or to lapse at least—in the early seventies. But Duncan had conscious justification for such misreadings. In a 1967 interview of which he sent me a transcript he expounded it in terms of what the writer him-self must do as reader of his own poem-in-process—but it is clearly what he was doing as a reader of my (and others') poems also:

*From "Life at War," *The Sorrow Dance.*

The poet must search and research, wonder about, consult the meaning of [the poem's] event. Here, to read means to dig, to let the forces of the poem work in us. Many poets don't read. For instance, take an awfully good poet like Robert Frost; while he writes a poem, he takes it as an expression of something he has felt and thought. He does not read further. It does not seem to be *happening to him*, but coming out of him. Readers too who want to be entertained by [or] to entertain the ideas of a writer will resent taking such writing as evidence of the Real and protest against our "reading into" poems, even as many protest the Freudians reading meanings into life that are not there. The writer, following images and meanings which arise along lines of a melody or along lines of rhythms and impulses, experiences the poem as an immediate reality. . . . I am consciously and attentively at work in writing—here I am like any reader. But I ask further, what is this saying? What does it mean that this is happening here like this?

This statement, as always with Duncan, contains, it seems to me, a valuable reminder of how closely writers must see what they do, to be responsible for it; and of how readers, similarly, should not be content with the superficial, the face value of a poem. But unfortunately, though his "digging for meanings" results in many felicities and resonances in his own work, the method often makes him a poor reader of others, a reader so intent upon shadow that he rejects, or fails to see, substance.

Meanwhile, if Duncan did not see what was obvious in that poem of mine, he certainly did see the war. Increasingly, from the mid-sixties on, its dark, dirty, oppressive cloud pervades his letters. In 1965, responding to a form letter I sent out to gather money and signatures for a full page ad in *The New York Times*—"Writers and Artists Protest the War in Viet Nam"— he had written,

> We feel as we know you and Mitch must feel—a helpless outrage at the lies upon which the American policy is run,

and at the death and suffering "our" armaments, troops, and bombers have inflicted upon Viet Nam. Count on us for all protests and write if the protest needs more money. We will tell you if we can't make it; but we want to do whatever we can.

And along with his sense of helplessness in the face of the outrage—where for all of us the horror itself was compounded by being committed *in our name*, as Americans—he began to worry about my increasing involvement in the antiwar movement.

> Denny, the last poem [it was "Advent 1966"] brings with it an agonizing sense of how the monstrosity of this nation's War is taking over your life, and I wish that I could advance some—not consolation, there is none—wisdom of how we are to at once bear constant (faithful and everpresent) testimony to our grief for those suffering in the War and our knowledge that the government of the U.S. is so immediately the agent of death and destruction of human and natural goods, and at the same time as constantly in our work (which must face and contain somehow this appalling and would-be spiritually destroying evidence of what human kind will do—for it has to do with the imagination of what is going on in Man) now, more than ever, to keep alive the immediacy of the ideal and of the eternal. Jess and I have decided that we will wear black armbands (as the Spanish do when some member of their immediate family has died) *always* and keep a period of mourning until certainly the last American soldier or "consultant" is gone from Viet Nam—but may it not be the rest of our lives? until "we" are no longer immediately active in bringing grief to members of the family of man. I started to wear a Peace button for the first time during the Poetry festival in Houston, and I found that it brought me to bear witness at surprising times—a waitress, a San Salvador millionaire, a Texas school teacher asked me what it meant. And I rejoiced in being called to my responsibility. Just at times when I was most forgetting myself and living it up.

Just over a year later, again, February 1967—

I have thought often how, if the outrage and grief of this war preoccupy my mind and heart as it does, the full burden of it must come upon you and Mitch with Nik so immediately involved. [Our son Nikolai was by now of draft age.] And I was fearful in January that you were having a bad time compounded with that other constant claim upon one's life the whole literary structure would make, and where you have a greater exposure in New York. . . . I think also of how much [anti] war groups and other organizations would lay claim. . . . it seems to me too that whatever is not volunteered from the heart, even goodness and demonstrations against the war, when it is conscripted is grievous.

There is, I feel, a confusion here. Certainly, as that poem "Advent 1966" and others attest, the ever-present consciousness of the war darkened my life as it darkened the lives of us all. Yet Duncan's affectionate anxiety about me and Mitch was in a sense misplaced. Duncan himself suffered, surely, a greater degree of frustration than we did, because we lightened that burden for ourselves by taking on the other burden of action. Duncan did bear testimony with his peace button and black armband; he attended a number of demonstrations, including the rally of writers, artists, and intellectuals at the Justice Department (which led to the conspiracy trial of Dr. Spock and four others, of whom Mitch Goodman was one) and the huge march on the Pentagon the following day, in the fall of 1967; and he participated in group poetry readings given as benefits for the Resistance movement. But he did not join with others on a day-to-day basis in organizing antiwar activities. Meanwhile, even though grief, rage, shame and frustration inevitably continued, and indeed even grew as my political awareness grew and I began to see how this war was only one facet of a complex of oppression, I nevertheless was experiencing unforeseen blessings. Not only was ongoing action a relief, an outlet for frustration, however small a drop in the bucket of resistance to that oppression one knew it to be; but—much more importantly—there was the experience of a new sense of community as one worked, or picketed, or even merely "milled around" with comrades. As a good Anarchist from his youth up, Duncan mistrusted group action; and he was just enough older than I to have a ready suspicion of "Stalinism" every time he confronted some action planned or carried out in a way that did not strike him as entirely "voluntarist." This habit of distrust had shown itself to me as far back as 1959, when he expressed hesitations concerning a magazine he otherwise liked (and which in fact was quite nonpolitical in its concerns) merely because of its "exaggerated estimate of Neruda . . . plus the poem by Celan where I suspected the reference to Madrid as standing for Spain in the Civil War" and added that he had sent "a prodding letter" to the editor, "to see if there was any neo-Stalinism going on there." This fear in him, by being a large factor in keeping him out of more involvement in the Movement during the sixties and early seventies, had two effects: one was that his political awareness, formed in the forties and early fifties, remained static; and the other, that he did not experience the comradeship, the recognition of apparent strangers as brothers and sisters, that so warmed the hearts of those who did feel it, giving us in the difficult present some immediate token of hope for a truly changed future—a comradeship which depended precisely upon a political awareness that was *not* static, but *in process of becoming*. Had he but realized it, the spirit of those days was (except in certain factions not central to the movement) not Stalinist, coercive, and regimented at all, but essentially as voluntarist as he could have desired. But we did gather together, and we did shout slogans—and it was perhaps due not only to ideological difference, but to temperamental distaste, that Duncan did not and could not do so. He was, therefore, isolated in his very real anguish; his blood pressure soared; and he could not see that there was nothing I was engaged in that was not "volunteered from the heart."

But the wedge driven between us by his supposition that I was acting coercively, toward myself and—possibly—towards others (a supposition which had, as I see it, no foundations in truth) had not yet gone very deep. In December 1968, a time of private troubles for me as well as of shared political ones, he wrote,

> . . . to reassure you my thoughts are with you. And a prayer . . . not to something I know, yet "to," but *from* something I know very well—the deep resources I have had in our friendship, the so much we have shared and share in what we hold good and dear for human life, and the service we would dedicate our art to. My own thought has been dark this year and in some part of it I have been apprehensive of how much more vulnerable and involved you are: I mean here about the crisis of the war and then the coming-to-roost of the American furies. What we begin to see are the ravening furies of Western civilization. And it corresponds with our own creative generation's arriving at the phase when the furies of our own art come-home-to-roost. Denny, just as I have been carried in my own work to a deeper, grander sense of the ground, I have begun to be aware of gaps and emptinesses—in my being? in the ground?—and I have now to turn next to work again on the H.D. book where I had begun to dread having to do with the inner conflicts I sensed at work there. The *World Order* essay, as I wrote, was written in phases of inertia, dread and breakthrus.
>
> Does it help at all to consider that in part your affliction is the artist's? The personal pain is compounded in it.
>
> Well I couldn't speed this off. My sense that I was doing no more than identifying a brooding center in my own feeling with your inner pain halted me in my tracks. Only, this morning, to find that my thought as I woke turning to you still revolved around or turned to the concept of inner trials belonging to the testing of the creative artist, which we as poets and artists come to, as surely as the fairytale hero or heroine comes to some imprisonment or isolation—to dwell in the reality of how the loved thing is to be despaired of. I am thinking of the story of

the forgotten bride and groom dwelling close to her or his beloved in despised form.

Only, in this fumbling, to try and say that your dread, pain,
and being at a loss—personal as it must be, is also the share of
each of us who seeks to deepen feeling. Not an affliction in and
of itself but belonging to the psychic metamorphosis—we cannot direct it, or, it is directed by inner orders that our crude and
unwilling conscious self dreads. Eros and his Other, Thanatos,
work there.

That beautiful letter, in which the feeling-tone of an earlier
time in our friendship resounds at a deeper, darker pitch, and
which sums up, or rather, is representative of, the rich, the
immeasurable gift given me by this association, seems almost
valedictory. Yet it was not yet so, in fact, for a month later
Mitch and I arrived on the West Coast to spend six months at
Berkeley. During this period, though my teaching job and
participation in current events (this was 1969, the spring of the
Third World strike and of People's Park) prevented me from
seeing Robert as often as I had hoped, there were some quiet
times of reading current poems to one another (and to Mitch
and Jess) and at least one or two walks in the mimosa- and
eucalyptus-scented lanes above Berkeley, a terrain he knew
intimately and seemed curiously at rest in.

It was not until after that, in the early seventies, that our
correspondence faltered and jarred to a halt. I will not deal here
with the way every negative element that had ever arisen between us, but especially the false interpretation begun in his
questioning of "Life at War," began to take over in our letters,
each of us taking fierce, static, antagonist "positions," he of
attack, I of defense. It is a conflict still unresolved—if this is in
some sense a narrative, the end of the story has perhaps not yet
been reached. But I think of my Duncan letters as a constellation rather than as a linear sequence. And in that constellation
the major stars are without question the messages of instruction

228

by means of which my intelligence grew keener, my artistic conscience more acute; messages of love, support, and solidarity in the fellowship of poetry. None of my many poet friends has given me more; and when I look back to Florence, 1948, I know I came then upon what was for two decades a primary current of my life.

AFTERWORD, 1991

Sadly, Robert Duncan and I were never properly reconciled during his lifetime. I wrote to him when I heard of his illness (he was on dialysis for some years before his death of kidney failure in 1988) but he had, I knew, given up all letter-writing and I did not expect to hear from him—nor did I. Exactly a month after his death I had an extraordinarily vivid dream about him, however, which left me with a strong feeling that we were, in fact, truly reconnected. I sent "To R.D., March 4th 1988"* to Jess, who assured me that Robert's affection for me had remained intact. I subscribe to that old tradition which claims that sometimes the souls of the recently dead hover around the living for a short while, taking care, in some way, of unfinished business.

To R.D., March 4th 1988

You were my mentor. Without knowing it,
I outgrew the need for a mentor.
Without knowing it, you resented that,
and attacked me. I bitterly resented
the attack, and without knowing it
freed myself to move forward
without a mentor. Love and long friendship
corroded, shrank, and vanished from sight
into some underlayer of being.
The years rose and fell, rose and fell,

*From *A Door in the Hive*, 1989.

229

and the news of your death after years of illness
was a fact without resonance for me,
I had lost you long before, and mourned you,
and put you away like a folded cloth
put away in a drawer. But today I woke
while it was dark, from a dream
that brought you live into my life:
I was in a church, near the Lady Chapel
at the head of the "west aisle." Hearing a step
I turned: you were about to enter
the row behind me, but our eyes met
and you smiled at me, your unfocussed eyes
focussing in that smile to renew
all the reality our foolish pride extinguished.
You moved past me then, and as you sat down
beside me, I put a welcoming hand
over yours, and your hand was warm.
I had no need
for a mentor, nor you to be one;
but I was once more
your chosen sister, and you
my chosen brother.
We heard strong harmonies rise and begin to fill
the arching stone,
sounds that had risen here through centuries.

From *Robert Duncan: Scales of the Marvelous*, ed. Robert J. Bertholf and Ian W.
Reid (New York, New Directions, 1979).

Rilke as Mentor

(1975/1981)

I HAVE ONLY A smattering of German, and consequently know Rilke's prose far better than his less satisfactorily translatable poetry, yet he has been for me an important influence. There is a depth and generosity in his perceptions that made them go on being relevant to me through the decades. I had already been writing for many years, and had been reading Rilke for seven or eight, when I first came to America and began to read Williams, Pound, and Stevens. Before long I met Robert Creeley and through him I encountered Olson's ideas. I remember Creeley's grimace of distaste for Rilke, or for what he imagined him to represent; but though I was excited by the new ideas, and open to their influence, I didn't give up on what Rilke meant to me, for I knew it was not the mere web of sentimentality Creeley accused it of being. It is true that Rilke could be pompous and sanctimonious at times—but those episodes are minimal in proportion to his strengths. Thus all the useful and marvelously stimulating technical and aesthetic tendencies that I came upon in the 1950s were absorbed into a ground prepared not only by my English and European cultural background in general but more particularly by Rilke's concept of the artist's task—a serious, indeed a lofty, concept, but not a sentimental or a smug one.

Although I went on to read other volumes, it was through my original encounters with him that his influence continued to hold. The first of Rilke that I read was the *50 Selected Poems* (from *Das Buch der Bilder* and from *Neue Gedichte*) translated with notes and introduction by C. F. MacIntyre (University of California Press, 1941), which my father gave me at Easter 1942—a bilingual edition. MacIntyre was a translator who exasperates most readers (he did versions of *Faust*, Verlaine and Mallarmé as well as of Rilke) but he did have the virtue, for which I honor his memory, of a passionate involvement with his subject and a willingness to take verbal risks to advance his peculiar, crotchety, but loving relationship to the chosen poet. This is particularly true in regard to Rilke's work: he loved it but he was not given to swooning over it; his notes have an acerbity of tone quite free of the *schwärmerei* that often surrounded Rilke both as man and writer (not without his collusion, no doubt) and which has continued to cause the kind of distrust Creeley expressed in 1950. MacIntyre helped me to place the poems in a cultural context, and also (quoting it in his introduction) first acquainted me with that famous passage from *The Notebooks of Malte Laurids Brigge* which tells, with only a slight degree of hyperbole, what a poet must have experienced in life in order to write a poem, or even a single line, of value. That was my first lesson from Rilke—*experience* what you live: to the artist, whatever is *felt through* is not without value, for it becomes part of the ground from which one grows. (Or as Goethe said—but I only read that years later—"In order to do something one must *be* someone.") Rilke's words reinforced my assumption that I did not have to undertake special (academic) studies to develop my poetry, but need only continue to read and write, and to be open to whatever might befall me; the rest must depend upon my native abilities and the degree of intensity and persistence that I was prepared to devote to the service of the art.

The next Rilke that I read was the *Letters to a Young Poet* in the Reginald Snell edition (London, Sidgewick and Jackson, 1945). Here, of course, it is in Letter I that he speaks at more length, and more specifically, about the needs of the poet than in any of the other ten (perhaps because it soon became clear to him that Herr Kappus was not destined for the life of art, and would be a receiver rather than a maker). That first letter in the series was my second lesson: again it was a reinforcement, a seal of approval for the instinct which had always told me not to run hither and thither seeking advice. Like everyone else I needed occasional reassurance, a word of approval, a warning against some weakness; but I knew, somehow, what Rilke's words now stated for me, that the underlying necessity was to ask not others but *oneself* for confirmation. And he specified the primary question not as "Is what I have written any good?" but rather, *"Must* I write?" I came at some point to recognize that when he says Herr Kappus ought to continue only if he could honestly answer "Yes," he meant the question (for every poet) to be a perennial one, not something asked and settled once and for all. Likewise, when, in the same letter, he states that "a work of art is good only if it has grown out of necessity," he is not merely repeating that injunction; the first imperative had to do with an initial sense of being inexorably drawn to the making of poems, while this second one demands that the poet apply the same standard to each separate work.

Rilke does not emphasize to Kappus the aesthetic, structural, needs of each poem; but his own *oeuvre* amply manifests that concern. Thus one is provided with a threefold basis for artistic integrity: scrupulous attention to three necessities— need as a person to write in order to fulfill one's being; the need of each separate poem to be written; and the aesthetic needs of each poem—each line. This implication of a standard of aesthetic ethics does not exclude the playful, the role of the artist as illusionist—it encompasses it. And it is important to remember, too, that Rilke did not scorn irony—goes out of his way to tell Kappus that it can be "one more means of seizing life," but that it is a dangerous resort in unproductive moments (leading then, he implies, to mere cheap cynicism) and that

233

it does not function at the profoundest depths of experience.

Another lesson from Rilke which reinforced something I knew already concerned the value of solitude. (Isn't all that we really learn the affirmation of what our experience already hints or what our intuition can assent to?) I had learned as a child to enjoy being alone; now I saw how Rilke pointed to solitude as necessary for the poet's inner development, for that selfhood which must *be* in order to experience all the multifold otherness of life. Later on, the phrase he used in relation to marriage or a comparable relationship, "the mutual bordering and guarding of two solitudes," dimly understood at first, became a cardinal point in my map of love; and still later in my life I came to see solitude, and the individual development for which it is a condition, as the only valid ground on which communion of the many, the plural Other of brother-and-sisterhood, can take place. (Rilke himself, of course, shunned the many in practice, and can scarcely be claimed as democratic in theory either; yet there are letters of his written in the revolutionary Munich of 1918 which show him to have been too open-hearted, apolitical and aristocratic though he was, to have been altogether irresponsive to that stir of new possibility, even if he soon became disillusioned with it.)

When I think of the *Selected Letters* (translated by R.F.C. Hull; London, Secker and Warburg, 1946) which was the third, and in many ways the most important, book of Rilke's that I obtained, it is as if of a palimpsest. So many passages, read at different times in my life, have yielded up so many layers of significance to me. Some I know almost by heart; yet there are others that I come upon as if for the first time. Early in 1947 I began making my own index for this volume, to supplement the ordinary one; and—like the wonderful poem-titles of Wallace Stevens—this list alone gives quite a strong, peculiar sense of the contents: *autumn the creator—standing at windows—as ready for joy as for pain—how can we exist?—the tower of fear—the savor of creation—each step an arrival—vowels of affliction—alone in cities—our conflicts a part of our riches—strings of lamentation—the mouse in the wainscot—further than work—open secret*—and so on. From each passage I received, of course, something specific; but they all combined—and not only those I indexed but, importantly and enduringly, others in which he described and evoked the working life of Rodin and Cézanne—to increase my understanding of the vocation of art, the obstinate devotion to it which, though it may not lead to any ordinary happiness, is nevertheless at the opposite pole to the morbid self-absorption often mistakenly supposed to be typical of artists. The models Rilke presents as truly great—even though he sadly reports on what he perceived as Rodin's decline from integrity in old age, and even though he did not underestimate Cézanne's mistrustful and surly personality—were heroically and exhilaratingly impassioned about art itself, and unflagging in its alluring, demanding service. "Work and have patience. . . . Draw your whole life into this circle," he quotes Rodin as saying. Rilke's emphasis on "experience," on living one's life with attention, is always balanced by an equal emphasis on the *doing* of one's art work, a zeal for the doing of it, not for the amateur's wish to *have done* it; an appetite for process.

Rilke's intense joy in the visual (whether in art or nature) recapitulated for me a direction towards which my mother had faced my attention very early in my life. "I love *inseeing*," he wrote in what I've always found a delightfully comic passage about *really looking* (for which "insight" has become too abstract a term):

> Can you imagine with me how glorious it is to insee, for example, a dog as one passes by—*insee* (I don't mean in-spect, which is only a kind of human gymnastic, by means of which one immediately comes out again on the other side of the dog, regarding it merely, so to speak, as a window upon the humanity lying behind it—not that)—but to let oneself precisely into the dog's very center, the point where it begins to be dog, the place

in it where God, as it were, would have sat down for a moment when the dog was finished, in order to watch it under the influence of its first embarrassments and inspirations, and to know that it was good, that nothing was lacking, that it could not have been better made. . . . Laugh though you will, dear confidant, if I am to tell you where my all-greatest feeling, my world-feeling, my earthly bliss was to be found, I must confess to you: it was to be found time and again . . . in such inseeing, in the indescribably swift, deep, timeless moments of this divine inseeing.

There is joy in so much of Rilke's letters, despite the early bouts of soulfulness and the later times of torment when (quickly recovering from his brief fall into collective pro-war hysteria in 1914) he perceived the frightfulness of WWI and intuited that it presaged the further horrors that we are witnessing (and the worse horrors we fear). It was not that he had any ordinary political astuteness; but his sensitivity to subsurface tremors, to ominous shadows (and also to the delicate counter-rhythm, the stir of seeds struggling into light) was acute. As a nonparticipant he did not undergo the daily bestiality of the war; but this peculiar sensitivity gives his overview a special kind of validity. And considering that that faculty made him highly vulnerable, it is remarkable that his sense of wonder and delight survive, so that, regaining Paris after "those terrible years," he is able to feel again "the continuity of [his] life": on October 20, 1920, he wrote, "here, here—*la même plénitude de vie, la même intensité, la même justesse dans le mal:* apart from political muddle and pother, everything has remained great, everything strives, surges, glows, shimmers—October days— you know them. . . . *One* hour here, the first, would have been enough. And yet I have had hundreds, days, nights—and each step was an arrival." The joy he found in his last years, in the Valais, in the little Chateau de Muzot where his wanderings came to rest, is not simple confrontation of an appreciative sensibility with the world's beauty, but the profounder joy of a struggle won, the lifelong struggle to transform "the visible into the invisible," that is, to *internalize* experience—and to use "the strings of lamentation" to play "the whole paean of praise which wells up behind all heaviness, anguish and suffering" (*"später auch den ganzen Jubel zu spielen"*). "Our conflicts," he says, "have always been a part of our riches"—and one feels he had earned the right to say that, for out of much inner conflict he had made works that give off energy and joy to others. In this way he provides an example for poets who follow him, just as a Cézanne or a Rodin, through their dedication and the work that resulted, provided examples for him. An example of persistence and of realism. He faced up to anguish and kept on creating: he could see both "Cézanne, the old man, [who] when one told him of what was going on, . . . could break out in the quiet streets of Aix and shriek at his companion: '*Le monde, c'est terrible* . . .'" and the Cézanne who "during almost forty years . . . remained uninterruptedly within his work, in the innermost center of it . . . the incredible freshness and purity of his pictures is due to this obstinacy. . . ."

This kind of influence, first on a young beginner, and then throughout the life of a working artist, represents one of the most deeply useful kinds of mutual aid. It is an influence not on style, not on technique, but on the attitude towards one's work that must underlie style and craft: it is out of that basic stance, a sense of aesthetic ethics, that they must develop (in whatever measure accords with the individual's innate and indispensible gifts). If the underlying attitude is shaky, the movements of style will be shaky too—desperate gestures made to maintain balance or hide the fear of falling. Rilke presents to any young poet an example of basic attitude that can remain relevant throughout a lifetime because it is reverent, passionate, and comprehensive. His reverence for "the savor of creation," as he calls it in a diary excerpt, leads him to concrete and sensuous images. His passion for "inseeing" leads him to delight, terror, transformation, and the internalization (or absorption) of experience. And his comprehensiveness, which makes no distinction between meeting art and meeting life, shows the poet a way to bridge the gap between the conduct of living and the conduct of art. Because he articulated a view of the poet's role that has not lost its significance as I have read and reread Rilke's prose for almost four decades, he remains a mentor for me now as he was when I was a young girl. No reiteration can wear thin such words as these:

> . . . to those who have not, perhaps, worked their way fully into their tasks . . . I wish that they may keep joyfully to the road of long learning until that deep, hidden self-awareness comes, assuring them (without their having to seek confirmation of others) of that pure necessity, by which I mean a sense of inevitability and finality in their work. To keep our inward conscience clear and to know whether we can take responsibility for our creative experiences just as they stand in all their truthfulness and absoluteness: that is the basis of every work of art. . . .

Adapted and revised, 1981, from a lecture given at a conference on religion in Chicago c. 1975.

A Poet's View

(1984)

THE BASIC QUESTIONS I have been asked to answer are, as I understand them: what is the relation between my religious and my intellectual position; is it satisfactory to me; and are whatever answers I can provide to these enquiries likely to be of use to others who may be searching to define their own condition? In order to respond I must first attempt to define what my beliefs are, and how they affect my work and other aspects of my life; as to the third question, it is probably answerable only by such other persons.

As a prelude to making an attempt at defining and summarizing my stance, it is necessary to point out that though I have a healthy respect for my own intelligence I am not—nor is any artist—specifically an intellectual. All the arts, and especially literature, have of necessity an intellectual component; and an honest artist is, and needs to be, conscious of having a point of view, a philosophy or a constellation of opinions and beliefs, which inform his or her work in some degree. But intellect and a conscious stance are not the mainspring of art work, which, as everyone knows (but sometimes forgets), draws upon a wider range of intelligence—sensory, intuitive, emotional— than the term *intellect* connotes. I must also emphasize that the subject of our enquiry appears to me to be a process, not a fixed quantity. For myself, at least, I feel I am focussing on an artificially isolated moment in a slow and continuing personal evolution. What I might write five years from now could be as different from what I say now as that is from what I might have written five years ago, although the direction of my development has, I believe, been consistent.

What, however, do I, an artist, consciously take as my intellectual stance, or as Myron Bloy has worded it, intellectual commitment? My intellectual creed, when I formulate it, turns out to be an aesthetic one, as befits an artist. I believe:

> in inspiration, to which intelligent craft serves as midwife; that the primary impulse of the artist is to make autonomous things from the materials of a particular art; and in the obligation of the artist to adhere to vision, to the inspired experience, and not make merely cosmetic "improvements." I believe in the obligation to work from within.

It will readily be seen that though I have called these commitments aesthetic, they merge, especially in the third instance, with the ethical; artistic quality appears to me to be bound up with artistic integrity. Furthermore, I believe:

> that artists, particularly writers, have social responsibilities, at least of a negative kind, i.e., even if incapable of undertaking social actions related to the implications of their productions, they should refrain, at least, from betraying such implications.

To conclude this list, I would add my belief that:

> creative gifts confer on those who possess them the obligation to nurture them in a degree proportionate to the strength and demands of the gift (which, paradoxically, cannot be determined unless the opportunity for its development be provided, which may mean sacrifices and imbalances in other areas of life).

I have designated these beliefs and opinions as "intellectual commitments" because they are consciously held and are conclusions arrived at by reflection. Because they concern aesthetic practice and the concept of artistic integrity—and I consider the latter to be linked to plain, common or garden, integrity—they clearly do not form a barrier to religious belief; that is, these intellectual commitments are not a system of dogmatic reasoning into which the a-rational nature of faith could not fit. To believe, as an artist, in *inspiration* or *the intuitive*, to know that without Imagination (and I give it the initial capital in conscious allusion to Keats's famous dictum) no amount of acquired craft or scholarship or of brilliant reasoning will suffice, is to live with a door of one's life open to the transcendent, the numinous. Not every artist, clearly, acknowledges that fact—yet all, in the creative act, experience mystery. The concept of "inspiration" presupposes a power which enters the individual and is not a personal attribute; and it is linked to a view of the artist's life as one of obedience to a vocation. David Jones wrote in one of his essays of the artist's impulse to gratuitously set up altars to the unknown god; and I alluded to the passage from what was then an agnostic standpoint. Later, that unknown began to be defined for me as God, and further, as God revealed in the Incarnation. Again, the rejection of merely cosmetic revisions in favor of the attempt to reach back and down to the origins of each image has to do with artistic morality, the ethics of the aesthetic, a platonic idea of integrity certainly not inconsistent with Christian (or other) religious belief, though not of course dependent on it.

I am more reluctant to define my own religious beliefs than I have been to list my convictions concerning "aesthetic ethics." The latter were formulated long ago, have long been a matter of record in my essays and other prose statements, and have not changed essentially, although in my teaching work I keep trying to refine them. In the matter of religion, however, I have moved in the last few years from a regretful skepticism which sought relief in some measure of pantheism (while it acknowledged both the ethical and emotional influence of my Jewish-Christian roots and early education) to a position of Christian

241

belief. Had I undergone a sudden dramatic conversion, I would probably find it easier to speak of this. But the movement has been gradual; indeed, I see how very gradual and continuous only when I look back at my own poems, my private notebooks, and the many moments throughout the decades when I stepped up to the threshold of faith only to turn away unable to pass over. Were the barriers I encountered emotional or intellectual? I think they were not emotional, for by temperament I was disposed to assent; and the experience, as a poet, of being at times a channel for something beyond my own limitations was, as I have suggested, an open door to specifically religious experience. Yet it seems somewhat exaggerated to call "intellectual" either my previous doubts (entertained since childhood, along with a sense of embarrassment at adult religious behavior) or my more recent sense of their irrelevance. I have not solved by a reasoning process the problems which had always stood in my way. Instead, I began to see these stumbling blocks as absurd. Why, when the very fact of life itself, of the existence of anything at all, is so astounding, why—I asked myself—should I withhold my belief in God or in the claims of Christianity until I am able to explain to myself the discrepancy between the suffering of the innocent, on the one hand, and the assertions that God is just and merciful on the other? Why should I for one moment suppose that I or any other human mind can comprehend paradoxes too vast to fit our mental capacities and, thus, never perceived in their entirety? Wasn't it as if I were scolding the Almighty, refusing my acknowledgement until provided with guarantees? What if I began to act as if I did believe, without waiting for intellectual clarity—that is, what if I prayed, worshipped, participated in the rituals of the Church? Might not faith follow? And with it some way to deal intellectually with the troublesome mysteries and paradoxes? These suppositions were accompanied by a strong, persistently occurring sense of awe and gratitude concerning the undercurrents of my own destiny—of a force I was conscious of at least by the early '60s, as a poem called *The Thread* testifies, and probably much earlier, although unable to name it.

At the same time, the important role in the struggle for peace and justice currently being played by certain branches of the church, whether Catholic or Protestant, and the accompanying movement away from stuffy respectability of social atmosphere, helped to dispel that sense of embarrassment and uncongeniality which previously had been one of the impediments standing between me and the experience of a fellowship of belief.

I have been engaging, then, during the last few years, in my own version of the Pascalian wager, and finding that an avowal of Christian faith is not incompatible with my aesthetic nor with my political stance, since as an artist I was already in the service of the transcendent, and since Christian ethics (however betrayed in past and present history) uphold the same values I seek in a politics of racial and economic justice and nonviolence. How does the wager interact with my creative work? There the question remains: does a position of even moderate orthodoxy threaten an artist's exploratory aesthetic freedom and "Negative Capability"? So far, from inside the creative work process, I have not found that it does; whether it will seem so for those who read the poems I write it is not possible for me to say. The public of a poet such as Margaret Avison, whose content and allusions are frequently unequivocally Christian, is certainly smaller than it would be if that were not the case. But a self-respecting poet does not court the audience but does what must be done to serve the art; so that is not a matter of concern. I have never felt that my *political* commitments were in themselves detrimental to my work, even though the challenge of incorporating politics in poems is one I have taken up with varying success—some good poems and some bad ones, no doubt, resulting. I have worked with and in behalf of many organizations which seek to promote justice and prevent war, and have even voted in state and national elections when there was at least a Lesser Evil to vote for, but I have never joined a party, nor even the Socialist or Peace and Freedom parties. And I believe this freedom from "party line" has helped me serve my poetic vocation in some work that is both engaged and has artistic integrity. By the same token, I see nothing inherently detrimental to my poetry in the fact that I participate in the Eucharist or that I read Julian of Norwich, Bonhoeffer, or Thomas Merton without skepticism. I am ecumenical to a degree no doubt scandalous to the more orthodox. Whether in St. Merri in Paris, a Presbyterian church in Palo Alto, or Anglican churches in London or Boston, if I discover spiritual fellowship and an active commitment to my political values I take it where I find it—and if liturgy and music are of a high order, so much the better (though if forced to choose between liturgical beauty and a manifest social conscience my loyalty would be to the latter—works over faith).

Drawn both by its rich traditions and by its present-day radical element (e.g., the Catholic Worker movement, the Bishops and Archbishops who have taken a radical stand against paying War Taxes, production of nuclear weapons, and support by our government of oppressive regimes in Latin America and elsewhere) to the (Roman) Catholic church, but resistant to its pyramidal authoritarian structure and rigid dogma, I have liked such individual Episcopal churches as combine a strong social awareness with decent music and some liturgical grace. These, however, are hard to find; more often there is either a style of "smells and bells" I can't help finding "camp" in its selfconsciousness—where (Roman) Catholic ritual is self-confident—or an evangelical tone that too often is excessively banal in language. The fundamentalist denominations are wholly alien to me even when they are not politically reactionary.

I perceive an element of vulgarity in my own "shopping around" for the right place of worship, which I regret; and I also perceive the danger of a personal ecumenical freedom degenerating into mere chronic fence-sitting. But I also see that one of the poet's tasks is, always, to maintain the delicate equilibrium which must exist between Negative Capability and passion, or creative energy. George MacDonald said that "When the desire after system or order degenerates from a need into a . . . ruling idea, it closes . . . like an unyielding skin over my mind, to the death of all development from impulse and aspiration." Martin Buber said, "To produce is to draw forth, to invent is to find, to shape is to discover." I cannot simply enter a ready-made structure; I have to find components and construct my own. The Protestant conscience and the spiritual power of Catholic rituals (which are sacramental *art*—I would refer the reader to David Jones' essay, "Art and Sacrament," in *Epoch and Artist*) both tug at me. And it is not to become, in a way foreign to my life's entire pattern, an "insider" of some cosy institution, that I seek a way to worship in communion. No doubt my sense of felicity at St. Merri in Paris was not unconnected with the fact that the Sunday mid-morning Mass there is part of a special ministry to the floating population of students, tourists, artists, street people which throngs the neighborhood. Though I own a house and have steady work, I am by nature, heritage, and as an artist, forever a stranger and pilgrim.

To return to the question of what utility, if any, my experience may have for others, which I began by saying was unanswerable except by others: if indeed there's a message here, it is perhaps that articulated in a dream-based poem I wrote in the 1960s, "The Novices." In this poem a man and a boy go into the forest to perform what they feel, without understanding it, is a duty; they are to tug out of the earth a great iron chain which is attached at the other end to an oak tree. But while they are attempting to do this the tutelary spirit of the place, the Wood Demon, appears, and tells them they need not perform this strenuous task: his purpose in summoning them was partially a test of responsiveness to a call (there are Biblical parallels here if one cares to find them) and even more importantly,

> . . . that they might look about them

> and see intricate branch and bark,
> stars of moss and the old scars
> left by dead men's saws,

> and not ask what that chain was.
> To leave the open fields
> and enter the forest,

> that was the rite.
> Knowing there was mystery, they could go.
> Go back now! And he receded

> among the multitude of forms,
> the twists and shadows they saw now, listening
> to the hum of the world's wood.

This acknowledgement, and celebration, of mystery probably constitutes the most consistent theme of my poetry from its very beginnings. Because it is a matter of which I am conscious, it is possible, however imprecisely, to call it an intellectual position; but it is one which emphasizes the incapacity of reason alone (much though I delight in elegant logic) to comprehend experience, and considers Imagination the chief of human faculties. It must therefore be by the exercise of that faculty that one moves toward faith, and possibly by its failure that one rejects it as delusion. Poems present their testimony as circumstantial evidences, not as closing argument. Where Wallace Stevens says, "God and the imagination are one," I would say that the imagination, which synergizes intellect, emotion and instinct, is the perceptive organ through which it is possible, though not inevitable, to experience God.

Response to a questionnaire from *Religion & Intellectual Life*, Vol. 1, #4, Summer 1984.

Work That Enfaiths

(1990)

WHAT A FRAUD I feel, sitting down to write about faith that works! What a fraud I shall feel when I am actually giving this paper to a gathering of people who, I know in advance, will each of them have a degree of faith not only far beyond my own but perhaps beyond anything I shall ever attain, or possess, or—since those verbs both seem ill-chosen—shall ever be blessed with! I know such faith only at second or third hand: that's to say, I have just enough faith to believe it exists. To imagine it. And to feel a kind of pity for people who can't imagine it at all, who *don't* believe it exists, who diminish its possibility in their minds by calling it self-delusion or superstition. Belief is something else. I can say the creed without perjury. But faith. . . . When my mother tried a few times to tell me about the faith she did indeed possess, she sought the right words in vain, although she was an articulate woman; and if she conveyed something of her experience to me so convincingly, it was more by her tone of voice than by the words she found. A singer (she was Welsh), she loved Handel's *Messiah* aria, "I know that my Redeemer liveth," and despised any performance of it which, though technically excellent, failed to give the emphasis of conviction to that word, "know": "I *know* that my Redeemer liveth." Such passionate knowledge, recurrent, intermittent, or in some cases even sustained, is what I know I don't have. "Flickering Mind"* confesses the fact:

*A Door in the Hive, 1989.

Lord, not you,
it is I who am absent.
At first
belief was a joy I kept in secret,
stealing alone
into sacred places:
a quick glance, and away—and back,
circling.
I have long since uttered your name
but now
I elude your presence.
I stop
to think about you, and my mind
at once
like a minnow darts away,
darts
into the shadows, into gleams that fret
unceasing over
the river's purling and passing.
Not for one second
will my self hold still, but wanders
anywhere,
everywhere it can turn. Not you,
it is I am absent.
You are the stream, the fish, the light,
the pulsing shadow,
you the unchanging presence, in whom all
moves and changes.
How can I focus my flickering, perceive
at the fountain's heart
the sapphire I know is there?

But if I feel fraudulent, why have I agreed to participate in
this event? To talk about "faith that works?"

Well, because I'm a poet, and I do have faith in what Keats
called the *truth of the imagination;* and because, when I'm following the road of imagination (*following a leading,* as the

Quakers say), both in the decisions of a day and in the word-by-word, line-by-line decisions of a poem in the making, I've come to see certain analogies, and also some interaction, between the journey of art and the journey of faith.

The analogies are recognizable if one thinks of the necessary combination in any artist of discipline and inspiration, work and luck, technique and talent, or craft and genius. Every work of art is an "act of faith" in the vernacular sense of being a venture into the unknown. The artist must dive into waters whose depths are unplumbed, and trust that he or she will neither be swallowed up nor come crashing against a cement surface four foot down, but will rise and be buoyed upon them. Every work of art, even if long premeditated, enters a stage of improvisation as soon as the artist moves from thinking about it to beginning to form its concrete reality. That step, from entertaining a project for a poem or other work of art, to actually painting, composing, dancing, writing it, resembles moving from intellectual assent to opening the acts of daily life to permeation by religious faith. I know the first from experience; I know the second only from a distance, but my experience enables me to imagine it, and to see that such permeation is "faith that works."

The *interaction* I perceive between the journey of art and the journey of faith necessitates my speaking rather personally. As I became, a few years ago, more and more occupied with questions of belief, I began to embark on what I'll call "do-it-yourself theology." Sometimes I was merely trying to clarify my mind and note down my conclusions-in-process by means of the totally undistinguished prose of journal entries. Sometimes, however, it was in poems that the process took place, and most notably in the first such poem I wrote, a longish piece called *Mass for the Day of St. Thomas Didymus* ("doubting Thomas"). The poem began as an experiment in structure. I had attended a choral recital for which the choir director had put together parts of Masses from many periods—medieval, renaissance, baroque, classical, and modern, not in chronological order. The program had a striking unity, nevertheless. It was obviously the traditional liturgical framework that not only enabled such a variety of styles to avoid clashing, but provided a cohesive overall effect, so that the concert was itself a work, a composed entity. And I thought to myself that it might be possible to adapt this framework, which had served such a diversity of musicians, to the creation of a poem. At the time—and even when, a couple of years later, I actually undertook this experiment—I still considered myself an agnostic. I thought of the poem as "an agnostic Mass" (using the word Mass merely as a formal description, as one might in saying of a Baroque composer, "He wrote over thirty Masses"), basing each part on what seemed its primal character: the Kyrie a cry for mercy, the Gloria a praise-song, the Credo an individual assertion, and so on: each a personal, secular meditation. But a few months later, when I had arrived at the Agnus Dei, I discovered myself to be in a different relationship to the material and to the liturgical form from that in which I had begun. The experience of writing the poem—that long swim through waters of unknown depth—had been also a conversion process, if you will.

Another instance of the interaction of artistic labor and incipient faith—shall I say, of the workings of the Holy Spirit, or is that too presumptuous?—concerns the way in which, writing a libretto about El Salvador for a composer who'd been commissioned to write an oratorio, I dwelt longer on the work and words of Archbishop Oscar Romero than I might have done otherwise, with my tendency to rush ahead too swiftly from one experience to another. Since I intended to quote directly from Romero, the thought of him remained constantly present to me and became a factor in my growing ability to stop making such a *fuss*, inside my mind, about various points of doubt. (If a Romero—or a Dorothy Day, an Anthony Bloom, a Raymond Hunthausen, a Jean Sulivan, or a Thomas Merton—

or a Pascal, for that matter!—could believe, who was I to squirm and fret, as if I required more refined mental nourishment than theirs?)

As to my more substantial stumbling block, the suffering of the innocent and the consequent question of God's nonintervention, which troubled me less in relation to individual instances than in regard to the global panorama of oppression and violence, it was through poetry—through images given me by creative imagination while pondering this matter—that I worked through to a theological explanation which satisfied me. God's nature, as Love, demands a freely given requital from that part of the creation which particularly embodies Consciousness: the Human. God therefore gives to human beings the power to utter yes or no—to perceive the whole range of dualities without which there could be no freedom. An *imposed* requital of love would be a contradiction in terms. Invisible wings are given to us too, by which, if we would dare to acknowledge and use them, we might transcend the dualities of time and matter—might be upheld to walk on water. Instead, we humans persistently say no, and persistently experience our wings only as a dragging weight on our backs. And so God remains nailed to the Cross—for the very nature of God as Love would be violated by taking back the gift of choice which is *our* very nature. It's an idea, or theory, undoubtedly familiar to many of you through works of religious philosophy; but *for me* it was original, not only because I hadn't come across such expositions of it but also because the concrete images which emerged in the process of writing convinced me at a more intimate level of understanding than abstract argument would have done. The poem I called "Standoff"* articulates this idea.

Assail God's hearing with gull-screech knifeblades.

Cozen the saints to plead our cause, claiming
grace abounding.

*Breathing the Water, 1987.

God crucified on the resolve not to displume
our unused wings

hears: nailed palms
cannot beat off the flames of insistent sound,

strident or plaintive,
nor reach to annul freedom—

nor would God renege.

Our shoulders ache. The abyss
gapes at us.

When shall we
dare to fly?

In a somewhat earlier, related poem called "The Task"* I
had pictured God as a weaver sitting at his loom in a vast
wilderness, solitary as a bear in the Alaskan tundra, listening to
the cries of anguish far off, audible above the clack of the loom
because all else is so quiet—and hastening his task; for the cloth
must be woven before the "terrible beseeching" can cease. A
friend's description of the heavenly but awesome quiet of the
wilderness near Mount Denali was one source for this poem.
Another source was what Julian of Norwich tells us she learned
in one of her "showings": that there is a divine plan, both temporal and transcendent, which will account for the unchecked
miseries of the world, a plan which our finite minds are incapa-
ble of grasping. God informs her, you remember, to trust this,
and tells her that "All shall be well, and all manner of thing
shall be well." The time is not yet ripe for us to comprehend
this mystery, she is told. But meanwhile all manner of thing is
not well, and "The Task" images the toil of a lonely God.

As if God were an old man
always upstairs, sitting about

* *Oblique Prayers,* 1984.

in sleeveless undershirt, asleep,
arms folded, stomach rumbling,
his breath from open mouth
strident, presaging death . . .

No, God's in the wilderness next door
—that huge tundra room, no walls and a sky roof—
busy at the loom. Among the berry bushes,
rain or shine, that loud clacking and whirring,
irregular but continuous;
God is absorbed in work, and hears
the spacious hum of bees, not the din,
and hears far-off
our screams. Perhaps
listens for prayers in that wild solitude.
And hurries on with the weaving:
till it's done, the great garment woven,
our voices, clear under the familiar
    blocked-out clamor of the task,
can't stop their
            terrible beseeching. God
imagines it sifting through, at last, to music
in the astounded quietness, the loom idle,
the weaver at rest.

    In other poems I have explored passages of Julian of Norwich and passages of the Gospel—for example, the parables of the mustard seed, which have always seemed to me, for the simplest botanical reason, to be misinterpreted (it is not a simple assertion along the lines of "great oaks from little acorns grow!"). Or again, the sheer *daring* of the Virgin Mary in the Annunciation narrative, contrasted with her so often-alleged meekness; or what I imagined as the state of mind of St. Thomas before and after his meeting with the risen Christ. Before, I imagine Thomas as one "whose entire being had knotted itself/into the one tightdrawn question"—the question raised dramatically by such an encounter as that of Jesus with the possessed child in Mark 9, which I assume he witnessed.

> Why,
> why has this child lost his childhood in suffering,
> why is this child who will soon be a man
> tormented, torn, twisted?
> Why is he cruelly punished
> who has done nothing except be born?

Thomas identifies with the father's cry of "Lord, I believe, help thou my unbelief"; but his harrowing doubt remains with him despite all the miracles he witnesses, for they do not address the profoundly disturbing matter of the suffering of the innocent. Even his meeting with the risen Christ does not suffice to give him certitude as long as it is visual alone; it is the concreteness of touch, of flesh and blood, which frees him at last. He is moved from tenuous belief to an illuminated conviction in which he can rest, like Lady Julian, from the nagging need for explanation, recognizing that (as Robert McAfee Brown has said) "puzzles are to be solved, but mysteries are to be experienced."

> But when my hand
> led by His hand's firm clasp
> entered the unhealed wound,
> my fingers encountering
> rib-bone and pulsing heat,
> what I felt was not
> scalding pain, shame for my
> obstinate need,
> but light, light streaming
> into me, over me, filling the room
> as if I had lived till then
> in a cold cave, and now
> coming forth for the first time,
> the knot that bound me unravelling,

254

I witnessed
> all things quicken to color, to form,
my question
> not answered but given
>> its part
in a vast unfolding design lit
> by a risen sun.*

The writing of each of these poems has brought me a little bit closer to faith as distinct from mere shaky belief. Thus for me the subject is really reversed: not "faith that works" but "work that enfaiths."

I was encouraged to be "as personal as you wish"—but what has all this personal history to do with the other issue we were commissioned to address? Has it any relevance to "the world of higher education and learning" and to "the problems of our wider world"?

My partial response has to do with the fate of poems after they leave the writer's desk. In writing, I was of course following personal imperatives, as any artist must. But it could not fail to occur to me that, once these poems of religious quest were published, I was likely to lose some of my readers. This proved not to be true. In fact, the positive response I've had to them from people I'd have expected to be hostile or disappointed has amazed me. Of course, there have been some who have said they just "couldn't get into" poems of Christian content and terminology; but the reverse has more often been the case. My Jewish readers, for instance—while not subscribing, of course, to whatever is specifically Christian in the poems—responded to them without hostility, and with solidarity in the basic interfaith assumption of belief in God. We often hear it said that there is much spiritual hunger in our society—but I have been surprised by how much quiet, unadvertised religious *commitment* there is among people one can loosely charac-

*"St. Thomas Didymus," *A Door in the Hive*, 1989.

terize as intellectuals—the people who constitute the audience for contemporary poetry in twentieth-century America.

This being so, one becomes aware that in so secular a society little in contemporary literature articulates the beliefs or yearnings which such people hold almost secretly. Just as I was shy about frankly uttering my beliefs in print, and did so with a resigned anticipation of negative response, yet was relieved and indeed exhilarated at the consequences, so, I think, do many crypto-Christians experience relief and pleasure when a poet whose work they already know, and with whose politics they are familiar and sympathetic, turns out to be one of themselves.

In recent years, the impulse to search for or return to cultural roots has been a factor in making religious practices less "uncool" for Jewish intellectuals than for their Christian counterparts. For Gentile intellectuals with Christian roots or leanings, a great deterrent is the disgusting vulgarity of "born-again" hucksters and their poisonous alliance with militarism and repression. Catholic intellectuals have an easier time, because despite many conflicts, within the Church and about it, regarding a number of very important issues, many non-Catholics as well as Catholics find inspiration in the heroes and martyrs of Latin America and elsewhere and in the church's leadership in peace and justice concerns in many places. Moreover, the Catholic Church has modern traditions of high intellectual discourse and major artistic contributions. One thinks of Messiaen in music, David Jones in poetry, Rouault in painting, Flannery O'Connor in fiction—to name a few off the top of my head. These are artists whom even avowed atheists respect and admire (often with a certain wistful envy), without fear of being considered naive and stupid by their peers.

Yet there is not a whole lot of contemporary poetry—in English, anyway—which articulates a faith-life (or quest) parallel to that of the many readers who appear to welcome such poetry when they do find it. The appeal of Wendell Berry's work is partly due, surely, to the way in which his land ethic has more and more seemed to draw on underlying Christian themes. (The converse is probably also true: readers drawn first to his ecological concerns are led through those concerns to an assimilation of his spirituality.)

Of course, attempting to supply a demand would be fatal to artistic integrity. But supply sometimes happens, by surprise, to meet demand; and in my own case I think the fact that my poems have been addressing doubts and hopes rather than proclaiming certainties has turned out to make them accessible to some readers, letting them into the process as I have engaged in building my own belief structure step by step. They are poems written on the road to an imagined destination of faith. That imagination of faith acts as yeast in my life as a writer: in that sense I do experience "faith that *works*" as well as "work that enfaiths." If the results sometimes attain their own autonomous life in the world, as every artist hopes will happen, it is possible that they may contribute to the life of other people. If they do, it must be first and foremost as works of art, on the same basis as any others, regardless of content. But since content evolves its forms and permeates them, each work that satisfies formally will bring with it the character of its content.

Finally, a poet speaking from within the Christian tradition and using traditional terms (though not necessarily upholding every orthodoxy) may have more resonance for our intellectual life than is supposed. The Incarnation, the Passion, the Resurrection—these words have some emotive power even for the most secular minds. Perhaps a contemporary poetry that incorporates old terms and old stories can help readers to reappropriate significant parts of their own linguistic, emotional, cultural heritage, whether or not they share doctrinal adherences.

This essay was written for a Consultation on "Faith That Works," organized by the Association for Religion and Intellectual Life in 1990. The papers were published in the summer 1990 issue of *Crosscurrents: Religion & Intellectual Life*, which is a quarterly.

Autobiographical Sketch

(1984)

"WHO ARE YOU? AND how did you become what you are?" are questions which, when I try to answer them honestly, increase my awareness of how strong, in my case (where in others place and community often play a dominant part), were inherited tendencies and the influence of the cultural milieu— unsupported by a community—of my own family. My father's Hasidic ancestry, his being steeped in Jewish and Christian scholarship and mysticism, his fervor and eloquence as a preacher, were factors built into my cells even though I rarely paid conscious heed to what, as a child, I mostly felt were parts of the embarrassing adult world, and which during my adolescence I rejected as restrictive. Similarly, my mother's Welsh intensity and lyric feeling for Nature were not just the air I breathed but, surely, were in the body I breathed with. Reading, at 60, the out-of-print or manuscript pages of my father's theological writings, or the poems my mother took (shyly) to writing in her late 70s and 80s, I see clearly how much they, though not dedicated to the vocation of poetry, were nevertheless protopoets.

When I say the cultural atmosphere of our household was unsupported by a community I refer to the fact that my parents—he a converted Russian Jew who, after spending the First World War teaching at the University of Leipzig (though under semi-house arrest as an "enemy alien"), settled in England and was ordained as a priest of the Anglican Church; she a Welshwoman who had grown up in a mining village and later in a North Wales country town, and subsequently travelled widely—were exotic birds in the plain English coppice of Ilford, Essex. Even though our house was semi-detached and exactly like its neighbors architecturally, it looked different because it had no half-curtains or venetian blinds like the others, only side-curtains on its large windows, so passers-by could look right in. What they could see included bookshelves in every room, while in the bay window of my father's upstairs study was an almost life-size stone statue representing Jesus preaching, which caused strangers to stare and cross the street to get a better look at it. And my mother's front garden, though more restrained than the larger back garden, was never prim like many of the others along the street but suggested a foreign opulence, especially when the California poppies—later to delight homesick G.I.s billeted down the road—were in full orange glory.

The Levertoffs lived in Ilford because my father had been given (in the mistaken supposition that he would want to proselytize a Jewish neighborhood) a church in Shoreditch that had no vicarage and no local congregation. Ilford, though in Essex, was then at the eastern extremity of London; its own western end was still country, though rapidly being "developed" into monotonous row upon row of small "mock-Tudor" houses I early learned to despise as jerry-built architectural monstrosities.

I didn't go to school, nor had my sister (nine years older) done so except briefly, another thing which set our household apart from others. Dissatisfied with my sister's one year at a convent boarding school during my infancy, and unimpressed by local day-schools, whether private or council, my mother (who had been teaching at a Constantinople high school run by the Church of Scotland when she met my father in 1910) taught me herself until at 12, enamored of the de Basil Russian

259

Ballet to which my sister had taken me, I began daily classes at a school of ballet on the other side of London. At that point I was put on my honor to continue reading some history, and went also for weekly French, piano, and art lessons in London; my other formal education ceased.

Romantic and beautiful Wanstead and Valentines parks, frequent expeditions into the Essex countryside with my sister, and my mother's very strong sense of history, developed in me a taste for seeking-out and exploring the vanishing traces of the village Ilford which London had engulfed. The reading I did myself, and the reading aloud which was a staple of our family life, combined to give me a passion for England—for the nuances of country things, hedges and old churches and the names of wildflowers—even though part of me knew I was an outsider. Among Jews a Goy, among Gentiles (secular or Christian) a Jew or at least a half-Jew (which was good or bad according to their degree of anti-Semitism); among Anglo-Saxons a Celt; in Wales a Londoner who not only did not speak Welsh but was not imbued with Welsh attitudes; among school children a strange exception whom they did not know whether to envy or mistrust: all of these anomalies predicated my later experience. I so often feel English, or perhaps European, in the United States, while in England I sometimes feel American—and certainly as a poet have been thought of for decades as an American, for it was in the United States that I developed, though my first book had been published in England before I crossed the Atlantic. But though I was quick to scornfully protest anti-Semitic remarks, or references to the Welsh language as a "dialect," these feelings of not-belonging were positive for me, not negative. I was given such a sense of confidence by my family, *in* my family, that though I was often shy (and have remained so in certain respects) I nevertheless experienced the sense of difference as an honor, as a part of knowing (secretly) from an early age—perhaps by seven, certainly before I was ten—that I was an artist-person and had a destiny. I did not experience competitiveness, because I was alone. The age gap—nine years—between me and my sister was such that my childhood was largely that of an only child. I was given a great deal of freedom to roam about outdoors as soon as I'd learned to cross streets safely; only the loneliest depths of Wanstead Park were out of bounds. The house was full of books, many of them late seventeenth- and eighteenth-century volumes. Everyone in the family did some kind of writing; my mother and sister always seemed to be helping my father correct galley proofs. My mother sang *Lieder*, my sister was a really fine pianist. The church services I attended were, despite the frequent childish embarrassment I've mentioned and my teenage doubts, beautiful with candlelight and music, incense and ceremony and stained glass, the incomparable rhythms of the King James Bible and the Book of Common Prayer.

All of this sounds idealized *ad nauseam*, I'm afraid. There were also tremendous domestic arguments and periodic full-scale "rows" and even real tragedy (my gifted but erratic sister's life and her conflicts and reconciliations with my parents were complex). But all in all I did grow up in an extraordinarily rich environment which nurtured the imaginative, language-oriented potential I believe was an inherited gift; and gave me—or almost seduced me into—an appreciation of solitude. Since writing poetry is so essentially a solitary occupation this has always stood me in good stead and perhaps I would not have developed it if I'd gone to school (unless I'd *hated* school, of course) for I have a sociable, gregarious tendency too, that might have taken away too much time and concentration and necessary daydreaming. Or I might have become caught up in aggressive competition, to the certain detriment of my creative possibilities.

While it is true that I was not competitive because I had no peers to compete with (my playmates, whether neighbors or kids I met in the park, were altogether separate from my beginnings in literature), I did, once I'd read Keats's letters, have hopes of Fame; but I thought of this as posthumous, and thus was saved from careerist ambition. And misinterpreting, to some extent, the gists of Mann's *Tonio Kröger*, I rather luxuriated in the protagonist's wistful alienation—though it was really his friend Lisaveta Ivanovna, the painter, the artist who was getting on with *doing her art*, who most excited me; especially since when I first read the story at 13, I had the *chutzpa* to believe I would be a painter as well as a poet. (I never deeply believed I would be a dancer despite the five years of my life when I took two ballet classes a day, shedding many tears in the process.)

Though my favorite poets were all men, I had enough faith in myself, or more precisely enough awe at the magic I knew sometimes worked through me, not to worry about that. Boys seemed, in fiction, to have more adventures; but in the "pretend-games" I made up and got my sister to play with me in my later childhood, some daring young female spies and messengers worked to combat Fascism and Nazism and to assist the government side in the Spanish Civil War (which was then going on). I didn't suppose my gender to be an obstacle to anything I really wanted to do.

Humanitarian politics came into my life early—seeing my father on a soapbox protesting Mussolini's invasion of Abyssinia; my father and sister both on soapboxes protesting Britain's lack of support for Spain; my mother canvassing long before those events for the League of Nations Union; and all three of them working on behalf of German and Austrian refugees from 1933 onwards. When I was 11 and 12, unknown to my parents (who would have felt, despite their liberal views, that it was *going too far*, and was inappropriate for my age, as indeed it was), I used to sell the *Daily Worker* house-to-house in the working-class streets off Ilford Lane, down towards Barking, on Saturday mornings. Oddly enough I was never questioned, despite knee-socks and long plaits (or pigtails, as one said then) though I had many a door slammed in my face.

I've written here only about my childhood, and not at all about the rest of my life and all its experiences of people, places, events; nothing about the mind's later journeys in literature and the other arts which mean so much to me; nothing about "intellectual stance," aesthetics, philosophy, religion. But there is, after all, no mystery about all of that: it's either in my poems or of little interest beyond the merely anecdotal. All that has taken place in my life since—all, that is, that has any bearing on my life as a poet—was in some way foreshadowed then. I am surprised to sound so deterministic, and I don't mean to suggest that the course of every life is inexorably set, genetically or by childhood experiences, for better or worse; nor that my own life had no options. Possibly I might have been a better person, and certainly a more efficient one in several respects, if I'd had a more disciplined and methodical education, more experience of economic struggle (never rich, and not extravagant, our household nevertheless never lacked for anything), and had not so early felt a sense of vocation and dedication to the art of poetry. But since I *did* have a vocation, to which some interesting genes contributed, it seems to me that I was fortunate in an upbringing favorable to their development; and this strongly affected my response to subsequent events and opportunities.

Poets owe to Poetry itself a loyalty which may at times be in conflict with the demands of domestic or other aspects of life. Out of those conflicts, sometimes, poetry itself re-emerges. For example, the impulse to reconcile what one believes to be necessary to one's human integrity (such as forms of political action) with the necessities of one's inner life, including its formal, aesthetic dynamic, motivates the attempt to write engaged or "political" poetry that is truly poetry, magnetic and sensuous—the synthesis Neruda said was the most difficult of any to attain (but which our strange and difficult times cry out for). Yet sometimes the poems one is able to write and the needs and possibilities of day to day life remain separate from each other.

263

One is in despair over the current manifestation of malevolent imbecility and the seemingly invincible power of rapacity, yet finds oneself writing a poem about the trout lilies in the spring woods. And one has promised to speak at a meeting or help picket a building. If one is conscientious, the only solution is to attempt to weigh conflicting claims at each crucial moment, and in general to try to juggle well and keep all the oranges dancing in the air at once.

In 1984 Jeni Couzyn asked each of the living poets included in her anthology, *The Bloodaxe Book of Contemporary Women Poets*, to provide an autobiographical sketch and some sort of statement about poetry.

Acknowledgments

Grateful acknowledgment is made to all those who gave permission to reprint in these essays quoted material from previously published sources: "The Olive" by Harlow Clark, reprinted by permission of the author; "One Day" by Yarrow Cleaves, reprinted by permission of the author; "john" and "good friday" from *good woman: poems and a memoir 1969–1980* by Lucille Clifton, Copyright © 1987 by Lucille Clifton, reprinted with the permission of BOA Editions Ltd., Brockport, New York; "Of Earth" and "A Voice" from *Common Ground* by John Daniel, Copyright © 1988 by John Daniel, reprinted by permission of Confluence Press; "Right Now" and "A Time for Peace" from *A Book of Peace* by Catherine de Vinck, Copyright © 1988 by Catherine de Vinck, reprinted by permission of Alleluia Press, Allendale, New Jersey; lines from *Heavenly City, Earthly City* by Robert Duncan (Copyright © 1947 by Robert Duncan), reprinted by arrangement with the University of California Press; "Horologium" by Reidar Eknar, reprinted by permission of the author; "Covenant: Saying Hello to the Land We Will Live With" from *Keeping Faith* (Grey Spider Press, Seattle, Washington) by Sam Green, Copyright © 1990 by Sam Green, reprinted by permission of the author; "Prayer to the Snowy Owl" from *Winter News* by John Haines, Copyright © 1966 by Wesleyan University Press, reprinted by permission of University Press of New England; "Black Marsh Eclogue" from *A Dragon in the Clouds* (Broken Moon Press) by Sam Hamill, Copyright © 1989 by Sam Hamill, reprinted by permission of the author; "I do not know whether each believer" from *The Wandering Border* (Copper Canyon Press, 1987) by Jaan Kaplinski, translated from the Estonian by Jaan Kaplinski and Sam Hamill, reprinted by permission of Copper Canyon Press; "Tulips," "To Speak" and "The Novices" from *Poems 1960–1967*, Copyright © 1964, 1967 by Denise Levertov Goodman; "Four Embroideries: (III) Red Snow" from *Poems 1968–1972*, Copyright © 1972 by Denise Levertov Goodman; "A Son" from *Life in the Forest*, Copyright © 1978 by Denise Levertov Goodman; "The Task" from *Oblique Prayers*, Copyright © 1981, 1982, 1983, 1984 by Denise Levertov; "Making Peace" and "The Stand-Off" from *Breathing the Water*, Copyright © 1987 by Denise Levertov; "To R.D.," "Flickering Mind," and "St. Thomas Didymus" from *A Door in the Hive*, Copyright © 1989 by Denise Levertov: all Levertov material reprinted

JAN 1 4 1993

Levertov, Denise,
1923-

New & selected
essays.

21.95

DATE			

6/93-4

6/93-4

φ PLC

1 of 3 vi New

BAKER & TAYLOR BOOKS